MAKE NO BONES

MAKE NO
BONES

Aaron Elkins

OPEN ROAD
INTEGRATED MEDIA
NEW YORK

Copyright © 1991 by Aaron Elkins

ISBN 978-1-4976-4311-6

This edition published in 2014 by Open Road Integrated Media, Inc.
345 Hudson Street
New York, NY 10014
www.openroadmedia.com

336140575295299

MAKE NO
BONES

Acknowledgments

The idea behind Make No Bones sprang from the wonderful "Mummies, Mayhem & Miseries" exhibit put on by the San Diego Museum of Man under Curator of Physical Anthropology Rose Tyson. Later, Dr. William D. Haglund, Chief Investigator, King County Medical Examiner's Office, took, a morning to help me work out a "perfect" murder (and then helped me solve it). Sergeant of Detectives Greg Brown filled me in on how things work in Deschutes County, Oregon. Dr. Ted Rathbun of the Anthropology Department, University of South Carolina, provided insight into the trickier aspects of reconstructing faces from skulls. Dr. Walter H. Birkby of the Anthropology Department, University of Arizona, spent a sunny hour beside a swimming pool cheerfully filling me in (so to speak) on the ins and outs of burial and exhumation.

I am extremely grateful to the tolerant and good-natured scientists of the Mountain, Desert & Coastal Forensic Anthropologists, who welcomed me among them at their 1990 annual meeting, and in particular to Dr. J. Stanley Rhine of the Department of Anthropology, University of New Mexico, who first suggested the idea of a murder set at a gathering of forensic scientists, provided technical assistance at several points along the way, and helped me in even more ways than he knows.

CHAPTER 1

From: Miranda Glass, Curator of Anthropology, Central Oregon Museum of Natural History.
To: Members of the Western Association of Forensic Anthropologists.
Subject: Sixth Biennial WAFA Conference
Esteemed Fellow Body-Snatchers:
June 16-22, the week of our eagerly anticipated bone bash and weenie roast, is fast approaching. As this year's host I hereby bid you a genial welcome.
Fittingly enough, this year's enlightenment and jollification will be held where it all started: the decaying but still scenic Whitebark Lodge...

* * *

Nelson Halston Hobert, president of the National Society of Forensic Anthropology, Distinguished Services Professor of Human Biology at the University of Northern New Mexico, and at sixty-four the undisputed dean of American forensic anthropologists, frowned as he read the letter. The breakfast dishes had been cleared to one side, his third cup of coffee was freshly poured, and his morning pipe was newly lit and fragrant. His posture was one of thoughtful repose, his mood benign but troubled.

"Damn," he murmured, "that's going to stir up a few old anxieties."

Across the table from him his wife appraised him and found him wanting.

"You have something in your beard," she told him in a matter-of-fact tone. "Banana bread, I believe."

"Mm," he said abstractedly, "I suppose." He continued to read.

"Honestly," Frieda Hobert said, not unfondly. She reached across the pile of mail and used the tip of her folded napkin to dab the offending crumb from her husband's bristly gray beard. Another flick removed a shred of tobacco from his old brown jogging suit. She looked him over once more, this time approvingly, and sat back satisfied.

If Hobert was aware of these attentions he gave no sign. "Miranda's set up this year's WAFA meeting," he told her. "The week of June sixteenth."

"You can't make it. Pru is getting married on the sixteenth. In Fort Lauderdale."

"I know, but couldn't I—"

"Absolutely not. You were rooting around in Ethiopia when Vannie was married. You're not going to miss this one." She dipped her chin and looked at him over the top of her plastic-rimmed glasses so he would know she meant it.

"No, I suppose I shouldn't," he said reluctantly. "Well, we could see about flights out of Fort Lauderdale that evening—"

"Nellie, I am not sitting up in an airplane all night long, not after what is bound to be an exhausting day. We can leave the next day, after a good night's sleep. Believe me, WAFA will manage to survive without you for a day or two."

Nellie scratched his gleaming scalp and frowned. "Normally I'd have no doubt about that. But...all right, we'll get a flight the next day."

The "we" was a foregone conclusion. For a dozen years, ever since she'd quit her job teaching, Frieda had accompanied him to his conferences and conventions. Occasionally this was annoying, but not often. She was extremely helpful on his trips, making airplane and hotel reservations, arranging his appointment calendar, even packing his clothes, and relieving him of a hundred bothersome details. He had become, he realized, a substitute for the generations of grade-school kids she'd nurtured for twenty-five years, but that was all right with Nellie. If not him, then who?

Besides, the truth was that he liked having her with him, liked starting and ending the day with her. They'd been married a long time now, and although there were plenty of ups and downs, a day without Frieda put him off his stride, made him feel not quite whole.

"You know why you need me?" she'd once asked when they were discussing the subject. "Because without me you tend to forget you're an august personage and have to behave accordingly."

Well, she certainly had a point there. It wasn't easy remembering you were an august personage.

She lowered the envelope she was opening. "What do you mean, *normally* you'd have no doubt?"

"Frieda," he said, "Miranda's arranged the meeting for Whitebark Lodge."

"Whitebark Lodge!" Her expression was pained. "What an absolutely rotten idea. What on earth was she thinking of?"

"Well, you have to remember, Miranda wasn't there the night that...well, the night of the party. No guilty memories for her."

"I hardly think guilt is the right word, Nellie. How could any of you even dream how it was going to turn out? You can't hold yourselves responsible for Albert Evan Jasper's—for what happened to him."

As she spoke he nodded along with her, drawing on his pipe. "I know, Frieda, I know." It wasn't the first time he'd heard her say it, and in general he agreed with her.

"Still," she said, tapping the envelope against her longish chin, "it's going to stir up some rather unpleasant associations, isn't it?"

"That's for damn sure." Nellie swallowed the last of his coffee, sucked hard on his pipe to make sure it was still lit, and abruptly stood up, not wanting to go into it with her just then. "It's not even nine, and I'm not due at school until one I'm going to put in the thyme and cotoneaster out front. What do you think of that?"

"I'm utterly astounded, my dear. They've only been sitting out there three weeks."

* * *

One week, actually, but that was Frieda for you. She enjoyed her little digs. Kneeling in the sun, working from his knees at a lazy pace, Nellie mixed the potting soil with earth from one of the planting holes in the prescribed three-to-one ratio.

"In the magnificent fierce morning of New Mexico," D. H. Lawrence had written, "one sprang awake, a new part of the soul woke up suddenly, and the old world gave way to the new."

If you asked Nellie, Lawrence had gotten it wrong. For him the high desert morning was relaxing, not energizing; very nearly anesthetic, in fact. The thin, dry air, the crisp, brilliant light, the rolling, open, pinyon-dotted foothills of the Sangre de Cristos, all made him feel sleepy and content, as sleek as a pampered house cat. Sleek and reflective and, on this particular morning, a shade melancholy.

He was reflecting on the first WAFA meeting, ten years earlier, as he worked the soil. "Rather unpleasant associations," Frieda had said, and she'd been putting it mildly. Damn unpleasant was the way he would put it. What else could you call it when you'd been responsible, no matter how unintentionally, for the death—the violent, unnecessary death—of the man to whom you owed very nearly everything important you had?

He leaned back on his heels, trowel at rest. Miranda's letter would have gone out to all forty or so WAFA members. For four of them—and only four—the mention of Whitebark Lodge would create those same "rather unpleasant associations."

He wondered what they were thinking about right now.

* * *

Callie Duffer was thinking about—or at least talking about—the self-esteem needs and personal-growth potential of an anthropology student named Marc Vroom, who was in considerable danger of flunking out of Nevada State University in his first graduate semester. As departmental chair, she felt she was required to declare her opinions.

"Surely you see," she told the three faculty members gathered in her office, "that failing this young man would solve none of his problems."

"Well, it'd go a long way toward solving mine," Harlow Pollard grumbled.

Callie swallowed down a surge of irritation. Had he said it with a hint of humor, even sardonic humor, she might have smiled. But Harlow was about as humorous as a codfish, and not so very much quicker on the uptake. Still, what was the point of getting annoyed? The man was to be pitied, a simplistic dinosaur incapable of comprehending the new dynamics of the educational suprasystem and the role of academics as change-agents. Poor Harlow still thought that he was there to teach anthropology, period. A living argument, Callie thought, against the tenure system.

Marge Harris, one of the younger instructors, tentatively waggled her fingers for attention. "Callie," she said hesitantly, "we all understand how dedicated you are to the concept of the university as a social support network—"

Harlow made an unpleasant strangled sound.

"—but you haven't had him in any of your classes," Marge went on. "He's constantly unprepared. When he's not argumentative he's flippant. When we try to point out what we expect of *him*, he treats it as a huge joke—"

"Ah!" Callie said, seizing on this, "what *we* expect of *him*. Couldn't that be the problem right there? Have we tried to attune ourselves to *his* needs? Have we taken the trouble to understand where *he's* coming from?"

A telling thrust, Callie thought, but the three of them just sat there, dumb and resisting. You'd think that at least the younger ones would grasp the importance of structural flexibility when you were dealing with a dysfunctional—

"Can I tell you what happened Friday?" Harlow said, face down, mumbling, talking to all of them. "I was giving my 304 midterm. Mr. Vroom came in fifteen minutes late, sat there five minutes, handed in his paper, and left. Do you know what he wrote?"

"No, what did he write, Harlow?" Callie said with a wooden-lipped attempt at a smile. How strange it was, when you came to think of it, that almost everything she said to Harlow Pollard required this granite-willed attitude of indulgence on her part. At fifty-three, he was nine years her senior, and once upon a time he had been her major professor. She had gotten her Ph.D. under him, right here at Nevada State, and started immediately as a temporary lecturer when he was already a fully tenured associate professor.

And now, she thought, idly fingering the buttery brown leather arm of the chair she'd inherited when she'd taken over the department, now here she was a dozen years later, a full professor and department chair to boot. And soon to be dean of faculty, if she didn't screw things up. And poor, plodding, shortsighted

Harlow? Harlow was still an associate professor. He would be an associate professor when he retired. (Soon, God willing.)

"Well, here's what he wrote," Harlow droned on. "'Sorry, prof, not my day.' This was in big block letters, then he drew one of those, what do you call them, one of those Happy Faces, and wrote 'Have a nice day.'"

He looked up, thick-witted and impenetrable. "Can anyone tell me what to make of that?"

Callie was weary of the conversation, but she leaned forward with what she hoped looked like eagerness. "But can't you see that, looked at in the right way, that's his attempt—faltering, tentative, to be sure—to open up communication? This is our chance to respond, to show him that we care, that we can be nurturing as well as censuring."

"Nurturing…?" Harlow echoed opaquely. He really, truly didn't get it, didn't even understand the words. The others weren't much better.

"He is twenty-eight years old," ventured Will Martinez, who couldn't have been more than a couple of years older. "You'd think—"

Callie decided it was time to assert her authority. Enough was enough. "I'm glad you've all shared your thoughts with me," she said briskly. "I've learned a lot from listening to you, but it's clear to me we have a way to go here. I think we should devote our team-building session Thursday to some hands-on training in nondirective counseling. I'll ask Dr. Mehrabian from human resources development to put us through some problem-solving role play. Does that make sense to everyone? Does anyone see any problem with that? Is there any feedback?"

Aside from the resigned, almost imperceptible slumping of three sets of shoulders, there was no feedback.

* * *

It hadn't been one of her better faculty meetings, Callie thought with irritation as the door closed behind them. She hadn't elicited enough response, as exasperating as that invariably turned out to be. She hadn't made them feel that the training was *their* idea. Well, what could she expect? The letter from Miranda had arrived only an hour earlier, and of course it had upset her. She was a high-strung person; she'd never claimed she wasn't.

Harlow must have received his copy in the morning's mail too; that would be more than enough to account for his having looked even more gray-faced and dyspeptic than usual.

She pulled it out of the desk tray and scanned it again. Whitebark Lodge. What a host of wretched memories that name stirred up.

Not that it had started badly, of course. It had been Nellie Hobert's idea in the first place, as she recalled: an informal conference-cum-retirement-party-in-the-woods for Albert Evan Jasper, put on by the celebrated anthropologist's grateful and adoring former students. Never mind that Callie had felt neither grateful nor adoring toward the chauvinistic old bully; never mind that she had left him after two maddening years to come and study with the less demanding Harlow Pollard, himself a browbeaten former student of Jasper's. The facts were that she had learned a lot from Jasper, that she'd been flattered to be invited to the meeting, and that some sort of send-off seemed his due.

Well, the old man had gotten a send-off, all right. Straight out of this life. She couldn't claim to be sorry about that even now, but it had been a miserable experience for her all the same. For a long time she had dragged around a burden of guilt, as if it had been her fault, her personal doing, that had driven him to his death.

Which it hadn't been, of course; hers or anyone else's. The therapeutic-psychodrama group at Esalen had helped her get that unwholesome idea out of her mind, and the marathon encounter weekend with its follow-up week of transformational body-mind work had put things in their true perspective: Albert Evan Jasper had been "driven" to nothing; he had made his own decisions, followed his own course, and marched—decisively and arrogantly as always—to his own violent end.

And now, even in death, even ten years later, even after she'd gotten it out of her system—or so she'd believed—here he was, still blighting her life. And no doubt doing the same to Nellie Hobert, and poor old Harlow, and the rest of them.

Damn him, she thought.

* * *

In his smaller, dustier office two floors below Callie's, Harlow Pollard stared hollowly at Miranda's letter. He was filled with a sense of impending doom, of a fateful circle coming closed. Whitebark Lodge. When he'd first read those words a few hours ago, his immediate reaction had been an instinctive aversion. He wouldn't go. How could he? How could Callie, how could any of them? But then a sort of desperate, horrible resignation had come over him. Oh, yes, he would go back. A part of him had always known that one day he would, that his long ordeal would be resolved there.

He frowned, probing with his middle finger at the spot below his sternum where the familiar pain was focused, where he was sure he could feel the acid eating through his stomach lining. He took a couple of chewable Pepto-Bismol tablets from the family-sized box in his lower desk drawer and forced them down a dry throat with a gulp of herbal tea that had been on his desk since yesterday.

My God, my God, Whitebark Lodge.

Not that he bore the responsibility for what had happened there. No one could say that. Of all of them, he was probably the least to blame. Whose fault was it, then? Well, that depended on how you looked at it. On the one hand, you might say it was everyone's, in an indirect sort of way, of course. On the other, wasn't it really Jasper himself...

Harlow passed his hand over his eyes. With puffy, unsteady fingers he tore the plastic wrapper from two more pink, heart-shaped Pepto-Bismol tablets.

* * *

A few hundred miles to the east, in a similar office in a similar building on the campus of the Colorado Institute of Technology, Professor Leland Roach was suffering no such distress. Happily engrossed in his work, his spare and narrow-shouldered form hunched over the laptop computer on his desk, he clicked away at his latest contribution to the *Southwestern Journal of Paleopathology*. His own words, elegant and authoritative, blinked comfortingly into existence on the screen:

...these fecal samples were then rehydrated in an aqueous trisodium phosphate solution, resulting in the recovery of four oocysts of a parasitic

protozoan identified as belonging to the genus Eimeria; most probably E. piriformis. This provocative burning...

The steady clicking faltered, then stopped. *Burning?* A tic of annoyance jogged his old-fashioned, pencil-straight mustache. Leland moved the cursor back and hit the *delete* key. *Burning* vanished, to be replaced by *finding.* Leland consulted his notes, flexed his fingers, and hunched forward again. But further words did not appear on the screen. His thought processes had been disrupted.

He'd read Miranda's letter when it arrived that morning, clipped a note to it instructing Eloise to make airline and lodging reservations for him, and put it out of his mind. Or so he'd thought. But now, here was burning popping up when he'd meant *finding.* A Freudian slip, he thought with distaste. Leland disapproved of Freudian slips as not being in accord with his notions of the way one's mind ought to work. To his way of thinking, they represented a sort of mental disloyalty, a sneaky double cross by some perverse corner of one's own brain. Leland prided himself on how infrequently he made such slips.

It particularly bothered him that he would make one now. There was no reason for his mind to play tricks on him. He was repressing nothing, hiding nothing from himself. What was there to hide? Terrible things happened to people. Nobody could be blamed.

Some of the others looked at it differently, of course, but that was their problem, not his. No sackcloth and ashes for Leland Roach, no rending of garments, no chest-beating and mea culpas. Life was difficult enough without taking responsibility for things that had not been under one's control.

Calmed by these eminently reasonable reflections, he mentally opened a drawer in an imaginary cabinet, filed away the disturbing thoughts—the metaphor was his own—and slammed the drawer shut. Then he returned more calmly to the intellectual pleasures of the subject on which he had been expounding. The quiet clicking resumed.

This provocative finding serves to highlight the potential contribution of feces to a greater understanding of...

* * *

"Screw you, buddy!" Les Zenkovich yelled, responding to the curses just hurled at him. For emphasis he brandished his middle finger out of the window of his Porsche.

The driver of the other car, leaning across his seat, opened a mouth already twisted with rage, but then got his first good look at Les: *Shit, the guy was built like the Incredible Hulk.* With a gulp he clamped his mouth shut, hurriedly braked, and drifted back. If that monster wanted the whole bridge to himself, he could have it, and welcome to it. "What do you give an eight-hundred-pound gorilla?" ran the old joke. Answer: "Anything he goddam well wants."

In the Porsche, Les adjusted the volume on the Creedence Clearwater tape and continued threading his way eastward through the ossified traffic on the Oakland Bay Bridge. The exchange had not perturbed him. By the time he got home to Kensington it would be forgotten altogether. People were jumpy these days, that was all, especially on the bridge. It had been that way since the earthquake, and according to the psychologists it was going to be that way for a while yet.

Not that it had made much of a dent in Les's psyche. Few things did. Les prided himself on a laid-back approach to life, "Mr. Mellow," they had called him in graduate school, and not just because he'd been a pothead back then. Take things as they come, that was his motto. Nobody gets out of this world alive, and you might as well enjoy things while you're here. A good part of the enjoyment, he'd learned, was watching other people unnecessarily screwing up their lives every which way they could.

Life was complicated enough without inventing problems, but sometimes he seemed to be the only person who understood that.

Now take Miranda's letter, for example. He'd received it that afternoon at his office on Mission Street. Assuming the others had gotten it today, too, there were four people who were pulling their hair out over it right now: Nellie, Leland, Harlow, and Callie. Well, not Nellie. No hair to pull. But none of them could be real happy about going back to Whitebark Lodge. Talk about bad karma.

If they'd just come out right at the start and told everybody what had happened, it'd all be ancient history by now. Les had said so at the time, but everyone else had shushed him, and so he'd gone along, dumb as it was. And now, for ten years, whenever they met, there had been this undercurrent, this squalid, crummy little secret between them.

They'd played it so close to the vest, in fact, that even Miranda hadn't been told what had happened. She lived in Bend, not far from the lodge, and she'd been lucky enough to be at some kind of family affair that night—probably getting married or divorced; she did a lot of both. All she knew was that Jasper had decided to leave suddenly, no explanation, which was true enough. Obviously that was still all she knew about it, or she'd never have arranged another meeting at Whitebark.

At the end of the bridge he turned north onto the still more clogged Highway 80. Even in the Porsche he had no maneuvering room but had to wait out the crush like everyone else. All the same, there was a half smile on his face as he tapped out time to "Rollin' on the River" on the steering wheel.

He could hardly wait to see how the old farts were going to deal with this.

"Twelve o'clock already?" Nellie looked up from where he was kneeling, his nostrils filled with the sharp, sweet smell of thyme.

"Yes," Frieda said. "You'd better think about getting ready. Here, I've brought some tea."

"I can't believe I've been at this almost two hours," Nellie said, brushing dirt from his thighs. He pushed himself up and winced as his knees unlocked. "Oh, my. On second thought, maybe I can."

He sat gingerly beside Frieda on the stone bench and took the mug she offered. "Ah," he said with pleasure, "just what I needed. What do you think of the plants?"

"They're just lovely. Nellie, I was wondering about something." "About what?"

"About Albert Jasper. About his remains. Don't I remember some problem about what to do with them? Whatever became of them?"

Nellie, who had recovered his customary cheerfulness as he'd worked, grinned. His short gray beard stuck jauntily out. "Ah, well, that's an interesting question. As it turns out, I think we're going to have a little surprise in store for everyone on that score. You too."

"What kind of surprise?" she asked distrustfully.

"If I told you, it wouldn't be one, now would it?" As he gulped tea, Frieda studied him with that over-the-tops-of-her-glasses stare. "I don't like that look on your face."

His eyes opened wider. "Look?" he said predictably.

"I can see that morbid sense of humor glinting away in there," Frieda said.

Nellie drew himself up. "Why, Frieda, what a thing to say."

CHAPTER 2

"Let me get this straight," Julie said, swabbing up cream-cheese dip with a carrot stick. "You want me to use up a week's vacation so I can go listen to a bunch of anthropologists mumble in their beards about the place of Marapithecus in hominid evolution? Like last year in Detroit?"

"That's *Rama*pithecus," Gideon said unwisely. "And those were evolutionary anthropologists. True, they can get a little stuffy. But these are forensic anthropologists. Chardonnay or Chablis?"

"Which one's open?"

"Chardonnay."

"That's what I'll have."

He poured glasses for both of them, the cold wine clucking into the bottoms of the hollow-stemmed glasses, then carried Julie's to her.

"Fancy glasses," she said. "I almost forgot we had them." "Fancy dinner," Gideon told her. "As you'll soon see." Julie was in the living room, browsing through the day's mail, while Gideon worked in the open kitchen, talking to her over the wide counter. Thursday was one of his nights to make dinner, inasmuch as he had only a 10:00 A.M. class, and an easy one at that, while she worked her usual 8:00 to 5:00, winding up with the dreaded weekly staff meeting. Today's, from what she'd told him, had been even more lunatic than usual, and he was happy to see her start to relax.

"Anyway," he said, "forensic anthropologists are a much looser crowd, more lively, more irreverent."

"Oh, I'll bet. I can just imagine all the great 'topics of conversation: handling decomposed remains, time-of death estimates..."

"Well, yes, but it's not all business. A lot of people bring wives and husbands. There'll be plenty of time for taking in the sights and just being lazy. Look, read the letter, will you? The one from Miranda Glass, with the Museum of Natural History letterhead."

Julie foraged in the plate of raw vegetables and came up with a broccoli stalk. Then she fished the letter out of the pile of mail. Behind her, the big bay window looked out onto a wet, somber world. It had been a typical early-May day in Port Angeles, Washington: raw, overcast, and drizzly. The sky at 6:00 P.M. looked exactly the way it had at 8:00 A.M., a featureless and dismal slaty gray. According to the KIRO weather report, it was going to look much the same tomorrow.

"'To Members of the Western Association of Forensic Anthropologists,'" she read aloud. "'Esteemed Fellow Body-Snatchers. June 16-22, the week of our eagerly anticipated bone bash and weenie roast, is fast approaching. As this year's host I hereby bid you a genial welcome.'"

She looked up at him from under lifted eyebrows. "Bone bash and weenie roast? Well, you're certainly right about them not being stuffy."

He smiled. "Miranda's a little more irreverent than most. Read on."

"'Fittingly enough,'" she continued, "'this year's enlightenment and jollification will be held where it all started: the decaying but still scenic Whitebark Lodge near Bend, Oregon. I must tell you that the lodge is not quite what it was ten years ago (who among us is?), but the management promises to do its best. Dinner and continental breakfast will be provided daily, and those of you who wish more variety will find the restaurants of Bend and Sisters just a short drive away. In addition, the general store in nearby Camp Sherman stocks an ample supply of gourmet comestibles (bologna, American cheese, tuna fish), which you may prepare in the privacy of your cottages. As usual, we'll set up a kitty to take care of lunch and beverages so that we are not unnecessarily torn away from our scholarly pursuits. Naturally, potables stronger than Diet Coke are the responsibility of the individual. As always, cocktail hour begins at sunrise.'"

Smiling, she glanced up again. "Maybe I ought to go, just to keep an eye on you. Don't you guys do any work?"

"Sure, we do. Don't let Miranda's style throw you off. We may be informal, but WAFA is a dignified, professional organization, and we work damn hard. Listen." He had come into the living room to get some vegetables and dip for himself, and he took the letter from her, turning to the second page.

"Here. 'Round-table topics will include the adjustment of aging standards in light of today's accelerating maturation rates; race-linked differences in sexual dimorphism; blunt-force skull fractures; and new developments in computerized forensic data nets.'"

"Very impressive."

Gideon accepted this with a magisterial nod. "'In addition, we're trying to scare up an FBI agent or high-level working cop to put on a session on crime-scene do's and don'ts, which, it pains me to say, most of us can sorely use. (Contact me if you know any likely candidates for this. No honorarium, but we'll cover expenses.) As usual, one of our conference highlights will be...'" He coughed and folded up the sheet. "Well, you get the idea."

She snatched it away from him. "'...will be our competition for the wildest, weirdest case of the last ten years. Present the most bizarre, off-the-wall doings you've had the good (?) fortune to be associated with in the last decade. Winner will receive a T-shirt with an appropriate and meaningful WAFA slogan, such as "Ten Years of Beer for Breakfast."'"

Julie nodded soberly. "'Dignified' hardly does you justice."

"Didn't I say it wasn't all business? Forensic work can get pretty grim. You need some comic relief."

"Right," she said, beginning to read aloud again as he went back to the kitchen. "'Another highlight,'" she said hopefully, "'will be the opening, after almost a year of feverish preparation, of the Murder, Mayhem, and Miseries exhibit in the Central Oregon Museum of Natural History. This, as you know, is the country's first permanent, large-scale forensic anthropology exhibit, and if I do say so myself, it's going to knock your socks off!

"'Sunday afternoon is reserved for unwinding, greeting old friends, hoisting a few, and similar intellectual pursuits. In the evening, please plan on being the guests of the museum for an open house and reception. On Monday we roll up our sleeves and get down to business with our first working session. Spouses/lovers/friends/whatever can soak up some rays around the pool, or play tennis, Ping-Pong, or basketball, or go horseback riding or hiking—or, if desperate enough, can always sit in on our sessions.

"'An extra treat this year will be a chuck-wagon breakfast to break up things at midweek. On Thursday morning we'll have a three-mile group horseback ride to a rustic picnic spot where the works—bacon, eggs, coffee, and so forth—will be waiting for us, compliments of the lodge.'"

Julie sipped her wine pensively. "I'll admit, it sounds like fun."

"Of course it does," he said, heartened. "And don't a few days in central Oregon sound good? Blue skies, warm sun, dry air—"

"Not really, thanks."

Naturally not. Raised in the Pacific Northwest, she thrived on the cool mists and lush, wet green of the Olympic Peninsula. So, amazingly enough, did Gideon, a native Southern Californian. All the same, by the time May arrived—after half a year of dark days and endless, drifting gray rain, with two more months of it yet to come—he was ready to bargain away his soul for a few days of hot, flat, cloudless sunshine. It was hard to remember that anyone could feel otherwise.

Glass of wine in hand, she began reading again, then lifted her head as he turned up the heat under some olive oil. "Mm, it's starting to smell good. What are we having, anyway?"

"Rock shrimp with garlic-basil sauce and pine nuts over fettucine."

She was patently impressed. "That sounds wonderful. How long will it be? I'm starving."

"I don't know, I'll see what it says on the can." "No, seriously."

He peered at the recipe and did some quick arithmetic. "Oh, should be no more than half an hour. Say seven o'clock at the latest."

Julie sighed. "Say eight o'clock," she murmured more or less to herself.

Julie was an amazingly fast cook. Her stints in the kitchen were blurred, efficient flurries of activity, with everything seemingly done at the same time. Gideon had a more leisurely approach, slicing, chopping, and arranging things well ahead of time, so he could putter pleasantly through the cooking with his own glass of wine beside him. The result, they both agreed, was that he enjoyed it more, but what took her forty minutes was likely to take him two hours.

"Say seven-thirty," he told her. "Have another carrot stick." He poured her some more wine and went back to cutting basil leaves.

Julie returned to the letter. "'The Annual Albert Evan Jasper Memorial Weenie Roast, Singalong, and Chugalug Contest will begin at its time-hallowed hour of 7:00 P.M., Friday, and end God only knows when.'" She looked at him quizzically. "Do you really have a singalong?"

"Absolutely. It's great fun."

"And a chugalug contest?"

He laughed, dumping the basil into the blender along with some garlic and Parmesan cheese. "Poetic license."

"And who's Albert Evan Jasper? I know the name…"

"One of the pioneering physical anthropologists. A student of Hrdlicka's. He was one of the first ones to really get into forensic work. The whole idea of WAFA came out of a sort of retirement party for him, put on by some of his own ex-students. They all got together at this Whitebark Lodge for a few days and talked forensic anthropology."

"Yes, I've heard these retirement parties can get pretty wild."

He smiled. "I guess some good discussion came out of it, and they decided to expand it and make it an every-other-year thing. I've been to a couple of them so far, and they've been useful. Fun too."

"I gather Jasper himself is dead now?"

Gideon flicked the blender on and off a couple of times.

"Yes, he died right there in Oregon, as a matter of fact. Never got to enjoy his retirement."

"He died at his own retirement party?"

"Well, not exactly *at*, but right after. He was killed in a bus crash on the way to the Portland Airport."

"And now," she said reflectively, "he has an annual weenie roast and chugalug contest named after him. I wonder how he'd feel about that."

"Oh, he was an eccentric old bird. From what I know about him I think he'd have gotten a kick out of it." He dipped a wooden spoon into the basil-garlic mixture, tasted it, and added a few more shavings of Parmesan. "What do you say, Julie? Will you come? It'd be something different for you."

"Gideon, I'd like to, but that third week in June is a real stinker for me. I already have four meetings set up."

"Couldn't you put them off a week? Move them up a week?"

"Impossible, it's quarterly review time."

"What about asking Don to take them for you? You could use some time to relax."

"Would you want me to do that? Slough off my responsibilities?"

Julie was a supervising park ranger at Olympic National Park headquarters, there in Port Angeles. As Gideon well knew, she took her increasingly pressure-laden job seriously.

"No. Yes."

"Thanks, that's helpful."

"Ah, Julie, it's just that—well, I hate being away from you if I can help it. Nine days…"

She softened instantly, leaning forward to put her hand on the back of his. Her black eyes shone. "Well, why didn't you put it like that in the first place, dopey? What was all that stuff about relaxation and sunshine?"

He hunched his shoulders. "I was embarrassed. Mature people aren't supposed to be so damn dependent on other people."

"I couldn't agree more." She tilted her head, smiled. "So do you want to make the flight reservations, or should I?" Gideon laughed. "I'll do it."

He started spooning the basil mixture into the hot olive oil. "You know what I was thinking?" he said over his shoulder.

"What? My God, that smells good."

"I was thinking of asking John if he'd like to do that session on crime-scene do's and don'ts. It'd be fun to have him along, don't you think?"

"John *Lau? Our* John? You're kidding."

"What's wrong with the idea? He's a bona fide FBI agent, isn't he? He's a first-rate cop, and he knows crime-scene procedure—he's sure given me hell when I've messed things up. I think he'd love the chance to tell an audience of professors to watch where they put their feet."

"I think he'd hate it. He can't stand giving lectures. Not that it wouldn't be nice to have him there."

"Oh, I bet I can bring him around."

* * *

"What are you, kidding me? You think I'm gonna stand up and give a speech to a bunch of Ph.D. professors with long gray beards? You're out of your mind."

Gideon smiled into the telephone. "What is it with beards? I'm a Ph.D. professor. Do I have a beard?"

"I'm not doing it, Doc. Find somebody else."

"I'm doing you a favor, John. You're always complaining that forensic types don't understand police work. This is your big chance. You'll have a captive audience."

"No way."

"You can have four hours if you want it."

"Thanks a heap."

"The meeting's not far from Bend."

"Bend?"

"Bend, Oregon."

"What's in Bend, Oregon?"

"Sunshine."

Silence. Gideon waited.

"People ski in Bend, Oregon."

"Only in the winter, John. The climate's high desert. Yesterday's temperature was almost seventy, humidity eighteen percent. Sunny. I checked it in the paper."

What hadn't worked for Julie, Gideon knew, was likely to do the trick for John, a native Hawaiian whose idea of good weather was a July day in Yuma, Arizona. Even Hawaii had been too cool to suit him, and too wet. The FBI, with bureaucratic caprice, had assigned him to Seattle, with its two months of sunshine (in a good year) and ten months of bone-penetrating drizzle.

"We could probably justify two or three days there for you," Gideon said. "You'd be welcome to sit in on the other sessions if you wanted...or you could just lie around the swimming pool."

"Three days?" John said, and Gideon knew it was settled. He could picture John on the other end of the line at his fifth-floor desk in the Federal Building, wistfully looking out on the rainy streets of downtown Seattle and the gloomy, fog-drenched Sound a few blocks away. In a way, Gideon had cheated, or at least stacked the deck; he'd waited a few days before calling, letting a brief spell of relatively tolerable weather pass, until another truly miserable day came along.

"Might be nice," John said. "Who pays?"

"We do. And if you want, I can have a letter sent on WAFA letterhead requesting your services."

"That'd be good. Applewhite would probably let me do it on work time."

"Great, I'll take care of it right now." He started to hang up.

"Wait, wait!"

Gideon brought the receiver back to his ear. "What?"

"Don't *you* sign it, Doc."

"Why not?"

"Because you make Applewhite nervous," John said with his usual candor. "Nothing personal. He just says every time we use you, things get weird."

"I report what I find," Gideon said. "I'm sorry if it makes things difficult for you."

"Hey, don't get mad at me. Applewhite just likes nice simple cases, no complications."

"Well, this isn't a case; this is just a bunch of graybeards getting together to talk about bones, remember?" "Yeah. But all the same, do me a favor, okay?" Gideon sighed, then laughed. "All right, I'll have Miranda Glass sign it, how's that?"

"Fine. Just keep your name out of it altogether, okay? No offense, Doc."

* * *

When it came time to book their airline tickets, they changed their minds and decided to drive. Eight or so hours in a car would be a sort of floating, between-two-places decompression period for Julie, whose job wasn't being made any easier by the usual freezes, cutbacks, and other hysterics that traditionally went along with the federal government's fourth fiscal quarter. They took their time, not that there was any choice in this part of the world. Port Angeles was situated at the very top of Highway 101, where it narrowed to two lanes and looped around the Olympic Peninsula, and you could go either east or west and still wind up in Los Angeles three days later, presuming of course that that was what you wanted to do.

They drove east and then south, skirting the Olympics, down along the Hood Canal, dawdling through sleepy towns built around oyster beds, down past Duckabush and Liliwaup and Dosewallips, none of which looked as if they gave much of a damn about fourth-quarter reallocation problems. They stopped for lunch at Tumwater and did their duty as tourists, touring the brewery and enjoying it.

Then it was out of the mistiness and ferns of the peninsula and onto Highway 5, a genuine freeway, where the country opened up and flattened out. South of Chehalis, Mount St. Helens reared into view, colossal and unmistakable, its scooped-out summit obligingly trailing a monumental, picture-postcard plume of white steam.

They spent the night at a motel in Portland, relishing the quiet sense of adventure that went along with being in a place where no one in the world knew they were. In the morning they stopped in Salem for a late, unhurried breakfast and took the Santiam Pass road up into the Cascades, over the weird, black volcanic crest of the pass itself, and halfway down the wooded eastern slope, covering in three easy hours what had taken the wagon trains ten grueling, dangerous days not so very many years before.

At two o'clock they pulled into the shaded parking area in front of Whitebark Lodge's main building. Miranda's letter had led them to expect a decrepit hulk of a place, and it was true that there were signs of neglect everywhere: forest-brown cottages unpainted for years or possibly decades; ample, once-lush lawns that now looked like goat-cropped meadows, hummocky and dandelion-infested; lavishly planted flower-borders half hidden by weeds; rust-colored algae thriving on the surface of the shallow pond that had been formed by diverting an arm of the creek that ran through the property. But the overall effect was of rustic comfort and rugged Western homeliness, of a relaxed and cordial matron (or better yet a madam), perhaps a little down on her luck right now, but with plenty still going for her.

Their three-room cottage had dust balls in the corners and a curling, soiled flyswatter lying on a windowsill, but there was also a fresh country quilt on the pine bedstead, a reasonably clean kitchen that dated back no further than the fifties, and a massive river-rock fireplace in one corner of the living room. There was thickly shellacked, gleaming, knotty-pine paneling on the wails, the doors, the floors, the cabinets, even the ceilings. Underneath the surface dust, which was easily gotten rid of with a broom from the closet, everything seemed clean, and all in all they thought it was just fine.

As far as Gideon was concerned, the sunshine slanting through the windows as if it were the most natural thing in the world didn't hurt either.

CHAPTER 3

The conference began much like any other. The attendees reported to the conference registration desk, where they picked up their badges (Gideon's said: "HELLO! My name is OLIVER GIDEON"), milled about with the other early arrivals, and renewed old acquaintances.

Among these cronies, there were predictable exclamations of wonderment at the number of new faces to be seen this year, along with fond talk of the old days when forensic anthropology was new and all of its practitioners could have fit—indeed, *had* fit— around a single medium-sized table in a Shakey's Pizza Parlor in Los Angeles. Now you had a hard time finding a familiar face in the mob. Who, went the refrain, were all these people?

In Gideon's case, as in many of the others', it was more than talk. For Gideon, forensic anthropology—the application of knowledge of the human skeleton to situations, homicidal and other, in which bones were all there was to go on—was a sideline; interesting enough on its own merits, but definitely secondary to his interest in hominid evolution, which alone took him to five or six meetings a year. As a result, he'd managed to make only two of the biennial WAFA conferences: the second, with twelve participants, and the third, with twenty. There had been no graduate students attending, and no family members.

This year, sixty-two had signed up, including twenty-one students, and at least a third had brought spouses/lovers/friends/ whatever. They had filled most of the aging lodge.

When Gideon came back with his registration packet the cottage was empty. He found Julie outside, sitting peacefully under a couple of pine trees beside the pond. She was in a bulky wooden lawn chair, her feet up on a second chair and crossed at the ankles, with a paperback Anne Tyler novel on her lap. Swaying branches broke the light that fell on her into shifting, watery shards, as it, an artfully out-of-focus Victorian photograph—all glowing, indistinct highlights and soft outlines; a sweet, sad memory of something loved and lost. His throat suddenly constricted.

She closed the book and looked lazily up at him. "Boy, do I feel relaxed."

He cleared his throat. "Boy, do you look pretty." She smiled. "Kiss," she said, "please."

He knelt and kissed her gently on the mouth. When he moved back, she tipped his head to her again, kissed him again, softly nibbled his lip. "I love you."

"You know," he said huskily, "we have time to—"

"No, we don't. We have to be at a museum reception at five."

"We have time if we hurry."

"Who wants to hurry? I'm free this evening after the reception. How about you?"

"Well, I'm pretty busy, but I'll try and work you in." He kissed her once more, stood up, and took the remaining chair. "Good book?"

"Uh-huh." She stretched, put the book on the table, and pointed at the registration packet. "Anything interesting in there?"

"I doubt it."

But the topmost item proved him wrong: a letter from Nelson Hobert, anthropology chairman at Northern New Mexico and president of the National Society of Forensic Anthropology, WAFA's parent organization. He scanned it silently.

Dear Colleague:

As many of you know, Albert Evan Jasper's prodigious contributions to our field did not end with his death. Dr. Jasper's will provided for the donation of his remains to NSFA, the organization over which he presided for so many years, with the provision that they be used "for the furtherance of knowledge and/or education in the science of human skeletal identification."

Ironically, the particulars of his tragic death made such application problematical, and for ten years his remains were stored while awaiting appropriate disposition. Recently, however, an opportunity to fulfill his wishes presented itself, viz, the installation of a major forensic anthropology exhibit by the Central Oregon Museum of Natural History in Bend.

Contacts with Miranda Glass determined that the exhibit included no material on identification from burned skeletal remains, and that she would welcome those of Dr. Jasper for that purpose. While this would appear to have happily resolved the matter, you will understand that it raised issues of delicacy and taste, particularly in regard to Dr. Jasper's family. Therefore, family approval was requested before taking the matter further.

I am pleased to report that Dr. Jasper's son and executor, Dr. Casper Jasper, has wholeheartedly approved the disposition of his father's remains in this manner, and they were transferred to Bend some two weeks ago. Miranda assures me that they will be permanently installed in time for Sunday's preview reception for WAFA members. As a longtime associate of Albert Evan Jasper, I can assure you that this final outcome of his bequest is fully in line with his wishes.

On behalf of NSFA, welcome to the fifth biennial WAFA conference. I regret that personal business will prevent my arriving until Monday evening, but I look forward to greeting you all then.

"Well, I guess you'd have to say this is pretty interesting," Gideon said, handing it to her.

She had hardly begun to read it when she looked up, frowning. "'Ironically, the particulars of his tragic death made such application problematical...' What does that mean? Didn't you tell me he was killed in a bus crash down here?"

"It means there wasn't much of him left, and what there was was in pretty bad shape. Burned to a crisp, in fact. Him and thirty or forty other people. The bus ran into some kind of fuel truck and pretty much exploded into flames. It was really horrible, I understand. There wasn't much left of anybody."

"How do they know which one was Jasper, then?"

"It wasn't easy. Nellie and the others worked on the victims for days, and they never did positively identify everyone. In Jasper's case, the jawbone and some of the teeth were still left, and they were able to match them up with his old dental charts."

The sounds of cars starting up drifted to them from the parking area in front of the main building. Gideon looked at his watch.

"We probably ought to get going ourselves. Reception starts at five."
He smiled. "You're right, we wouldn't have had time."

Julie glanced at the letter again without getting up. "Nellie
Hobert? The man who wrote this letter actually worked on the
body?"

"They all did. Nellie was one of Jasper's ex-students too; the
very first, I think. He was here at the lodge for the meeting. As I
understand it, they had no idea Jasper was even on that bus. They
didn't know he'd left. In the morning they got a call from the
state police saying there'd been this awful traffic accident, and
could they possibly help identify the dead? Everybody pitched in,
of course, and it was only after they got down to work that they
realized he was probably one of the victims." He stood up. "The
dental records made it definite."

"Yuck."

Gideon shrugged. "It's what forensic anthropologists do."

"I know, but the idea of his own students, people who were
celebrating his retirement with him the day before—handling his
teeth, poking at his bones…" She shivered. "I repeat: yuck."

"Oh, I don't know about that. I've always thought there was
something highly appropriate about a forensic anthropologist
winding up as the subject of a forensic analysis."

"Maybe, but it's highly creepy too. If you ask me, you should be
glad you weren't there."

Gideon couldn't argue with that. Jasper's remains aside, being
up to his elbows in a morgue room full of the ghastly remnants of
people who had been crushed and burned to death a little while
before was an experience he was glad to have missed. He'd had
his share of similar ones, but it wasn't something you got used
to. It wasn't that he didn't enjoy working with bones—nothing
fascinated him more—but the older they were the better he liked
it, with ten thousand years being just about right.

He held out his hand. "Come on, let's get going. I'm sure you
wouldn't want to miss the unveiling. You can read the rest of the
letter in the car."

"I don't know…" she began doubtfully.

"Believe me, with Miranda MC'ing things, there won't be
anything morbid about it."

He was turning their car out of the lodge in the wake of a bus hired for those who didn't have cars, when Julie looked up from the letter with a spluttering laugh. "He named his son *Casper Jasper?*"

"I told you, he was a bit of an oddball."

"Well, I guess he was. *Dr.* Casper Jasper. Is his son an anthropologist too?"

"I think he's an internist."

"Oh, a real doctor."

"Ha," Gideon said, "most amusing. I met him once, you know."

"Casper?"

"Uh-huh. He was still in medical school—I was just out of grad school myself—and his father brought him along to a conference. A big lanky guy, about six-seven; nice enough but a little, well, spacey. Some of us were walking along a street—I think it was in Tucson—and Casper, being as tall as he is, ran smack into one of those metal awning rods in front of a store. Caught him right across the forehead. Very disconcerting."

"I should think so."

"I mean for the rest of us. One second he was talking along with us, chattering away, and the next he was out cold and flat on his back. At first nobody could figure out what happened. The rod was way above everybody else's head."

"What did you do?"

"His father took over, and very efficiently too. Wouldn't let anybody move him until we got an ambulance there to run him in for x-rays. And he was fine. They didn't even keep him overnight." He shook his head. "You should have seen that rod, though."

For most of the short trip to Bend they followed the bus in silence, content to take in the immense views. They were in what Oregonians called the High Country, but dominating the sky to their right was the even higher country of the eastern Cascades: Mount Faith, Mount Hope, and Mount Charity—the wind-scoured, volcanic peaks better known as the Three Sisters, from which the town of Sisters to the north had taken its name. Below and on their left, at the base of the shoulder along which the road traveled, was a totally different landscape: the wheat-gray desert country of central Oregon, seeming to spread out forever, flat and featureless except for dusty, cinder-cone volcanoes and the strange, black, fan-shaped forms that Julie told him were ancient lava flows.

The highway itself traveled through a kind of buffer zone, a pleasing countryside of gnarled junipers, gently rolling rangeland, healthy-looking cows, and occasional ranch houses. Bend itself arrived with a bang. One moment they were in open, unspoiled country, and the next moment Mountain View Mall, an honest-to-God suburban shopping mall, popped up in front of them, right out of the sagebrush, and they were in the city. Highway 20 became Third Street, an undistinguished, trafficky thoroughfare of malls, motels, and all-you-can-eat buffets, varied by an occasional body shop or auto-parts store.

They had lost the bus by now, but Julie had the directions. "Right on Greenwood," she told him. "Follow the signs to the college. Tell me some more about Dr. Jasper—the father, I mean."

"Let's see…I guess the first time I ever saw Albert Evan Jasper was at the AAA meeting in Boston. This was maybe sixteen or seventeen years ago. There was a banquet in one of the hotels, and Jasper was sitting up at the head table with the bigwigs. I was way in the back with the other graduate students. Well, a waiter asked us what kind of a conference it was, and one of the guys at our table said we were phrenologists—we told people's personalities by the bumps on their heads."

"Not that far from the truth," Julie observed.

Gideon lifted an eyebrow in her direction but otherwise ignored this. "Well, the waiter said how about a reading, and my friend told him we were mere students, but if he wanted one from the world's greatest living practitioner, just go up and ask Jasper. So up he marches to the head table. We couldn't hear anything of course, but we could see the waiter talking and Jasper listening with a funny look on his face, just blinking slowly back at him."

Once off Third Street they were back in rural Oregon. They passed the Elks Lodge, complete with a bronze elk on the roof, crossed over the Deschutes River, and went by a little white church that would have been right at home in Vermont. At College Way they turned right to head uphill toward Central Oregon College, where the museum was located.

"And?" Julie prompted.

"And," Gideon said, laughing as he remembered the long-ago scene, "Jasper motions him to bend down, feels his head all over, and gives him a reading, a five-minute one. The waiter was absolutely delighted."

Julie laughed too. "He sounds nice."

"Well…"

"But definitely a character."

"That for sure."

Julie folded the letter, meditatively brushing it against her lips. "I suppose I'm not looking at this the right way, but doesn't this thing tonight strike you as rather…well, macabre? I mean, there's Jasper, identified after his death by his own friends and colleagues—"

"Colleagues," Gideon said. "I don't know about friends. From all I've heard, he really was a hard guy to like."

"All the same, it's pretty grisly. And then ten years later, what's left of him ends up in a glass case right back where he got killed, with the—the exhibit being unveiled right in front of those same colleagues. Brr. That doesn't seem downright gruesome to you?"

Gideon thought it over while he turned into the parking lot beside the low, modern, stained-wood museum building.

"No," he said. "Creepy, yes. Gruesome, no."

* * *

For almost an hour the fifty-odd people had attentively followed a cheerful and outgoing Miranda Glass through the Lucie Kirman Burke wing of the Central Oregon Museum of Natural History, beneath murals of bears and cougars. They had trooped slowly by glass cases illustrating the principles, problems, and oddities of forensic anthropology: skulls punctured with bullet holes, or with axes or arrows still embedded in them; skeletons twisted by rickets or achondroplasia; trephinations, scalpings, beheadings; fractured bones, split bones, crushed bones, cannibalized bones; murder victims from two thousand years ago and from two years ago; pelves, mandibles, vertebrae, and long bones that demonstrated the criteria of aging, sexing, and racing skeletal material.

It was all very well done; eye-catching and grisly enough to grab anyone's attention, but thorough enough to teach something to those who had the patience to look and to read.

But it was in front of one of the least spectacular cases that the group gathered for the longest time: a sparse, gray-black assemblage consisting of half a mandible, the base of a cranium, a few vertebral fragments, and three or four cracked, misshapen long-bone segments, all of them embedded in an irregular mud-colored mass, like a set of fossil relics from the La Brea tar pits. In this case, however, the mass was known to be the melted-down plastic cushioning material from Seat Number 34 of Bus Number 103 of Cascade Transport Lines.

On the wall beside it was a placard coolly detailing the effects of heat on bone and explaining how anthropologists analyzed burnt skeletal material. In small upper-case letters at the bottom were the words, "Bequest of A. E. Jasper."

Gideon had wondered how he would react to the display. He hadn't known Jasper very well, and their limited acquaintance hadn't done much to make him like the older man. A top-notch scientist, certainly, and a legendary wit and iconoclast; but to Gideon the jokes had seemed contrived, the personality beneath them mean and self-centered. Gideon had seen him publicly cut a hapless student to shreds—wittily, to be sure, but the student hadn't looked any happier for that.

Still, how often did you look into a glass case in a museum and see someone you'd shared a pepperoni pizza with? To his great surprise, sudden laughter bubbled up in his throat. He covered his mouth and converted it—unconvincingly, he was sure—to a cough. At the sound, there was a sudden splatter of similarly unpersuasive snuffles and throat clearings. Was it tension relief, the same nervous reaction one saw at funerals? Or simply the freakishness of the situation? Some of these people had known Jasper a lot better than he had. Some of them, as Julie had said, had actually handled and pored over these remains immediately after the bus crash.

Miranda Glass was one of them. He looked up and accidentally caught her eye. She stared fixedly back at him, eyes very wide and on the edge of fluttering, mouth pursed, soft chin tucked in, while her hand went to the nape of her neck to wrap a strand of hair around her index finger. *You bastard, don't make me laugh.* She couldn't have said it more clearly if she'd spoken.

An entertainingly freewheeling woman about fifteen years older than Gideon, with a round, deceptively cherubic face, she'd been a student of Jasper's once, but had never finished her doctorate and never gone on to teach. Instead, she'd drifted into museum work, where she'd established a solid and well-deserved reputation. Although she still served the local police as a forensic consultant, her paramount interest was the museum, and all but the simplest and most unambiguous cases were forwarded to the state medical examiner in Portland for analysis.

An unsettling tendency to say whatever came into her head made some people uncomfortable in her presence. Others, Gideon among them, found Miranda a bracing change of pace; something like being slapped in the face with a palmful of Aqua Velva.

She had successfully fought down her own urge to laugh and was now soberly finishing her reading of the official letter of transmittal from Nellie Hobert. "'...given his very bones to continue in the service of education, to which he so selflessly devoted his life. Surely Albert Evan Jasper would be pleased.'"

There was a spatter of polite applause, after which Miranda added some comments of her own.

"As most of us know. Dr. Jasper was also quite a showman; some might say an exhibitionist." She paused, pushing oversized octagonal glasses up on her nose and managing to look droll doing it. "If you ask me, the man would have died for an opportunity like this."

Those who didn't know Miranda glanced around them for cues on how to respond. Those who knew her laughed, or groaned, or shook their heads.

"In conclusion, folks, you have to admit that this is a pretty appropriate windup for a teacher of anthropology. So, when you get back home, remember us in your wills. There'll always be a place for you in the Central Oregon Museum of Natural History."

The laughter now was more general. "Don't get any ideas," Julie said to Gideon. "I'm not about to be the widow of a museum case, no matter how beautifully laid out."

"Ah, but there are advantages," said the spare, fiftyish man on Julie's other side. "I had a woman once—I speak figuratively, you understand—who donated her husband's skeleton—he'd died under somewhat ambiguous circumstances—to our lab on the condition that she be allowed to visit him monthly. She did, too. We'd pull out the drawer for her and she'd sit down and look at him for a while. We always made sure he was quite attractively displayed. After half an hour she'd leave, always with a sad, thoughtful smile."

Julie's mouth curled downward just a little.

"Personally," the man went on, "I've always been convinced she poisoned him. I suppose she needed the periodic reassurance that he was really dead."

"That's really touching, Leland," Gideon said. "That's a wonderful story."

"But seriously now," the man said, wide-eyed behind heavy, plastic-rimmed glasses. "Surely you wouldn't deny the world the bones of America's Skeleton Detective, the 'Quincy' of the bone labs, the darling of the media?"

Gideon laughed. Leland was Leland. It was the way he was made, and you couldn't take what he said personally.

The pale-eyed, amber-mustached Leland Vernon Roach was another of Jasper's students. Unlike Miranda he'd managed to complete his doctorate, but like her his main interests had strayed from the forensic. In Leland's case they were in the direction of the relatively new science of coprolite analysis—the study of fossilized excrement to determine food content and eating habits.

Once, when Gideon had asked him how it was that he'd gotten into so arcane a subfield, Leland had shrugged. "You happen to like bones," he'd said with his prissy, exquisite diction. "*I* happen to like shit." Gideon still didn't know if he'd meant it to be funny.

Now he clapped the smaller man lightly on the shoulder. "I'll give it some serious thought, Leland," he said. "Assuming I can talk Julie into it."

Julie muttered something as they moved on to the next exhibit with the others.

"What?"

She arranged her mouth to speak with Lelandlike precision.

"Fat," she said, "chance."

CHAPTER 4

Gideon was shaving the next morning, listening to Julie tell him from the shower about her plans for the day—she was driving to the Lava Butte Geological Area south of Bend to talk shop with the head ranger—when the telephone rang.

"Gideon, this is Miranda. Something peculiar's come up. Would you mind skipping the first session today?"

He had glanced at the schedule a few minutes before. The first session was *Recent Developments in Quantitative Microradiography and Histomorphometric Analysis.*

"Um, I think I could manage that," he said. "What's come up?"

"Albert Evan Jasper's disappeared."

It took a second to make any sense at all of this. "I don't—what did you say?"

"His skeleton—it's missing."

"Missing?"

"It's been stolen."

"Stolen?"

Miranda's sigh crackled in his ear. "As wildly enchanting as this conversation is, I need to break it off and make some more calls. I want to get the FMs together. Meet in the lounge in half an hour? I'll have coffee and stuff sent in."

"Yes, sure, be there." He hung up, replaying the brief conversation. Now how the hell could...

"Who was that, Gideon?" Julie called.

"Miranda," he said, walking abstractedly back to the bathroom. He used a towel to dab shaving cream from under his ear. "Jasper's skeleton is missing."

The shower door opened. Julie stuck her head out, looking puzzled. "Missing?"

* * *

"FMs" was shorthand for Founding Members, also sometimes called the Board of Directors, although this last was something of an exaggeration. As scientific organizations went, the Western Association of Forensic Anthropologists was more laid back than most. There were no officers, no formal chair, no standing committees. The people Miranda had gathered were, except for Gideon, simply those ex-students of Albert Evan Jasper who had come together ten years earlier to pay homage to their teacher and talk about their profession. After WAFA had sprouted from this nucleus, what little direction was necessary continued to be handled by this group, largely by default.

There were seven Founding Members. One of the original ones, Ned Ortiz of USC, had died a year earlier and Gideon had accepted an invitation to replace him, but 110 one had bothered to change the FM appellation to something else. Of the six others, only Nellie Hobert, who wouldn't arrive until that evening, wasn't there. The rest were all present in the lounge (the Tack Room, according to a tiny brass plate on the door), a roomy, comfortable, seedy place with well-worn chairs and sofas, roughly finished bookshelves stuffed with glittering rows of Reader's Digest condensed books, and a generally rustic atmosphere (more acres of knotty-pine paneling).

Miranda was in front of the empty fieldstone fireplace, explaining and gesturing. Gideon was in a scarred, cane-backed chair near an open window that let in the piney fragrance that still smelled like perfume to him. Another day, and he wouldn't smell it anymore. Next to him sat Leland Roach, looking like an undernourished turtle with his thin shoulders hunched up and his head pulled in, and giving off his usual aura of complacent disapproval.

Sitting earnestly—and not many people could sit earnestly—on a table in a corner near the television set was Callie Duffer, smoking furiously. A toothy, big-boned woman in her early forties, with wire-coat hanger shoulders and long, restless hands, she was a full professor at Nevada State University and department chair besides. Fidgeting at Miranda's eccentric and rambling recitation, she was clicking one lacquered fingernail against another, making fitful, insectlike snapping sounds. These brought pointed little mustache twitches of annoyance from Leland, to which she appeared oblivious.

More relaxed, if not overly attentive, was the youngest member of the board, Les Zenkovich, who had stationed himself on a decaying leather couch within easy reach of the sweet rolls. With a neck like a tree trunk, a stubbly blond beard, and kinky, receding hair tied into a short ponytail, Les looked more like an amiable, over-the-hill linebacker than a scientist, an effect heightened by the loose tank top and flimsy shorts he wore. His arm muscles bulged, his thickening midsection bulged, everything bulged.

When Gideon had left Northern California State for the University of Washington a few years earlier, it had been Les who was hired to fill in behind him, but the appointment had failed to work out. Academic considerations aside, this was no surprise to Gideon. He couldn't imagine Amanda Righter, the decorous and genteel head of the department, being much taken with Les's view on academic ceremony ("meaningless bullshit"), or the gold stud he wore in his right ear, or his weekend gigs as bass player with a country-western group in Oakland. Even Les's bulginess had probably been an affront to Amanda's well-cultivated sense of proportion. To the relief of all concerned, he had resigned after a year, opening his own consulting business—Golden State Forensic Services—and settling happily into life as an anthropological private eye. He had arrived at the meeting in a red Porsche with a DR BONES license plate.

On the couch next to Les was Harlow Pollard, a fiftyish associate professor from Nevada State. Once he had been Callie's doctoral committee chairman. Now he was her subordinate. Not a comfortable situation for either of them, Gideon imagined.

A gray-faced man who had stomach problems and looked it, Harlow sat perfectly erect, perfectly still, feet flat on the floor and close to each other, knees pressed together, hands on his knees. His anxious, somewhat vague gaze was fixed on Miranda with his familiar blend of misgiving and incomprehension. The total effect was something like that of a worried squirrel trying to make sense of an unfamiliar sound.

It wasn't dimness of mind that was Harlow's problem, or so Gideon had always believed, as much as an almost desperate need to have his facts ordered and classified, with every last ambiguity resolved. When they weren't, he fretted until he got everything straight, which could take a long time.

And what Miranda was telling them was particularly hard going. Sometime between five o'clock and ten o'clock the previous evening, while the museum was closed to the public for the WAFA dinner and reception, the charred partial skeleton of Albert Evan Jasper had disappeared from its case. On his seven-thirty round, the morning guard had discovered that someone had taken out the eight screws holding on the front of the case and removed the bones; an easy task inasmuch as they were wired to their backing, a breadboard-sized rectangle of white Styrofoam that was not itself firmly attached to anything. The case front had then been replaced and loosely attached with two of the screws.

A quick search of the museum this morning had not turned up anything. A more thorough search was now under way, but without much hope. The bones with their Styrofoam base weighed only a pound or so. Break the plastic in half, and they could have fit into an attaché case or a bag and been carted off anywhere.

When she finished, Miranda dropped into a chair. "So, somebody tell me. What's this all about? Where do we go from here?"

"Miranda," Gideon said, "if it didn't get discovered until this morning, how do you know when it happened? Why couldn't it have been after ten last night?"

"No, impossible. That's when we locked up the place. I saw to it myself. And we have a good security system on the doors and windows, and a guard with a dog inside. Nobody got in after ten."

Gideon nodded. "I see. And we know it didn't happen before five, because that's when we were all there in the room looking at it."

"Exactly. It happened between five and ten. Had to."

"Wait a minute," Les said. "If your security system is so great, why didn't the alarm go off when they opened the case?"

"Because there aren't any alarms on the cases. They're just on the doors and windows."

"So, whoever did it, you're telling me all they had to do was unscrew the front of the case and walk away with the bones? I mean, jeez, Louise."

"Don't look so amazed, Les. It's pretty standard in museum

work. In the first place, security costs money, something skeletal collections don't have, and—"

"And in the second," Leland interjected, "why worry, right? After all, who would want to steal a bunch of beat-up old bones?"

Miranda nodded with a wry smile. "That's about it."

The fingernail-clicking, which had gone on all this time, finally ceased. "If you have a night guard," Callie said, "why didn't he notice it was missing last night?"

"Because he didn't know it was supposed to be there. That case has been sitting empty for almost a week. The exhibit only went into it yesterday morning, and nobody told Security about it."

"Now wait, Miranda," Harlow said slowly, "if it happened when you say it did, and the museum was closed to the public, that means that one of us—that is, one of the WAFA people—must be responsible."

Leland raised his eyebrows at Gideon and tapped the side of his head with a forefinger. "Quick," he murmured, "the man is quick."

"Yes, I think we have to accept that, Harlow," Miranda said patiently. "Any one of us who wanted it had the run of the museum. With everybody wandering around chattering during cocktails, anybody could have disappeared for half an hour without being noticed."

"Honestly..." Callie uttered a disbelieving and unhumorous laugh. "Now really...I mean, the question is, who would..."

"No, Callie," Leland interjected. "The question is, *why* anyone would—"

"No," Les said, finishing the last of a raspberry Danish and licking his thumb, "the question is, who gives a shit? Oh, hey, sorry, Leland."

"Really, Les—" Leland began.

Les shrugged him off. "Look, we're not exactly talking about stealing Peking Man here, you know. What we've got here is a prank, no big deal. There was a lot of booze flowing last night. Some of the grad students had a few too many and figured it'd be funny. It is funny, sort of. They'll give it back, don't worry."

"God, I hope you're right," Miranda said.

"Well, I can't agree with Les," Callie said, jerkily grinding out a half-smoked cigarette. "I don't think it's a joke, I think it's a cry."

Leland regarded her sadly, emitting a long, audible sigh. "A cry," he said.

"A cry, a statement. For empowerment, for self-actualization. An appeal to be *noticed,* to be accepted as whole, valid individuals in their own right, not as, quote, students, end quote." She pushed herself heatedly up from the table. "Look, I'm not saying that's what it's about on a conscious level, but on a deeper level, yes. I see it as an attempt to shake up the existing status-role hierarchy, the distribution of power, or rather the nondistribution of power."

Empowerment. Self-actualization. Status-role hierarchy. From somewhere—the sociology department at Nevada? The business school?—Callie had appropriated these and similar terms, and made frequent and ardent use of them. She was reputed to run her own department using fearsome-sounding techniques like sociotechnical systems analysis and instrumented team facilitation. At the last WAFA meeting Gideon had attended, she had conducted a session called "Values Clarification for the Forensic Scientist: A Nonevaluative Simulation." He'd sat through all three hours of it and come away thoroughly baffled.

Generally speaking, he kept well clear of Callie. No matter how impassioned she got, there was always a part of him that hung back, unwilling to buy what she was selling. The jargon might be right, but somehow the behavior didn't quite jibe. And, genuine or not, all that concentrated earnestness could be overwhelming. After a conversation with her he tended to come away drained, while she seemed to go her way with more energy than ever.

"I believe the woman somehow *feeds* on one," Leland had once remarked along similar lines, "like a veritable goddamn vampire."

Her assessment of the theft left them in silence for several seconds. Harlow blinked nervously at her, one finger digging fitfully at a spot below his sternum. Leland stared out the window looking distantly amused. Les grinned more openly.

"Don't you just love it?" he said to Gideon.

"Have the police been notified?" Leland asked.

"Well, that's one of the reasons I wanted to talk to you," Miranda said. She mooched a cigarette from Callie and lit it like someone not overly familiar with the process. A choky little cough when she inhaled confirmed this. "The fact is, I haven't called them yet, and I'm not sure if I should. I think it's just a prank too—"

Callie, drawing deeply on a fresh cigarette, shook her head theatrically.

"—and I think the bones will be returned," Miranda went on. "At least, I'm hoping they are. Well, if that happens, I don't see the point of a lot of publicity and fuss, maybe even a police record for some of the kids."

"Call the police, Miranda," Leland said firmly. "For one thing, they're not 'kids'; they're in their twenties and thirties. For another, putting the fear of God into them just might have a salutary effect, even at this late juncture." Miranda looked uncomfortable.

"No, I just can't agree with that, Leland," Callie said tightly.

"Somehow," Leland said, "I fail to be astonished."

Callie flushed but said nothing. Unlike the others, Callie let Leland get under her skin. An ability to take things with a grain of salt was not one of her strong points.

"Come on, give them a chance to return them on their own," Les said. He scratched his short beard. Biceps bulged. "Come on, guys, let's be honest: we all did things just as dumb when we were going to school."

"I most certainly did not," Leland said.

Les grinned at him. "Hey, I believe you, Leland."

"Is there any insurance involved?" Gideon asked.

"No," Miranda said. "Just on the cases, not the contents."

He nodded, unsurprised. *Objets d'anthropologie* were not quite the same as *objets d'art*. What was the market value on a bunch of burned or otherwise mutilated human bones? What was the estimated replacement cost? And if you could arrive at one, just how would you go about replacing them?

"I'll tell you what's really worrying me," Miranda said. "What's the museum board going to say? And what about Jasper's family, for God's sake?"

"Ah," Leland said, "the estimable Casper Jasper, et al."

"As long as you're worrying," Callie said, "don't forget about Nellie Hobert. He'll have kittens when he hears."

"Gadzooks," Miranda said. "I hadn't even thought about Nellie.

Here he keeps the bones safe for ten years, gives them to us, and we lose them in exactly one day."

"Nellie Hobert's a good guy. He's not going to make a fuss," Les said, an assessment with which Gideon agreed. "And he's not going to blame you, Miranda." He wiped his fingers on a paper napkin and tossed it on the low table. "Look, why don't we do this: announce to everyone that a joke's a joke, but the bones have to come back. Tell them they have, say, two days to get them back to the museum, with no questions asked. If they're not back by then, the cops get called in."

After a few minutes' discussion this sensible recommendation was agreed to by everyone; somewhat reluctantly in Leland's case.

"All right," Miranda said, "at the ten-thirty break I'll make a general announcement about the theft and about what we've agreed to here. I just hope it all works out."

"I was thinking," Callie said, picking a shred of tobacco from the tip of her tongue. "It might help if I set up some voluntary encounter sessions this afternoon—give them an opportunity for some venting and catharsis. I'll facilitate," she added unnecessarily.

"Oh, do," Leland said. "If *that* doesn't do the trick, nothing will."

"Drop dead, Leland," Callie said.

* * *

John Lau arrived late that afternoon, delighted with the sunshine and glad to be out of Seattle. ("You want to guess what it was doing when I left?") He had dinner in the lodge dining room with Julie, Gideon, and the founding members, where the talk was mostly about the missing bones. John listened with the look of a man who didn't quite believe what he was hearing but was willing to be a sport and go along with it.

"Bone-napping," he mused gravely over apple cobbler. "I'd really like to help out, folks, but I don't think it's a federal crime. Unless," he added, as a smile finally broke through, "they cart the stuff across state lines."

Les laughed. "Hey, Callie, how'd the encounter group go? Anybody 'fess up?"

Callie had just lit up. She exhaled noisily, lower lip extended to blow the smoke upward, and shook her head. "How many showed up?"

"Well, there wasn't much lead time, and people had already made other plans—"

"How many? Three? Four? Anybody?"

"Three," Callie muttered.

"Plenty of venting and catharsis, though, I bet."

"No," she said defensively, "as a matter of fact there wasn't. You can't expect miracles at a first session. We're talking about counterintuitive risk-taking behavior here, and you can't build a conducive climate for that in a couple of hours. It takes time to establish new interactive norms."

Leland regarded her with open distaste. "I hate to change the subject," he said, "but need I remind anyone that the evening is slipping away? Are we going to play poker, or are we not? There are traditions to be upheld here."

John turned to Gideon, surprised. "You people play poker?"

Gideon laughed. "Do birds eat worms?"

John surveyed the table of academics with undisguised avidity. "For money?"

Miranda, on John's other side, waggled her eyebrows at him. "Care to join us, young man?"

"I wouldn't want to horn in."

"The more the merrier. You too, Julie."

"Well—sure," she said, then whispered to Gideon: "Will you make me one of those charts?"

"What charts?"

"You know, that shows which hand beats which hand." "Why do I foresee disaster here?" Gideon said. "Harlow, we'll use your cottage," Leland announced. Harlow hesitated. "I don't know, Leland. I think I'll sit this one out."

"Nonsense," Leland told him. "We don't want to keep other people up all night, and you have the most out-of-the-way cottage. Besides, I lust after your money." Leland had had a few glasses of wine by this time.

Harlow smiled wanly. "Couldn't I just give you ten dollars right now?"

"That," said Leland, "wouldn't be sporting."

CHAPTER 5

"Whuff," Gideon said, holding out his cup.

Julie refilled it for him from the ancient percolator. Making morning coffee was generally his job, but Julie had wisely quit the poker session early and been in bed by midnight. She'd won $9.50 too, which had mildly irritated him at the time, but in the end it made up for most of his losses. Leland, as usual, had been the big winner. Gideon had finally figured out why he was always so successful. With that perpetually joyless expression on his face, you couldn't help thinking that *this* time his cards really were awful.

"I just hope none of the students were trying to find somebody to confess to last night," she said. "All the professors were holed up in Harlow's cottage gambling and boozing until three in the morning."

"Two."

"Three. You woke me up when you came in. You were quite cheerful at the time. Playful, too, although I must say that didn't amount to anything."

"Don't remind me."

"Are you very hung over?" she asked sympathetically.

"No, I don't think so," he said, yawning. The coffee was beginning to clear his head. "I could've used a little more sleep, though."

"Well, I should think so." She leaned her elbows on the little dining-room table, holding her cup in both hands. "Gideon, maybe I'm getting paranoid from living with you too long, but the whole thing sounds fishy to me."

He scratched his cheek, playing her words back. "I think I missed something."

"What happened to Jasper's...remains, or whatever you want to call them. Why are you all so ready to assume it's just a student lark?"

"What else?"

"Wouldn't they have left a note or something to show it was a joke? They wouldn't leave you all worrying about what happened to the bones. No, I think there's more to it than that. I think somebody might not want them out there in full view with dozens of professional anthropologists peering at them."

"You are getting paranoid." He yawned again, sipped some more coffee, and shuddered. Percolators certainly made a powerful brew; you had to say that for them. "Or do you know something I don't?"

"Maybe one of you—one of your friends, I mean—liked it better when they were out of sight in a drawer somewhere. Maybe somebody has something to hide."

"Like what?"

"Like maybe Jasper wasn't killed in that bus crash."

Ah, he'd wondered if that was where she was heading. "That's Jasper, all right, Julie. Teeth are like fingerprints; when you get a match, it's a match. Besides, five highly competent anthropologists worked on that crash, and they don't come any better than Nellie Hobert—"

She was shaking her head. "No, no, I'm not suggesting it wasn't him, I'm suggesting maybe he didn't die in the crash. Maybe—who knows?—maybe he was already dead when it happened, and someone's afraid one of you bigwig experts will be able to tell it from the skeleton."

Gideon looked wryly at her. "That would have made getting on the bus a little tricky, wouldn't it?"

After a second she smiled. "Well, I didn't say I'd figured it all the way out. But I don't think you have either. I'm just surprised to see you jumping to conclusions, that's all. That's not like you."

"Well, maybe you're right."

"But you don't think I am."

"No, I think it was just some of the kids."

"Well, maybe *you're* right." She stood up. "Let's talk about something important. Any chance you can break away this morning for a short horseback ride?"

"Well, I hate to miss the sessions."

"We ought to get our muscles limbered up for Thursday."

"Thursday? Oh, God, the trail-ride chuck-wagon breakfast."

"You'll love it."

"I don't know, I'm a city boy. Getting on a horse makes me nervous. They're too damn high."

"Now look, you. I'm taking vacation time so we can be together and have fun and relax, and that means—"

"That I'm going on a horseback ride. Yes, ma'am."

"All right, then. I'll let you off this morning, though." She leaned over to kiss his cheek and winced. "Ouch. Take a shave, will you? Then let's go get some breakfast, I'm starving."

They got to the breakfast buffet at seven-thirty, drank some orange juice and some more coffee, and on Gideon's suggestion carried their plates of fried eggs, hash browns, and biscuits outside to look for a place to enjoy the slanting, high-country sunlight for a while. They had the grounds to themselves, the other attendees preferring to eat inside. Most of them were from the Southwest; catching up on sunshine was not one of their priorities.

They found a reasonably comfortable low wall—actually part of the rock-and-mortar foundation of an old building that had once stood there in a grove of ponderosa pine—looking out over the near-deserted road to a broad meadow with a few fat cows grazing in it. Happily vacant of mind (was there anything that made one more contentedly empty-headed than watching cows?), Gideon ate his breakfast enjoying Julie's quiet company and relishing the morning sun's warmth on the back of his neck. He could feel it, with pleasure, on the rims of his ears. It had been a long winter on Puget Sound.

After a pleasantly indeterminate time they looked around to see Nelson Hobert come tramping ebulliently up the path, arms pumping, wearing a T-shirt that said: "Young at heart, other parts a little older." Red bermuda shorts displayed lumpy knees and squat, bowed calves. With him were a group of half-a-dozen people, including three of his students from Nevada State, extraordinarily attractive females in their twenties, trailing behind him in a row. Gideon smiled, remembering something that a frankly admiring Les Zenkovich had once said: "I think the old geezer imprints them, you know? Like ducklings."

Despite his being five-foot-five, bald, potbellied, billygoat-bearded, and unashamedly into his sixties, Nellie Hobert had a remarkable knack for attracting a steady stream of worshipful and attractive young women students. To his colleagues (and to Nellie himself, Gideon thought) it was a source of wonder and amusement; to some of the more predatory among them a source of envy. Hobert's harem, they called them, which pleased Nellie immensely, patently unpredatory though he was.

Not that he didn't glow when surrounded by those fresh and adoring faces. Who wouldn't?

Nellie had arrived the previous evening, accompanied as always by his wife, Frieda. Tired from a long day, he had nevertheless joined the poker party at about ten and stayed almost to the bitter end. An enthusiastic but hopeless card player, he had contributed handsomely and without complaint to Leland's profits. And as Gideon had known he would, he'd taken the news of Jasper's disappearance in his stride.

"The old boy just won't stop making waves, will he?" had been his comment once he'd gotten over the initial shock. "Well, don't worry about it," he'd generously told Miranda, "we'll get the old crock back. Who'd want to keep him?" Julie had taken to him at once.

"Good morning, Julie, Gideon!" he called now. "Guess what! Meredith here has spotted what she thinks are some cremains on the National Forest trail along the meadow. We're going out to have a quick look before things get going. Care to come?"

"Cremains?" Julie repeated.

"Cremated remains," Nellie said.

"*Human* remains?"

"Yes, but don't excite yourself. We're talking about ordinary, legal funerary cremations. People scatter the ashes everywhere, you know. Want to see?"

She jumped up. "Sure! Gideon?"

He declined with a wave. "Go have fun. I'll pass."

For one thing, it felt too good to sit without moving in the warm high-country air. For another, as Nellie had said, the finding of cremated remains—Gideon still resisted calling them cremains, but it was a losing battle—had become an everyday occurrence. Regardless of laws to the contrary, people were always emptying urns filled with white ashes and chalky fragments in scenic areas—deserts, mountains, beaches, parks. He'd come across two in the past year himself: one in Mount Rainier National Park, the other near a dig on a beach along Washington's wild Olympic Peninsula. No doubt, if he was in the habit of keeping his eyes on the ground when he walked, he'd have spotted more. Even the police shrugged them off these days.

Still, it was good for the students to know what they looked like—Julie too, being a park ranger—and Nellie, more power to him, never passed up a chance to teach anybody about anything, even after forty years as a professor.

As they left, Gideon mopped up the last of the egg with his biscuit and looked around him. Many of the resort's outlying buildings had been razed, mostly in the last few years from the look of them, and in the fall the rest would come down. Not that the owners were hurting. The manager had explained that the lodge was being bulldozed out of existence, older, unused structures first, in preparation for its transformation by a developer. Somehow, what had once been an out-of-the-way tract of useless meadows and woods had become two hundred acres of prime country land in the booming resort district west of Sisters. By next year at this time, the rambling, aging lodge would have metamorphosed into "Witch's Butte Estates, Forty Prestige Ranchettes in Central Oregon's Newest and Most Exclusive Golfing Community."

Well, things changed. The departed building whose foundations he was sitting on now, for example; it had been older than the lodge itself, dating back to the time when there had been a working ranch here. The rough old rock-and-mortar foundation suggested this, as well as some photographs that were in a scrapbook in the lounge. They had been taken in the sixties and they showed this structure as one of several ramshackle, tottery old sheds crammed with moldering, ancient ranch equipment, long disused. Black, split yokes and harnesses, and rusty, spiked implements of metal, sinister and inscrutable. All gone now.

He yawned, stretched, and got up, his eyes roving instinctively over the ground. The building had been almost a hundred years old, more than enough to spark his anthropologist's curiosity. Not much to see, though. No intriguing bits of history poking up out of the soil. The floor of the shack, once probably hard-packed earth, had reverted to a softer soil, covered with pine needles and dotted with spindly tufts of rabbit brush, little different now from the surrounding countryside.

Still, as always, there were a few things. The scraping off of the topsoil by the bulldozer along one side had revealed the ghostly vestiges of a row of postholes running diagonally through the building. So there had been an even earlier structure here, perhaps from Indian or pioneer days. Well, that was mildly interesting, he thought lazily, squatting down to take a better look.

But there wasn't much to see. The darker soil of the filled-in postholes disappeared into a nest of straggling brush growing out of the corner of the foundation. Without getting up, he turned on the balls of his feet to see if he could tell where they met the other corner of the foundation. Abruptly, the ground gave way beneath his left foot. He managed to keep from tumbling over by grabbing for the foundation, and as he did so he realized that he had been squatting on the very edge of a depression, the rim of which had crumbled under his weight.

More interested now, he pulled the trailing brush out of the way, tucking the branches into the irregular rocks of the foundation. And there, just inside what had once been the wall of the shack, was a...was a what? He got up and stood for almost a full minute, hands on his hips, staring intensely at the ground.

At his feet was a flat, shallow trench, roughly oval, about four feet long, three feet across at its widest, and two or three inches deep, scantily grown over with strawlike grasses. The sides had mostly collapsed, but here and there they could still be seen; vertical, now disintegrating walls with convex rims, like the top of an old-fashioned bathtub. Less apparent, but still noticeable—if one knew to look for it—was a smaller depression within the outlines of the first, a slight sinking of the soil, as if someone had scooped out a few more handfuls of dirt from the middle of the larger cavity.

A historical archaeologist must have guessed he was looking at the filled-in entrance to a root cellar. A casual visitor might have guessed, if at all, at hidden treasure.

A forensic anthropologist didn't have to guess. Gideon hunkered down again, elbows on his knees to examine it more closely. In the profession, this was what was routinely referred to as a soil-compaction site, a nice bland term that might have had to do with something comfortable and homely, like composting techniques or solid-waste landfills. But it didn't. A soil-compaction site was what you eventually got when you buried a body and tried to leave the ground looking the way it had before, with no mound to give it away. And that, ninety-nine times out of a hundred, meant homicide.

The larger depression was the result of the dug-up, redeposited soil slowly settling; it happened when you dug a grave, it happened when you planted a rosebush. The convex rim resulted from excess soil on the edges of the hole. The smaller sunken area in the center, and this is what gave it inescapably away, was a "secondary depression"—another one of those nice neutral terms—which typically formed a few weeks after burial, when the abdominal cavity bloated, burst, and finally decomposed, allowing the soil above to sink down into it.

The body, he guessed, was about two feet below the surface. Any shallower than that, and the decomposing tissues would have provided a burst of organic fertilizer to the root zone, making the plant growth above it noticeably denser, which it wasn't. And it wasn't much deeper than two feet, because they never were. People disposing surreptitiously of unwanted corpses didn't like to spend any more time digging than they had to. You didn't find neat, rectangular six-foot-deep graves in places like this. Generally they were a foot or two deep—enough to cover them over with a few inches of soil—and no roomier than they absolutely had to be.

Gideon guessed that the body inside would be folded into the smallest possible bundle, which was on its side, arms and legs pulled up. Years ago, archaeology texts had offered various ingenious theories as to the religious reasons prehistoric people so often buried their dead in the fetal position. Now, forensic anthropology had provided a simpler, more likely explanation: It was the fastest, easiest way to get somebody into the ground and covered up.

He looked up, at the sound of Nelson Hobert's rattling laugh. Nellie had dropped off Julie and the students somewhere and was on his way to the meeting room for the first session of the day, telling Harlow Pollard about the cremains and waving the last of a glazed donut for emphasis.

"There are *two* sets of cremains out there," he announced, "probably more. It's a pretty site, that's why. The stream, the meadows. One's a classic sling-and-fling job—are you familiar with Willey's typology?—the other's a pump-and-dump..."

He saw Gideon squatting by the side of the trench. "Gideon, Julie's gone riding. She'll see you at—ha, what do we have here?"

Gideon stood up and moved out of the way. "Have a look."

Nellie clambered over the foundation. "Oh, dear," he said with sharp interest. He poked the rest of the donut into his mouth and leaned over from the waist, hands on bare, hairy knees. "Well, well." After a moment he slapped his thighs and straightened up, eyes bright. "By cracky, look what we have here."

"What is it?" Harlow asked, hanging back. "Soil-compaction site."

"Soil-compaction site?" Harlow was one of the more narrowly trained people at the meeting. Although a de-greed physical anthropologist, he had made odontology his specialty long ago, as a graduate student. Now he was one of the best when it came to teeth, but he had little familiarity with burial sites or crime scenes. His specimens came to him, he didn't go to them.

"There's a body under there," Nellie said happily. "A body?"

"A homicide," Gideon said. "You can bet on it." Harlow looked from one of them to the other. "A *homicide?*"

"Yes, a homicide," Nellie said through square brown teeth. "For Christ's sakes, Harlow!"

"A homicide," Harlow repeated dimly. "You mean a human body?"

Nellie let his breath out. Like many good teachers, he was endlessly patient with his students, but testy with others whose minds didn't move quickly enough to meet his standards. "The last I heard," he said dryly, "human bodies were the only kind you could commit homicide on."

"But that's—no, I don't—why would—"

Gideon gently intervened, explaining about soil-compaction sites. Not that he expected it to do much good. Explaining something to Harlow could be like talking to a tree. He listened quietly but it was hard to say how much got through.

"All right then," he said, "it very well might be a burial..."

But, thought Gideon.

"—but why in the world would you want to say it's human? Anyone could have buried a dog here, or a goat…"

"A *goat!*" Nellie exclaimed, his cheeks reddening. "What kind of a damn fool—"

"True, Harlow, it could be anything," Miranda Glass said kindly. With eight or nine others she had drifted over. "It'll have to be dug up to know for sure. But I will bet you dollars to dumplings that by tonight there's going to be a set of Homo sapiens choppers for you to do your stuff on."

Harlow shook his head emphatically. "Not me. I have to catch a three o'clock plane; Callie and I both. We have to go back to Carson City. The biological sciences curriculum committee meets tomorrow morning."

"You're leaving early?" Miranda said with a groan. "What about your odontology round table Thursday? Christ, Harlow, if I have to revise the whole schedule I'll kill myself."

"No, no, we'll be back early Thursday morning. I'll do the session, all right." Harlow seemed tense and distracted, the way he got when his stomach acted up. "Didn't I say I would?"

Nellie cleared his throat, impatient with the diversion.

"Now then," he said, very much in authority despite his T-shirt and lumpy knees, "the police have to be notified. Miranda—"

"The police—!" Harlow exclaimed.

"Miranda," Nellie continued, "I assume they know you around here, so you're probably the best one to call them."

"Right," Miranda said, starting for the main building. After a few steps she stopped and turned back with one of her rosy smiles. "This is going to be a switch. *They* usually call *us* about mysterious bodies in shallow graves."

CHAPTER 6

Twenty minutes later, a white, brown-striped Chevrolet with a Deschutes County Sheriff's Office emblem on the door pulled into the main parking area. By this time, there were fifty people milling about the burial site, the attendees having decided with the briefest consideration that being in on the start of an actual exhumation beat all hell out of the scheduled morning session on bilateral nonmetric cranial variation.

Deputy Debbie Chavez, skinny and weather-bitten, walked with a cop's confident lope and seemed very much at home in her uniform of brown shirt, snug tan trousers, and boots.

"All right, folks," she said after talking briefly to Miranda, "here's the drill." She swung around so the sun was behind her, took off her sunglasses, and stuck them under the flap of a shirt pocket. Gideon heard them click against her plastic chest-protector. An unexpected dusting of little-girl's freckles flowed over the bridge of her nose and along the untanned skin under her eyes.

"First off, if Mrs. Glass here says we've got a body down there, that's good enough for me."

"It was the consensus," Miranda said modestly.

"Whatever. So what I'm going to do is get on the horn and call the sergeant. Till he gets here, I'm going to seal the area, and I'd appreciate it if you people wouldn't do any more tromping around here."

"We're not *tromping*, young woman," Leland Roach said. "For your information, we happen to be forensic anthropologists— which means we are quite experienced in just this kind of thing— and we're thoroughly familiar with crime-scene protocol."

"Uh-huh," the deputy said, looking down at the muddle of scuff marks and footprints—Gideon could see his own—around the oval depression. "You betcha."

She was right, Gideon knew. They hadn't been thinking. As soon as the soil-compaction site had been recognized for what it was, they should have kept everyone away. It was sheer luck that no one had stepped right *in* the thing. Well, at least John would have an attentive audience when he gave his session.

Nellie Hobert cleared his throat. "True, we may have been a little careless, deputy. On the other hand, this site's obviously been out in the open for years. I can't imagine we've ruined any evidence. Ahum."

Nellie was embarrassed. He was one of the country's two or three leading authorities on crime-scene exhumations. His *Exhumation Techniques* had been a police-science standby for over a decade, and it came down mercilessly on careless tromping.

"Well, all the same, I just think I'll go ahead and secure the area," Debbie Chavez said pleasantly. "Sergeant likes it that way. Why don't y'all just go about your business and come back in an hour if you want to?" She smiled, a quick up-and-down jog of the corners of her mouth. "We could maybe use a few experts about then."

* * *

By 9:00 A.M. the excavating operation was humming along like a demonstration out of Nellie's manual. Ordinarily, forensic anthropologists take care not to intrude on each other's territory, but in this case Miranda had readily deferred to Nellie's status and experience, and the NSFA president, with a shapeless tan fishing hat on his bald head and a stubby, unlit pipe between his teeth, was atoning for his earlier sins of carelessness with a vengeance, directing Deputy Chavez, another deputy, and several anthropology students with equal vigor.

A thirty-by-thirty-foot square had been cordoned off with yellow plastic tape and gridded. The "artifactual material" on the surface—a couple of rusty bolts, a corroded paper clip, the worn rubber heel of an old shoe, none of which anybody really thought would amount to anything—had been staked with engineering pins, mapped, and photographed from every conceivable angle, then gathered up by Dan Bell, the sheriff's evidence officer. A crime-scene log had been established, and a line of entry had been delineated from the perimeter to the suspect depression. By means of this narrow path, those very few people permitted to enter made their way in—but not before having the patterns on the soles of their shoes recorded by Deputy Chavez.

Nellie himself had deftly exposed the edges of the pit with a whisk broom, and the digging itself was now under way, being carried out by two earnest graduate students under Nellie's exacting supervision and the close attention of the forty or fifty people who now ringed the cordoned-off area.

John Lau had slept late, as he'd said he would, barely getting in on the dregs of the buffet. Then, seeing the crowd, he'd wandered over just as things had gotten started, looking mopey and preoccupied.

"That Leland's like a shark," he grumbled at Gideon. Gideon laughed. "How much did you wind up losing?" "Eighteen bucks." He shook his head. "I still don't think he had that flush. I should have stayed in."

"Cheer up, John. Look at that sun. It's supposed to be ninety today. Enjoy yourself."

"How can I enjoy myself when I've got that session tomorrow?" He sighed. "I wish it was today, so I could get it over with."

Sleepily, he looked around at the activity. "What's this, a practice dig?" Then he saw the police uniforms and the POLICE LINE DO NOT CROSS tape and his eyes opened all the way. "Hey, what's going on, Doc?"

"It's a burial. At least I think it is." He'd begun to feel less sure of himself. The police activity, the excitement, had made him edgy. If there wasn't a body there after all this fuss, he was going to look awfully silly. Leland was probably preparing one of his juicier little epigrams right now, just in case it was needed.

"How do they know?" John asked.

"Well, it just looked to me like a classic—"

John tilted his head toward him. "You're the one who found it?"

"Yes, why?"

"No reason," John said. "Just asking."

"Look, John," Gideon said a little tartly. "I didn't go looking for the damn thing. I practically fell into it, over there—"

"While minding your own business..."

"Well...yes, damn it—" He laughed. "Sorry, I guess I'm starting to get nervous. Maybe I was wrong about it."

"We'll find out pretty soon," John said sagely.

A few minutes later Nellie took a break and walked over to chat. "How are we doing here, John?"

"You're doing great," John said. "I don't know why you guys want a lecture from me."

Nellie beamed. "Well, it always has more weight coming from someone outside the fold. Besides, you should have seen us an hour ago."

"Nellie," Gideon said, "does it still look to you like there's a body in there?"

"Oh, sure, no doubt about it, none at all."

Gideon was reassured.

At a little after ten o'clock Julie returned from her ride. "What in the world is this all about?" she asked. She looked wonderful, tousled and healthy, and she smelled of horses.

Briefly, Gideon explained.

"How did anybody even think to look for a burial here?" she wanted to know. "Who found it in the first place?" "Guess," John said.

Julie laughed. "That's what I thought. Well, I better go get cleaned up."

But she stayed where she was, engrossed by the scene. "Uh, if they do find a body, it'll just be dry bones, won't it? Not some kind of awful, messy...you know."

"Let us fervently hope so," Gideon said sincerely. "It's been there a while, so I think decomposition is long past. If not, you'll smell it before you see it."

But the only smells were clean ones: pine needles and pine bark, sweet and spicy, and the coarse, dry soil. It hadn't rained for weeks, so with each scoop of the trowel a puff of red-brown dust rose and floated off. Gideon could feel it in his nostrils and at the back of his throat. Above, through the branches, the sky was enormous and beautiful, a clean, washed-out blue, marred only by the occasional silent, bright speck of a jet plane floating by. As predicted, the temperature had risen rapidly, and the humidity with it, but they were still in dappled shade. Even the diggers had hardly worked up a sweat. It was all very pleasant and unhurried, more like an archaeological dig than a forensic exhumation.

And Gideon had stopped worrying about whether they'd find

anything. What if they didn't? He'd been wrong before, and he'd be wrong again. So had all of them, and everyone was accustomed to it. That, in fact, was one of the healthiest things about forensic anthropology; its practitioners were willing to be proven wrong. They had to be. It was an applied science, and your hypotheses and guesses were always being put to practical tests. And since nobody could be right all the time, people either learned to live with being wrong or they got out of the field.

Nothing like theoretical anthropology, where scholars could barricade themselves behind unverifiable pet theories for decades, ready to fight off dissenters with an old broom handle if need be. Who, after all, could prove one way or the other whether Neanderthal Man walked fully erect, or if Oreopithecus was a hominid ancestor or just another Miocene ape?

But in forensic work, either a particular bone you examined was female or it wasn't, was Caucasian or it wasn't. And if you said a distinctive conformation of the soil meant that a body was buried under it, either a body would be there or it wouldn't.

It was. At eleven o'clock one of the students, using the trowel in the Hobert-sanctioned manner, horizontally scraping off about a few inches of soil at a time, caught the tip in a bit of tattered gray clothing. The rotted cloth tore, but not before dragging a bit of bone to the surface.

"Ha!" Nellie said, and Gideon was relieved in spite of himself.

Nellie dropped to his knees and leaned over to peer at the fragment through his bifocals, his stiff gray beard fixed on it like a pointer's snout. There was a surge against the tape as anthropologists and student anthropologists jostled forward. Everyone seemed to be in a jolly mood. From the point of view of the attendees this was turning into quite a conference; one that would surely take its place in WAFA legend.

"This must be a new experience for you," Julie said. "Bones coming up out of the ground, and you can't do anything but watch from behind a barrier, just like the rest of us."

"It's awful," Gideon agreed. They were about fifteen feet from the digging. "I can't even make out what the hell it is. A bit of fibula? No, ulna."

Nellie was sympathetic to his colleagues' plight. Still on his knees, he straightened up, took the unlit pipe from his mouth, and made a terse announcement. "Proximal left ulna. And…" He leaned down again to blow away some soil. "…medial epicondyle of the humerus. Disarticulated but in anatomical apposition. Quite dessicated. Good condition." He stretched out his hand without looking up. "Chopsticks."

Julie turned to Gideon. "What?"

"A left elbow joint, without any soft tissue—"

"Come on, Gideon, I can understand that. But didn't he say—"

"Chopsticks. He was talking to one of the students. When you get near the bones, you don't want to dig with anything metal, even a trowel. Nellie favors slightly sharpened chopsticks. He sent someone out for a few a little while ago. Also some small paintbrushes to use for whisks."

"Chopsticks," Julie repeated. "Do you use them too?"

"Yes, I do. Sometimes a piece of bamboo. A dental pick, if nothing else works."

"How odd," she murmured. "All those times you've gone running off to dig up some murder victim in the woods the last thing I pictured was you poking around with chopsticks, like a man in pursuit of an egg roll."

He grimaced. "Well, not quite."

Nellie's probing, assisted by follow-up whisking by the students, was producing quick results in the loosely packed soil. Every few minutes his head would come up again. "Coracoid process," he announced. "Acromion…Left iliac crest…Male, on his right side, legs sharply flexed…Fine condition, just beautiful…"

He was, of course, going about it right, not just digging away at it, but first clearing the surrounding dirt a few vertical inches at a time. This the students would do with trowels, so that the skeleton, embedded in its matrix of soil, slowly emerged, mummylike, on its own pedestal of earth. As it did, Nellie would carefully go to work with his chopsticks, in effect dissecting out the skeleton.

By this time, many of the nonanthropologists had drifted away, Julie among them. "I smell like a horse," she said. "I want to take a shower before lunch."

Gideon nodded, absorbed in the digging. Nellie had made a preliminary determination as the bones came into view: Caucasian male of middle size, over forty, under seventy. No sign of cause of death. Finer distinctions would have to await removal and cleaning.

A little before noon, a rumpled, bearlike man with a pouchy, anxious face made his way toward Gideon and John.

"Dr. Hobert there tells me you're FBI," he said to John.

This, they knew, was Sheriff's Lieutenant Farrell Honeyman, who had arrived several hours earlier to supervise the investigation. "Oh, boy, this is all I need," had been his very first words, murmured despairingly at Deputy Chavez as he climbed out of his car.

They had not made a favorable initial impression on John, who had been standing nearby with Gideon. "That's Homicide?" he'd said under his breath. "Good luck."

Gideon shared his reservations. The crestfallen Honeyman, with his baggy suit and his face like a plate of runny scrambled eggs, had stood off to the side of the grave for most of the morning, uncommunicative and abstracted. In addition to repeated forlorn sighs, there were frequent glances at his watch and various other signs that he was a man of many worries. He had briefly questioned Gideon about the finding of the site, but even then his mind had seemed to be elsewhere.

But now, having found a colleague, he had perked up, at least to the extent of becoming more talkative. "God, I'm up to my earlobes," he told John. "I have a multi-team interagency task-force meeting coming up this afternoon. This is the last thing I need."

"What's up, lieutenant?" John said, ready with sympathy for a fellow cop's caseload problems. "Drug bust going down?"

"Drug bust?" Honeyman answered, his droopy eyes widening. "No, I'm talking budget restructuring, personnel reallocation, the whole schmeer."

"Oh," John said after a fractional pause.

"I'm the administrative lieutenant," Honeyman explained. "Our detective sergeant's on vacation. He's really screwed me. I'm telling you, John, I'm really glad you're here. If you've got any ideas, I wish you'd just pitch right in."

"Oh, I'm sure you can handle it without any help from me," John said gracefully.

"No, I mean it. I'll take all the help I can get."

"Hey, I'm here to get away from this stuff," John said. "This is your show all the way." But Gideon could see that he was grateful to be asked, something FBI agents learned not to expect from the locals.

"Not a bad guy," John said when Honeyman moved off. "I just hope he knows what he's doing."

"Why don't you take him up?" Gideon asked. "He could probably use some friendly advice."

John shook his head. "Doc, the guy was just being nice. He doesn't want my help, believe me. I know these people."

After that, John spent a few more minutes restlessly shifting from one foot to the other while the exhumation inched along, punctuated by Nellie's osteological bulletins. Finally, he gave up. "I'm gonna go sit by the swimming pool," he grumbled. "I gotta work on my lecture notes."

"John, you'll do fine. They'll love you. I'll be there. I'll shill for you from the audience."

But John, not persuaded, went away talking to himself.

The exhumation proceeded. Even with frequent pauses for photographs and careful piling of the dislodged earth for later sifting by the evidence unit, much of the skeleton was exposed by twelve-thirty, its arms and legs folded up like a sleeping child's. The small bones of the hand had been slightly scattered. Shirt, trousers, and underwear were almost completely rotted away, no more than some stiff, gray-brown scraps, but the one foot that was visible was still encased in a sturdy, well-preserved lace-up shoe.

As things wound down, Gideon found himself standing next to the solitary, woebegone Honeyman again. "Do you have any open cases that might fit this?" he asked, as much out of sympathy as anything else.

"What? Well, we haven't even established how long that body's been there yet."

"Oh, I think five to ten years would be a pretty reasonable guess. The body's completely skeletonized, so that tells us it's a few years old anyway. And it's not too old, or there wouldn't have been any signs of the burial left to see in the first place."

"Oh. Well, I suppose that makes sense. No, we don't."

"I beg your pardon?"

"We don't have any open cases from five to ten years ago that could fit this. Some of that was before my time, but I've had the files checked, and there's nothing. No missing white males, not that age, not from around here. Hell, I don't know what they expect me to do with this." He nodded and moved despondently off.

Les Zenkovich, who had come up and listened in on the last few sentences, watched him go. Like most of the others, he had left for a few minutes to get something to eat from the lunch buffet, and he was now using a toothpick with an air of well-fed serenity. He looked expressively toward the burial, and then at Gideon.

"Well, somebody's sure as shit missing from somewhere," he said, sucking a bit of food from between his teeth. "You can bet on that."

CHAPTER 7

For someone who knew as much as he did about the joints and what could go wrong with them, Nellie Hobert cracked his knuckles often and with relish, extending thick-wristed, fuzzy forearms with his fingers interlocked, bending them backwards, and snapping the lot with a long, rolling crackle. It generally meant he was feeling good.

As usual, Gideon flinched. "Damn, I wish you wouldn't do that, Nellie."

"Ah, nothing like feeling those synovial bursae pop," Nellie said happily. "No harm to it, you should know that. Now then. You are probably wondering why I asked you here, yes?"

"Well, yes."

It was late in the afternoon, and the two men were in the basement of the Central Oregon Museum of Natural History, in a workroom crowded with partially constructed museum "boulders" made of chicken wire, papier-mâché, and wallpaper glue. In one corner a library table had been draped with heavy polyethylene plastic, and on it was the skeleton, laid out on its back.

Not literally on its back, of course, inasmuch as it didn't have a back to lie on, but in a supine position, skull tipped gently to the side, as in sleep, its disarticulated bones arranged in anatomical order. Except for a few of the smallest bones—the hyoid, a few phalanges, and some carpals and tarsals—they were all there and all in good condition, with no damage worse than some abrading and a few gnaw marks here and there. Cleaned now, they were tinged a reddish-brown, like the soil they'd come from, and they smelled faintly of earth and decay.

It wasn't a putrid odor—active decomposition was long past—or even unpleasant, really, but simply the way bones smelled after they'd been in the ground a long time, after even the tallowy odor of the fat had disappeared: musty, foresty, a little mildewy. A peaceful, undisturbed smell, the way old, dead bones ought to smell.

The skeleton had been removed from its grave and put in marked paper sacks at about 1:00 P.M. that afternoon. From there, according to Nellie, it had gone to the mortuary at the Saint Charles Medical Center for a pro forma autopsy by the medical examiner's pathologist.

"The ME just looked at it and laughed," Nellie said. "He told me: 'With forty goddamn forensic anthropologists hanging around looking over my shoulder, you think I'm crazy enough to stick my neck out on some bags of bones?' It was the shortest autopsy on record, let me tell you."

"So he turned them over to you for analysis?"

"Yes, this morning. To Miranda, officially, but she asked me if I wouldn't take charge." He smiled. The unlit, metal-stemmed pipe between his teeth bobbed up and down. Nellie's sudden, wide smile was one of his most disarming features; his lips seemed to disappear, his face to split into two equal parts, like a Muppet's.

"And you know me," he said, "taking charge is what I love to do. Anyhow, we bagged it up again, brought it over here, and Miranda and I worked the thing over. She's good, Miranda. Just doesn't get enough cases to give her any confidence. She needs to get her hands dirty a little more."

"Uh-huh. So what am I doing here, Nellie?"

Nellie had telephoned him at the lodge half an hour earlier, at three-thirty, and asked if he could drop by the workroom. Gideon had left the conference session on forensic data nets and driven to Bend. He still didn't know what for.

"Well, I asked you to come over because I need your help, Gideon. I'm pretty sure I found something, and I want you to tell me if I'm right."

Gideon was honestly surprised. "You want me to tell you?"

"That's right. Between us girls, you're the only one of 'em that's worth a damn, whippersnapper though you are."

"Well, I wouldn't say—"

"Yes, you would. Who's better? Harlow knows everything there is to know about teeth but damn-all about bones. Callie's off in never-never land—and anyway, they're both back in Nevada right now. And as for—"

"All right, but what—"

"—Leland, he doesn't have time anymore for anything but his precious turds; Les wouldn't know a—a—well, who else am I going to ask?"

"Ask what? Nellie, you're the president of the association. You're the dean of American forensic anthropologists. If you're sure you found something, then that's good enough for me. It's there."

"Think so?" He leaned his rump against the table, crossed his arms, took the pipe from his mouth, used the stem to scratch the side of his short, gray beard, and peered at Gideon from under disorderly eyebrows. "Well, now."

Here comes a shaggy-dog story, Gideon thought.

"That reminds me of some testimony I gave in a case in Gallup," he said, "and the defense attorney was trying to make me look bad, the way they do. Punching holes in my credibility, you know?"

"All too well." Gideon had put in some uncomfortable hours on the expert-witness stand himself.

"Well, sir, this attorney, he says to me, 'Now, then, Dr. Hobert,' he says..."

Shaggy-dog story, all right, Gideon said to himself. He settled down to wait it out.

"'Dr. Hobert, who would you say is the most expert forensic anthropologist in the state of New Mexico?'

"Well, I didn't quite know where he was going with that, so I just told him, nice and humble, that it was me. 'I am,' I said.

"'I see,' he says. 'All right, then, Dr. Hobert, who would you say is the most highly regarded forensic anthropologist in the United States?'

"'I am,' I said, but I was starting to get nervous. I didn't like this guy.

"'I see,' he says. 'Now then, could you tell the court, who in your opinion is the most expert forensic anthropologist in the *world?'*

"I look him in the eye, take a deep breath, and say: 'I am.'

"He leans over at me with that smirk they get. 'No one in the entire world is as good as you are?'

"'Not...even...close,' I tell him, "Well, the prosecuting attorney asks for a recess and gets me aside. 'Nellie,' he says, 'how could you say those things? You know that kind of thing puts the jury's back up.'

"So I said—you want to know what I said?"

"Do I have a choice?" Gideon answered, but he was already smiling. Here it came.

"I said: 'Well, *hell*, man, I was UNDER OATH!'"

Nellie banged his hand on the nearest table, rolled back his head, and shouted laughter at the acoustic-tile ceiling. He stuck his pipe back in his mouth. "Did I have you going there, or didn't I?"

"Not for a second," Gideon said, laughing along with him. "Now: What was it you wanted my help on?"

The older man sobered. He turned back toward the skeleton. "Tell me what you see."

"Well, as you said, it's male, Caucasian—"

"Yes, yes, of course. We've done all that. Caucasian male, average build, estimated stature of 69.3 inches, plus or minus 1.18—"

"You used the Trotter and Gleser equations?"

"For femur plus tibia—and Suchey-Brooks for aging from the pubic symphysis. It's a textbook Phase 5, completely rimmed, which gives us a range of say, thirty to seventy, and most likely forty-five to sixty-five. Throw in the vertebral lipping, the atrophic spots on the scapula—"

Gideon picked up the right scapula and held it up against the light from the fluorescent tubes on the ceiling. There were milky patches of translucence where the bone had thinned in its normal, unstoppable progression toward disintegration.

"—the sternal rib changes," Nellie continued, "the general bone density and so on and so forth, and you get an age of around—"

"Fifty-five or so," Gideon said, putting down the scapula. "Say fifty to sixty."

"On the money, my boy. As for possible features of individuation, we have a healed fracture of the left ulna, probably from childhood, and an extracted first molar, also old. A few fillings. And some arthritis in the metatarsophalangeal joints, but nothing worse than any other old geezer. And that's it. Nothing much to go on. For that matter, nothing very interesting. *But...*" He paused weightily. "...in cause of death I think we have something else entirely."

"Cause of death?" Scanning the bones, Gideon had seen nothing to suggest what it was.

"Yes. How was the dastardly deed done? That's what I want your opinion on. I think that we have something unusual here; a—well, I better not give you any hints. Wouldn't want to bias you. Go ahead, tell me what you think." He bestowed a split-faced grin on Gideon and used the stubby pipe to make a gesture at the skeleton: *It's all yours.*

Intrigued, Gideon picked up the skull, most likely of all bony elements to tell a story of death by violence. Until now, he had seen only the front and the left side, which showed no fractures, no entrance or exit wounds. He turned it over and there on the rear, just to the right of center, was an inch-and-a-half-long horizontal crack just above the lambdoidal suture. Gideon ran his finger along it.

"Oho," Nellie said quietly, chewing on his unlit pipe.

Gideon looked at him, puzzled. The crack was an uncomplicated linear fracture of the right parietal. No depression of the bone, no radiating fracture lines. Textbooks described this kind of injury as the probable result of an "accelerated head impacting on a fixed surface"—and not the other way around, which would have had more sinister implications. In other words, a simple fall; hardly proof of dastardly deeds.

"Nellie," Gideon said cautiously, "I'll grant you that this *could* have caused death—maybe a contre-coup brain contusion, subdural hemorrhage—"

"Yes, yes." Nellie gestured impatiently. "Could. But didn't."

"Well, then—"

"Keep looking. You haven't found it yet."

Gideon turned the skull, millimeter by millimeter. He shook his head. "I don't see anything else on the skull."

"Not on the skull."

"Below the skull?"

Nellie cocked his head. "Is there another way to go from the skull?"

Gideon smiled. "Okay, below the skull." He lifted the sternum. Nellie shook his head. "Higher."

Gideon put down the sternum and picked up the first cervical vertebra, the atlas, so named because the globe of the skull rested on it.

"Lower," Nellie said.

Gideon put it down. "I'm sure glad you're not giving me any hints." He moved to the second cervical vertebra.

Nellie shook his head. "Nope, but you're getting warmer."

Gideon sighed. "Nellie, how about just—all!"

Inconspicuous as it was, it seemed to leap out and catch his eye. On the sixth cervical vertebra, located just below the level of the Adam's apple—a minuscule break zigzagging its way across the front of the right transverse process, one of two small, winglike spurs jutting out from the body of the vertebra.

Gideon leaned closer, nudged the bone with a forefinger. The crack was perhaps a quarter of an inch long. "Hinge fracture," he said, using the conventional term for a break that went only partway through the bone, something like what happened when you snapped a fresh twig.

"Exactly," Nellie said with enthusiasm. "Precisely. And you'll also notice, on the posterior root—"

"Another fracture," Gideon said. "Hairline. And as for the adjacent vertebrae..." One by one he lifted them and carefully examined the convoluted surfaces.

Nellie nodded vigorously, urging him along.

"...nothing," Gideon said. "No sign of trauma." Another crisp nod from Nellie. He paused in lighting his pipe. "So? What's your conclusion, doctor?"

Gideon leaned against a lab stool. There wasn't much room for doubt. Injuries like these, in these particular places, meant that enormous squeezing force had been applied to the neck. One saw them in hangings, or even in manual strangulations if the killer happened to be built along the lines of King Kong. But in such cases, the wholesale wrenching of the neck muscles generally produced injuries to more than one vertebra, often to four or five. To have only a single vertebra cracked, and that one in two places, meant that the constriction had been extraordinarily localized.

It wasn't something one came across often; in Gideon's experience only twice. And each time it had been caused by the same thing.

"Garrote," he said.

"Aye, mate," Nellie said with satisfaction as he got his pipe going. "The old Spanish windlass."

The technique dated back at least to the time of Christ. In its basic version a cord—in ancient times it had been made of animal sinew—was looped twice around the neck, and a stick or other firm object inserted between the loops. Rotating the stick would then twist the cord, much like a tourniquet, and create terrific pressure, first closing the windpipe and then, with a few more twists, snapping the spinal column; thus combining the virtues, so to speak, of strangling and hanging. When applied at the level of the sixth cervical vertebra, it would also compress the carotid sheath, thereby shutting off blood flow to and from the brain. Just for good measure.

The Spanish Inquisitors, who used the method as a merciful alternative to the stake, claimed that it was painless, but there was a lack of definitive data on this point. What it demonstrably was, however, was simple, efficient, and silent. And, if the cord was knotted at close intervals, bloodless.

Gideon touched the crack in the skull. "You think he was knocked out by a fall, then garroted?"

"Let's hope so," Nellie said, "for his sake."

Gideon hoped so too. He stood looking down at the table in an odd reverie. What an enormous difference there was between the livid, flagrant corpses a pathologist had to work with and this, the anthropologist's quiet and unassuming skeleton. This man's life had ended horrifically, yet the bones gave no signs of upset or fright. Or even of pain. Just two clean, inconsequential-looking little cracks in one tiny, inessential-looking bone. The skull grinned like any other skull, no different from that of a man who had died peacefully in his bed. There were no bulging eyeballs, no purple and protruding tongue, no cruelly bruised and swollen flesh.

A good thing too, or he'd have been out of this business a long time ago.

Nellie smacked his hands together. "Well, then, if that's settled, let's lock up and get out of here. If you've got time, let's stop by Honeyman's office and give him the good news."

He took off the lab apron he'd been wearing and tossed it onto a coat hook. Today's T-shirt was a bright and cheerful blue. "Our day begins when yours ends," it said. "Dallas PD, Homicide Unit."

* * *

"So," a sweating, shirt-sleeved Honeyman said bleakly, turning the stub of a pencil end-over-end on the big old desk that took up a full third of his tiny office. "It's definitely homicide. There's no doubt about it anymore."

"Was there ever?" Nellie asked. "Or did you seriously consider that he might have buried himself?"

Honeyman glared at him, then permitted himself a baggy smile. "I could always hope."

"What about you?" Gideon asked. "Making any progress?"

"Progress!" Honeyman said with a snort. "The budget meeting was a total disaster! They actually expect us—"

"I meant on the burial," Gideon said.

"Oh, the burial. Well, there are these." From an ink-stained shirt pocket bulging with half a dozen pens he pried out a small yellow envelope, which he opened and upended on the desk. A quarter and two nickels rolled out. "These came out of the grave after you finished. Right under the body, about an inch below."

"Must have rotted out of his pocket," Nellie said.

"Yes, or somebody dropped them while they were burying him. Same difference."

Gideon turned the coins over to read the dates: "1981, 1972, 1978." He looked up. "So at least you know something you didn't know before. He couldn't have been buried before 1981."

"No, or after, either. Not that I know what that does for us.

"Or after?" Nellie repeated. "Why the devil not? Just because a 1981 coin—"

"Well, it's not the coin," Honeyman said, "it's the shed." "The shed," Nellie said.

"Yes, the shed."

Gideon tried helping things along. "The shed that used to stand where we found the grave?"

"Sure, what else are we talking about? I talked with the management, and they said part of it blew down in a huge windstorm we had in October 1981, and they bulldozed away what was left of it a few days later. So there you are. That body was buried in 1981. Before October."

"*Where* are we?" Nellie demanded. "So the shed blew down in October. Who's to say the body wasn't buried later?"

Surprisingly, Honeyman was ready for him. "It's always possible, but what would be the point? It would have been right out in the open, only a few feet from some of the guest cottages. And you can see it from the road. You'd have to be crazy to try to bury a body there."

"Well, yes…"

"But…" Honeyman said, and Gideon began to think he might actually be enjoying himself. Not many people got a chance to lecture Nelson Hobert. *"But* while the shed was still standing, it was perfect. Easy to get into, a nice dirt floor to dig in, plenty of junk in it to hide the grave—and with the open side facing away from the cottages and the road. What more could you ask? The chances of that grave ever being found were just about zero."

Gideon nodded his agreement. If Honeyman ever decided to get out of administration and into detective work, he just might do all right.

"Not quite zero," Nellie pointed out. "It *did* get found."

"Oh, certainly," Honeyman said with another of his sad-eyed smiles, "but only because our poor, dumb perp never bothered to calculate the probability of a convention full of forensic anthropologists showing up and crawling all over the place ten years later. Just goes to show the limitations of the criminal mind."

"Nineteen eighty-one," Gideon said slowly. "Wasn't that the year of the first WAFA meeting?"

"WAFA?" Honeyman said.

"Western Association of Forensic Anthropologists. Their first meeting was at Whitebark Lodge. In 1981." Honeyman laid down his pencil. For the first time a flicker of real interest showed in his eyes. "Is that so? All these same people?"

"Well, just a few of us," Nellie said. "We've grown quite a bit since then, you know. Back in 1981 there were only…"

He stopped in mid-sentence, forgetting to close his mouth, his head tilted as if he were listening for something.

"What?" Honeyman said nervously. "What is it?"

"By gum," Nellie said softly, incredulously. Jammed between the side of Honeyman's desk and the wall, he leaned as far back as he could in the straight-backed chair, locked his hands behind his neck, and stared, seemingly at the marked-up boxes of a big

"Executive Plan-Your-Month" calendar over Honeyman's head. But his eyes were unfocused and Gideon could see that his mind was racing. He sat like that for a long time, then lowered his gaze and faced them, still not altogether back from wherever he'd been.

"By gum," he said again. "I believe I know who that skeleton is."

CHAPTER 8

"Well...who?" Honeyman asked.

"Chuck Salish," Nellie said, and looked dreamily at Gideon. "Has to be. Think about it."

Gideon frowned back at him. "Nellie, I don't know who Chuck Salish is. Was."

It took a moment for this to register. "You don't—

No, of course you don't. You weren't there. Forgive me, I forgot. Chuck and Albert were going to go into business together when Albert retired, you know. Albert—"

"Albert, Albert, who's Albert?" Honeyman was growing increasingly edgy.

The interruption seemed to wake Nellie up. His eyes drifted back into focus. "Albert Evan Jasper, of course. They were going to open a forensic consulting outfit. It would have been one of the first."

"Chuck Salish," Gideon repeated. The name was completely unfamiliar. "An anthropologist? I've never heard of him."

"Anthropologist? No, what gave you that idea? He was an FBI agent, out of the Albuquerque office. He was—"

"FBI *agent?*" Honeyman stood up, opened his mouth, closed it, and opened it again. Still, it was a few seconds before anything came out. "You're telling me I've got a—a dead FBI agent, a *murdered* FBI agent, lying on a table in the museum?"

"Yes, that's right," Nellie said calmly. "He was retiring, too, at about the same time Albert was. They'd worked together on a case or two, you see, and they'd gotten along, and they'd decided to go into business together, so—"

"Dear God, why me?" With a pitiful groan Honeyman flung himself back into his chair. "Well, what was he doing around *here?*" he demanded accusingly.

Nellie looked mildly back at him. "Do you suppose we could get out of this room? I could stand a little fresh air. And, my word, I'd give my soul for a hot cup of coffee. Farrell, you look as if you could use something yourself, if you don't mind my saying so."

"What I could use is unhearing what you just told me," Honeyman muttered.

A few minutes later they were settled around one of the awning-shaded tables outside Goody's Soda Fountain on Wall Street, a block north of the Justice Building. Gideon was as glad as Nellie to be out of Honeyman's stuffy office. It was a relief, almost a surprise, to see that the air was still clean and fresh, and to be among people who weren't talking about buried skeletons and murdered FBI agents. Despite the temperature, which had now climbed into the promised nineties, Nellie had his hot coffee, a double espresso. Gideon had iced tea in front of him. Honeyman had bought a bottle of fruit-tinged mineral water.

Nellie tossed down half the coffee in two swallows and heaved a great sigh. He searched in the roomy pockets of his Bermudas, hauling out his pipe and two tobacco pouches, one a soft red leather, the other a cheap plastic one, cracked and dingy. He chose the plastic one, as Gideon knew he would. It contained the expensive, evil-smelling Latakia he loved. The red one held an aggressively perfumy blend that he smoked only when Frieda was around.

"Well, then," he said, completing his drawn-out lighting ritual, "the two of them had worked together and gotten to be friends, and Albert invited Chuck along to our get-together to meet some of the people in the field. But the unfortunate upshot of it was that he was killed in the bus crash too." His eyebrows came up as he glanced keenly at them. "Or so I thought until today."

"This is the '81 Santiam Pass crash you're talking about?" Honeyman asked.

"That's right. Gideon, you know what we're referring to?"

"I think so. The bus accident you and the others all worked on. The one Jasper was killed on."

Nellie nodded. "Albert and thirty-seven others. Maybe more— we had some *odds and ends of people* we never attributed for sure."

Odds and ends of people, Gideon thought. Was there any other profession where this would pass for everyday conversation?

"It was on an early-morning run between Bend and the Portland Airport," Nellie went on, "a service for people in the resorts around here." His coffee was black and sugarless, but he stirred it anyway. "Well, what I assumed at the time—what we all assumed—was that some of those odds and ends were Chuck Salish. We had every reason to believe he was on that bus, and no reason, none at all, to think he wasn't."

That sounded a little indefinite to Gideon. "Are you saying you actually identified some of those fragments as Salish?" he asked.

"Gideon, when I say odds and ends I mean odds and ends. I'm not talking about dentition, facial skeletons, nice big chunks of long bone and innominate—I'm talking about burnt, crumbling scraps so mutilated and tiny that they couldn't be positively attributed to anybody. Maybe they belonged with some of the people we'd identified for sure, maybe they didn't. The whole thing was a horrific jumble, just terrible. We examined what we had, we talked it out; and, where we had to, we made the best guesses we could, that's all."

Honeyman lifted both hands pleadingly. "Wait, wait, wait. Hold it, hold it, hold it. Did I just hear you say that you just guessed he was on that bus, and that was that? An FBI agent? Tell me that's not what you told me."

"Well, it was a little more than a guess," Nellie said with a bit of edge to his voice. "We knew those fragments were male, we knew they were Caucasian, we knew they were at least middle-aged, we knew—I forget what else we knew. It's been ten years."

"But thousands of people are male and middle-aged. *Millions* of people—"

"But millions of people hadn't made reservations on that particular bus. Chuck had. It's all in the files, Farrell, and I'll defend our decision as sound, based on what we knew at the time."

"But—" Honeyman clumsily poured mineral water into his glass and gulped it down. Gideon doubted that he was aware of doing it. "All right, but if you feel that way about it, why are you changing your mind now? What's different now? Why are you doing this to me?"

"What's different now is that we've turned up an unidentified body in an unmarked grave. That wasn't a factor, or rather not a known factor, in 1981."

"So? So? This person could be anybody, somebody we've never heard of. Why do you want to assume it's Salish, for God's sake?"

Nellie smiled. "You really don't want it to be Salish, do you?"

"You have no idea," Honeyman said unhappily. " I have no *time* for this. A nice unidentified John Doe, one more poor old drifter from ten years ago, with no leads—that I could cope with. But a murdered FBI agent? You don't know what you're doing to me."

"Well, I'm sorry, Farrell, truly, but I have two basic reasons for thinking that's Chuck back there in the workroom. First"—like the old professor he was, he began ticking them off on his fingers— "according to what you've told us, this happened in 1981, and 1981 is when he happened to be with us at Whitebark Lodge."

"Him and you and plenty of other people. It was a booming resort back then."

"Yes, but how many of those people are unaccounted for?"

He let this sink in, then moved to the next finger. "From what you say, there are no open missing-person files or unsolved homicides from 1981. So, whoever this is, apparently no one is even aware he's missing. Does it really take such a leap to wonder if it isn't someone we all thought was on the bus?"

Honeyman wasn't ready to give up yet. "But why Salish in particular?" he persisted. "What about some of the other remains? Didn't you say there were other people you couldn't identify for sure?"

Beneath Nellie's eye a muscle jumped. "That's true. In some cases we had to base identifications on a ring, a—a leg brace…"

"Well, then, that means other people could be 'missing,' too, without anybody knowing. Why couldn't it be one of them?"

Good question, Gideon thought.

"I'm sorry, Farrell, but I don't think so," Nellie said. "The possible whereabouts of every person who could conceivably have been on that bus were tracked. Your own department worked on it. So did the state people. IBM lent us a couple of computers. And yes, a few possibles were never run down, at least not to everybody's complete satisfaction—that's hardly surprising in a case like this. But there were only two guests at Whitebark who weren't accounted for, who were not demonstrably alive and kicking…Albert Jasper and Chuck Salish. Albert was identified beyond dispute. That leaves Chuck."

Good answer, Gideon thought. "Nellie, what about Salish's physical characteristics? What we have here is a male Caucasian, probably in his fifties, about five-nine, give or take an inch or so. Did Salish fit that?"

He thought for a moment, sucking on the pipe. "Oh, yes."

"So would half the people in Deschutes County," Honeyman said, but without conviction. However unwillingly, he had come around to Nellie's point of view.

Gideon had too. "If it's Salish," he said, "it ought to be easy enough to prove. That skeleton's almost whole, with a good set of dentition. A copy of Salish's dental records ought to settle it."

"That's a fact," Nellie said. "And unless I'm mistaken, we already have those. They'd be in the medical examiner's file from 1981. I'm sure we got medical and dental records on everyone."

He sucked on the pipe and blew out a turgid brown cloud. Two people who were in the act of sitting down at the next table wrinkled their noses, looked disbelievingly at each other, and quietly took their sundaes several tables farther away.

Honeyman was crunching ice between his teeth and looking depressed. "All right, let's say it is Salish. I don't suppose you'd have any idea who would want to kill him?" Gideon had the impression he was praying for a no.

Nellie blinked at him. "How on earth would I come to have any idea about that?"

Honeyman shrugged deferentially. "I only meant that you were there. He was one of your party. I just thought you might—"

"Farrell," Nellie said, "if that question means what I think it means, you're about twenty miles off base. Whoever murdered Chuck Salish, it wasn't somebody from WAFA. We're on your side, or have you forgotten?"

To his credit, Honeyman held his ground. "As far as you know, nobody in the group had any kind of grudge against him?"

"Nobody there even knew him before Albert showed up with him." Nellie was staring hotly at Honeyman, his bearded chin thrust out. "Now listen, Farrell, this is a respected organization of certified forensic scientists, and I'm privileged to head the national organization. There isn't a one of those people you're asking me about who hasn't had more experience working with law enforcement than you have, dammit, and I resent your implications."

Honeyman shifted impassively into the stolid copspeak that policemen used at such times. "I'm sorry you feel that way, sir, but I'd still like an answer to my question. To your knowledge, did any person there have a grudge against Mr. Salish?"

Gideon winced. It was probably the first time in Nellie's life that anyone had talked to him in that particular tone.

"No," Nellie said angrily, "nobody had a grudge against anybody."

"I see. Everything was sweetness and light," Honeyman said, continuing to show more backbone than Gideon had given him credit for.

Nellie scowled at him for a moment, then bent his head while he used a paper clip to jab ferociously at some clotted tobacco in the bowl of his pipe. "Yes," he muttered, "that's right."

Gideon stared at him. Nellie Hobert, ordinarily about as devious as a duck, was holding something back; he was almost sure of it. There was nobody whose forthrightness Gideon trusted more than Nellie's, and yet—

"Hell," Nellie mumbled as he got the pipe going again,

"I'm sorry, Farrell. I apologize. It's been quite a day."

"Nothing to apologize for, sir," Honeyman said, still stiff. Nellie's face split into its familiar Muppet grin.

"Then stop calling me 'sir,' all right? It makes me nervous."

Honeyman relaxed and smiled back at him. "Me too."

"It's just that I thought you were barking up the wrong tree, that's all."

"I probably was." He looked at his watch. "Five o'clock. Look, I better get a deposition from you. Would this be a good time to come on back to the office?"

"I don't see why not. I don't have anything pressing until eight. I've promised to report to the membership on the skeletal analysis." He smiled wryly. "It appears I'm going to have some interesting things to tell them." He glanced at Honeyman. "You have no objection to my telling them about Chuck Salish?"

Honeyman hesitated, then shook his head. "Go ahead, they may as well know. Christ, an FBI agent! Dr. Oliver, you're welcome to come on over to the office too. You might be able to add something."

"I can't see what," Gideon said. "Besides, I promised my wife I'd have a before-dinner drink with her. I'm already late."

"You'll be at the evening session?" Nellie asked him.

"I wouldn't miss it," Gideon said. He got up and made his good-byes, but his smile felt strained.

What was going on with Nellie?

CHAPTER 9

Boeuf Wellington, Whitebark Lodge's dinner entree, sounded dangerously ambitious to Gideon and Julie (the previous two main courses having been Rhoda's Meatloaf and Pineapple-Wiener Kabobs). It also failed to appeal to John, who was in the mood, as always, for a hamburger. Thus, with a little over an hour to spare before Nellie's eight o'clock report, the three of them drove to Sisters for dinner.

"Place looks like Dodge City," John observed as they pulled into a parking lot off Cascade Avenue.

He had a point. Ordinarily, when town fathers decide that their central area needs a face lift, they focus their resources on making it look bright and new. In Sisters they took a different approach; they made it look bright and old. Pokey tourist traffic and roaring logging trucks aside, driving down the main street of Sisters was like driving through a freshly painted Western movie set: wooden 1880—style storefronts, overhanging balustered porches that made half the buildings look like bordellos, and plank boardwalks. All this in a town in which no building predated the twentieth century.

Surprisingly, it had worked. The town's appearance, while undeniably cute, had managed to stay somewhere this side of cutesy. Perhaps it was the surrounding pine forests, perhaps the bare, lonely, upward sweep of the Three Sisters to the southeast. Or maybe it was the hard-to-miss presence of so many honest-to-God, red-suspendered, flannel-shirted, wire-whiskered loggers. On either side of the parking slot into which Gideon had pulled were battered pickup trucks with bumper stickers. The one of the left said: "Save a logger, eat an owl." The one on the right announced: "I love spotted owl—fried."

Whatever it was, the rugged Old West ambience clicked, and if the pre-1970 photographs in one of the shop windows were any guide, the new-old Sisters was a big improvement over the old-old Sisters.

John's state of mind at dinner was greatly improved. Farrell Honeyman, pleading shortage of manpower, had formally requested his assistance on the case, calling Seattle while Nellie was still in his office. And Charlie Applewhite, John's boss, had tentatively approved, at least until it was positively determined whether the murdered man was Special Agent Chuck Salish. If it was, and they had the killing of a federal agent on their hands, the FBI's involvement would become much more than tentative.

"There's one problem, though," John told them. "Applewhite says that if it looks like it's gonna take a lot of time, I better make my apologies on that lecture."

Gideon studied him. "Gee," he said, "I wonder if it's going to take a lot of time."

John peered gravely back. "Heaps," he said, and all of them laughed.

They were in the Hotel Sisters Restaurant, located in a yellow frame building dating from almost as far back (1912) as it had been made to look. Getting into the spirit of things, they had passed up the dining room to eat in Bronco Billy's Saloon, complete with a swinging-door entrance from the lobby, a dark, polished, authentically antique bar backed by a long mirror, and buffalo and deer heads mounted on the walls. The waitresses wore cowboy vests and bolo ties.

They had eaten lunch late and weren't hungry enough for the dinner plates, so they asked for sandwich menus. All of the entries, in accordance with what seemed to be the custom in this part of Oregon, had Western appellations: the Lone Star, the Barnyard Bird, the Buckaroo. Even the hamburgers had names: the Brama Bull ("smothered in mushrooms and melted cheddar cheese"), the Bullrider ("smothered in barbecue sauce").

John was having trouble finding what he wanted. "So what's a plain hamburger?" he asked the waitress.

She pointed with her pencil at the bottom of the menu. "Right there, hon."

"'The Roper,'" John read aloud. "'Plain and simple, no bull.—'"

He looked up at her and laughed. "Okay, I'll have a Roper. But with fries."

"They all come with fries, honey."

Gideon and Julie asked for Barnyard Birds—broiled chicken sandwiches with chili, jack cheese, and guacamole. The waitress jotted down their orders and brought back a plate of nachos and three mugs of the local Blue Heron beer.

"Gideon, how long will it take to prove whether that skeleton is Chuck Salish's or not?" Julie asked.

"That depends on what kind of file there is on him in the ME's office. If they already have dental records, medical records, photographs—"

"They do," John said. "I talked to them on the phone."

"Well, then, I'd say it'll take Nellie all of five minutes. This guy has a missing tooth and some fillings, so a look at Salish's dental charts should—"

"They don't have the dental charts," John said. "I thought you said—"

"Everything but. They had them, because they're listed on the file contents sheet, but they're not in the file."

"What about dental x-rays?"

John shook his head. "There's nothing at all from his dentist. Everything else's still there."

The three of them looked at each other. "You don't suppose they could have been accidentally lost?" Julie asked.

The others regarded her silently.

"No, I didn't think so," she said. "Gideon, why would somebody take just the dental records and leave everything else?"

"Well, I don't know just what else there is, but the dental stuff is your best bet for making a positive identification, so I'm assuming someone didn't want us to find out who this was."

"No, doc, we can't say that for sure," John said. "For all we know, somebody took those records out of the file years ago, long before anybody found the skeleton."

"But not before somebody buried it," Gideon pointed out.

John swallowed some beer. "Yeah, true."

After a few moments' silence, Julie said: "Interesting, but where does that get us?"

"Beats me," Gideon said. "Anyway, it shouldn't be too hard to get copies again." He worked a sticky, cheese-soaked tortilla chip free from the mass on the plate, loaded it with ground meat and salsa, and brought it carefully to his mouth.

John shook his head. "I don't know about that. The dentist's name isn't on the contents sheet, and Salish's wife is in a nursing home now. She doesn't remember who the hell Chuck Salish was, let alone his dentist. But I've got the FBI office in Albuquerque looking into it. They'll come up with him."

Gideon washed down the chip with a gulp of beer. "You've been busy, haven't you? When did you hear about this, a whole two hours ago?"

"Well, yeah, but we're talking about a murdered special agent here. The Bureau's funny about things like that. We take an interest."

"Let's say his dentist can't be located," Julie said. "Could Nellie make an identification anyway?"

"Well, there are some skeletal features that ought to show up in the medical records," Gideon said. "A healed fracture, a few arthritic joints in the foot. But that kind of thing is trickier, less definite. It'd probably depend on whether there are x-rays, and what kind of x-rays."

John had been staring down at his mug, slowly rotating it on its coaster. Now he looked up. "Doc, you realize that I have to look at all your old pals as prime suspects here."

Gideon realized it, all right. He'd been thinking of little else. "Including Nellie?"

"Well, I'm not real worried about Hobert. If he had something to hide, all he had to do was keep his mouth shut, and this'd be just another John Doe. Besides, from what I hear, everybody in the Bureau who's ever worked with him'll vouch for him personally, right up to the director."

Gideon drank some beer, began to say something, then took a slow second swallow. "I'll vouch for him too."

"Yeah, I like the little bugger myself. All the same, I asked one of the ME's deputies to sort of casually just happen to hang around the room with him while he's working on the skeleton tomorrow."

"What about when he's not working on it? That workshop in the museum isn't exactly secure. Anybody could get at it."

"I'm way ahead of you. The skeleton's being moved to a room in the Justice Building downtown. Nellie can work there just as easy." He used a chip to scoop up some salsa. "Just to be on the safe side, you know?"

Gideon nodded; he knew.

Julie didn't. "I can't believe what I'm hearing," she said. "John, all these people are forensic anthropologists. They work *with* the police. Surely there are other suspects?"

"Like who?"

"Well, like...it could be anybody. Somebody Salish once sent to jail, or one of the other guests at the lodge, or an employee, or a, a—"

"Julie, here's a guy who comes to a resort with a bunch of anthropologists, okay? He's an FBI agent, but he's not here on a case. In fact, he's out of his region. And he winds up killed and stuffed in a hole. As far as we know, the only people with any connection to him are these six anthropologists. So who the hell else is there that makes any sense? Where else do I start? You tell me."

"Well..."

"And there's something else," John went on. "Somebody knew enough to get rid of the dental records, right? And they needed access to the ME's files to do it, which you can't just walk in off the street and do. Doesn't that sound like one of the anthropologists who worked on the bus crash? Doc?"

"I suppose so, yes," Gideon said reluctantly. John's thinking was sound enough, but these were friends and colleagues who were being so blithely accused; people he'd known and respected for years. Agreeing with John didn't make him feel any happier about being co-opted.

"But what motive would they have?" Julie asked.

"What motive would anybody have?" John answered. "That's what an investigation's for."

She sighed and leaned back. "Well," she said, patently unconvinced, "you two are the experts."

"Hey, we better quit while we're ahead, Doc."

That was fine with Gideon.

The food came—big, messy, appetizing wooden platters loaded

with extras—beans, more salsa, french fries, pickles—and they found that their appetites were heartier than they'd thought. Gideon was halfway through his sandwich and surrounded by soiled paper napkins when a new thought surfaced.

"There weren't six anthropologists at that meeting, John. There were eight."

John looked up from his hamburger. "Eight?"

"Two of them are dead. Jasper, of course, and Ned Ortiz from USC."

John went back to the hamburger. "Yeah, well, I think I better concentrate on the live ones. Dead guys are tough to get anything out of."

"But Jasper's the only one with any kind of a real connection to Salish. The others didn't even know him before the meeting. And Jasper left suddenly, without telling anybody. Doesn't that make him worth checking out? If—"

He stopped abruptly. If he'd heard himself right, he had as much as suggested that the late, great Albert Evan Jasper was a murderer. And that really was overdoing it. "I mean," he finished lamely, "I thought that was the way the police mind worked."

"That's the way the police mind works, all right," John said. "All I have to figure out is how you check out a cigar box worth of burned bones."

"If you can find them," Julie said. "Nobody seems to know where they are at the moment."

She had said it casually, but her expression suddenly changed. She put down her sandwich and spoke quietly. "There's got to he a connection there."

John was studying her. "Well, now, that's something to think about."

Gideon considered the idea. "No, how could there be a connection? We're getting our causal sequence backwards. Jasper's bones disappeared Sunday night. The skeleton didn't even turn up until this morning—two days later. And Chuck Salish's name didn't come into the picture until just a few hours ago."

"Yeah, I know," John said slowly. "Far be it from me to argue with causal sequence, Doc, but I think Julie's got something there."

She smiled at him. "Why, thank you, John."

And maybe she did. Julie had a way of spotting connections that other people missed. it had happened enough times before.

"There might be something else worth thinking about, John," Gideon said heavily. He might as well get it out. "I know Nellie fairly well by now, and I get the impression he's holding something back."

"Huh? Twenty minutes ago you were vouching for him."

"I'm still vouching for him. I don't think he's killed anybody, I just think he's—look, Honeyman asked him if everybody got along at the 1981 meeting, and he said yes, but I got the feeling that he was—well, holding something back."

"What makes you think so?"

Gideon shrugged. "It was just in the air. A feeling. You'd have to know him."

John looked understandably doubtful.

Gideon banged his mug down, suddenly nettled. "Look, John, I'm just telling you the impression I got. If you want to follow it up, fine. If you don't want to follow it up, fine. All right?"

John glanced at Julie. "What's with him?"

"Nothing's with me. Come on, let's get out of here." He swiped irritably at the check and turned it over. "Twenty-six dollars."

John looked at Julie. "Did I say something to make him mad, or did you say something to make him mad?"

"Oh, he's not mad at us," Julie said, and then looked at Gideon with a smile. "He's feeling like a rat, that's all. These people are his friends, and he feels like a traitor to his own kind. We're just getting the brunt of it." She touched the back of Gideon's hand. "Not that I'd want you any other way."

Gideon reacted with silence and mixed feelings. It was damned irritating to have someone who knew what you were feeling before you did. On the other hand, if you were going to feel like a rat anyway, it was nice to have Julie there to understand.

"That's about it," he said gruffly, and squeezed her hand in return.

On the short drive back to the lodge, John chuckled to himself in the back seat. "Hey, guess what Applewhite said when I talked to him about this on the telephone."

Gideon thought for a second. "He said: 'I bet that sonofabitch Gideon Oliver is mixed up in this somewhere.—

John grinned. "You got it. Or words to that effect."

* * *

The evening session was held in Whitebark Lodge's meeting room, where the folding tables had been stowed along the walls and the seats arranged auditorium-style. Once at the lectern and into his subject, Nellie recovered all of his customary verve. His description of the skeleton was precise and dramatic, his account of the cause-of-death analysis—for which he gave Gideon generous credit—was detailed and suspenseful, if not altogether accurate in its minor points. ("Gideon looked at me. I looked at Gideon. What, we wondered, could have caused these bewildering little fractures? Our eyes met above that small, puzzling vertebra. 'Garrote,' we both whispered at the same time, as the grim implications...")

His audience, so engrossed that they forgot to fidget on the uncomfortable folding chairs, consisted of the forty-some-odd anthropologists and students. The spouses, et al., had long ago had their fill of the new skeleton and had found other things to do, as was attested by the clacking of Ping-Pong balls and bleeping of video games from the recreation room next door. The only "outsiders" at the session were Julie and John, sitting with Gideon in a row of seats placed along one of the walls, and Frieda Hobert, occupying pride of place on the aisle in the first row.

The news about Chuck Salish created the expected stir, and when it was noticed that John was in the room, there was a flurry of questions: "Did the police think it was Salish?" "Was there any idea as to the motive for the killing?" "Were there any promising leads?"

"Hard to say," John answered from his seat. Lieutenant Honeyman had barely gotten started. There were records to look at, people to talk to.

"Are you involved in the investigation?" Leland wondered. "I ask because you seem to be privy to the lieutenant's plans."

"I guess you could say that," John said. "The lieutenant sort of asked me to sit in. He figured, since I'm here anyway, I could be a go-between between the department and you folks. Sort of what I'm doing right now."

"I see," Leland said stiffly. "And tell me this, please. Are those of us who were here at the time to consider ourselves under suspicion?"

The underlying hum of whispered conversation stopped as suddenly as if someone had turned off a tap.

"I ask only out of idle curiosity, you understand," Leland said.

There were a few uncertain laughs, along with a head-thrown-back guffaw from Les Zenkovich.

"Let's make sure we know who's dead first," John said. "Then we'll think about who killed him."

"I see. So your decision to remove the skeleton to the safety of the sheriff's office is not to be taken personally?"

"By who?" John said pleasantly.

Leland made a small movement with his mouth and turned in his seat to face the front again.

One of the students raised a deferential hand. "Had anybody thought about making a facial reconstruction from the skull of the dead man? Couldn't that confirm the identification?"

There was a murmur of interest, mostly from other students.

Nellie, who was still moderating from the front of the room, made a face. "I doubt it, but why don't we ask our resident expert? Gideon, what do you think?"

Gideon started, caught by surprise. "Uh—well, I'm not really an expert—"

"Watch out now," Nellie said with a wink, something he could actually manage without being arch, "you're under oath."

Gideon laughed. "Seriously, I am not an expert."

Seriously, he wasn't. The science—or art; the issue was up in the air—of using modeling clay to build up a facial likeness directly on a human skull had few expert practitioners. There were perhaps two dozen in the United States, some of them anthropologists and some artists, often working together. None of them, however, was here at the meeting, and Gideon was. Two years before, he had attended a week-long workshop on the technique and had found he had a knack for it.

But he'd also found out how unobservant he'd been all his life. He'd had to learn, almost as if he'd never seen them, the way an eyelid was shaped, and an upper lip, and how people's ears were set into their heads. But he'd stuck with it, and since then he had used it in four cases; and although no one would ever confuse his work with an artist's, he'd been reasonably successful. Three of the four reconstructions had led to positive identifications, which put him well ahead of the national average.

Among professional anthropologists, the practice had as many scoffers as true believers, with Gideon somewhere in the middle. It was, as far as he was concerned, a helpful tool if used discriminatingly, by people who knew what they were doing, with full appreciation of its limitations. His own three-for-four batting average he put down to some extremely lucky breaks. One of the cases had been a woman with an easily recognizable bony hump on the bridge of her nose, another had had eyes set extraordinarily far apart, and a third had been a man with a jaw like Benito Mussolini's (that one, for better or worse, had gotten national media coverage). But the fourth had been just an everyday sort of skull, with no particularly distinctive features. And of course that was the one that was still sitting in a box in the King County Medical Examiner's Office in Seattle, unidentified.

He'd always been frank in his reservations about the process and about his own skills. All the same, when the WAFA schedule was being prepared, Miranda had asked him if he'd put on a demonstration, mainly for the students in attendance. She had offered to provide all the materials he'd need and he'd agreed. The half-day session was on the schedule for the following afternoon—and that, he supposed, made him the closest thing to an expert they were going to get.

"I think—" he began.

"Stand up so people can hear you," Nellie said, waving him up.

Gideon stood. He didn't have much to say. "My opinion is that there wouldn't be much point. When you already have a pretty good idea whose skull you've got, there are quicker, better ways to confirm it."

"Right you are," Les said from the audience. "What do we need to mess around with clay for? There are some good pictures of Salish in the file, and we can use video superimposition and computer-generated imaging to see if they match the skull." Since he'd become a consultant, Les had developed an appreciation for high-tech anthropology.

Nellie vigorously nodded his agreement. "I'll take it a step further than that. There's no need for any of this mumbo-jumbo here. Not only do we have virtually the man's entire skeleton, we have his complete dentition, which can be compared directly to Mr.

Salish's dental records, once Mr. Lau locates them. What more do we need?"

In the matter of facial reconstruction, Nellie was firmly on record as a scoffer. He had written several articles on the subject. The kindest of them was an article in the *Journal of Forensic Science* entitled, "Facial Reconstruction: Harmless Fun but Not to Be Believed."

"We'll know if it's Salish, all right," he said, "and we won't have to resort to facial reconstruction to do it."

"But what if it isn't?" one of the students asked; a mustached thirty-year-old in khakis and a scuffed slouch hat; one of several who seemed to have studied anthropological dress with Indiana Jones. "Maybe it'll turn out to be someone else. At least a reconstruction would give us a place to start."

"Not necessarily," Gideon said. "You have to understand, a facial reconstruction is a long way from an exact likeness. Nobody's going to look at it and say: 'My God, that's *him!*' All you can do is show it around and hope; see if it looks even a little familiar to anybody."

"But what's wrong with that?" asked another student. "Couldn't we do that?"

"Show it around? To whom? Who's missing that we know about?"

The student shook her head. "I don't follow."

"Well, reconstructions are like fingerprints. They're not any good unless you have something to compare them to—*somebody* to compare them to, and we don't have anybody we're looking for. Nobody but Salish, and as Les and Nellie said, there are better ways of proving it's Salish."

"But—"

"And if it turns out to be someone else, some other missing person, we don't have any idea of where he's missing from—according to the lieutenant, it's not from around here—so *where* do we show it around? And to whom?"

"Oh," the young woman said, and sank disappointedly back. "I see."

"Thank you, Gideon," Nellie said, pulling together his notes from the lectern. "And now I think—"

Gideon was still standing. "But on the other hand..."

He still didn't see any forensic point in it, but by now his teacherly instincts were engaged. Throwing cold water on any glimmer of student interest went against his grain. Besides, seeing how close the reconstruction came to Chuck Salish's face would make it interesting for him as well as them.

"On the other hand, I'm supposed to do a demonstration tomorrow afternoon anyway. I was going to use a skull from the museum collection, but I don't see why I couldn't demonstrate just as well on an actual murder victim."

"Yes, it does add that certain je ne sais quoi," Leland said, sotto voce.

"But if I'm going to go through the whole process for real," Gideon went on, "even if we just skim through it, it'll take more than an afternoon. I'd better get started in the morning."

"But how can you do that?" It was Miranda. "Nellie, aren't you still working on it?"

Nellie considered. "I'll tell you what. You go ahead and work with the skull tomorrow, Gideon. I still have plenty to do on the postcranial skeleton. Let's see, isn't tomorrow afternoon's general session going to be at the museum?"

It was, someone volunteered. The topic was blunt-force skull fractures, and they would be using Miranda's collection.

"Well, then, why don't we give you until...oh, four o'clock, Gideon? Since everyone will be in Bend anyway, we can all drop by and see how your work stacks up against the photos—and against the memories of those of us who remember Mr. Salish. An impartial evaluation of the art of facial reconstruction, done in the spirit of scientific inquiry."

The smile he directed at Gideon was somewhere between that of a friend for a friend, and of a frog for a fly.

"Not fair and you know it, Nellie," Gideon said. "A day isn't enough for a thorough job, especially if I'm supposed to be teaching while I'm doing it. Three or four days, maybe—"

There were a few good-natured boos.

"Come on, Doc, put your money where your mouth is," John murmured. "Give it a shot."

Gideon sighed. "All right, fine," he announced. "For what it's worth. But it's *not* a test of the method. And it means we'll have to get started early tomorrow. We'd better get the reconstruction going at seven."

The looks exchanged among some of the students suggested a slight diminution of enthusiasm.

"Miranda," Gideon said, "is there a problem getting the materials to me that early?"

"No, I'm usually at the museum by six. Quiet time, you know. I'll go on over to the sheriff, get a room set up for you, and see that there's coffee and donuts."

"Can you do that?"

"Sure, they owe me. And I can sign the skull over to you then."

Leland, looking dissatisfied, waved a finger at Gideon. "This means you won't be able to attend the regular morning session."

"No, I suppose not. What's on?"

"I am. I'm presenting an overview of recent developments in coprolite analysis and their applications to forensic archaeology. With slides and hands-on material."

There was a near-imperceptible pause. "Damn, Leland," Gideon said, "it looks like I'll have to miss it."

CHAPTER 10

"I think I'm getting bones on the brain," Julie said.

Yawning, Gideon flipped another pebble into the creek. "Who wouldn't?" *Ploop*.

They had gotten up early to spend some time together. With Gideon committed to the all-day reconstruction and Julie planning to pay a working visit to Lavalands National Monument, they wouldn't be seeing each other until late afternoon. They'd had a quick cup of coffee and then walked along the nature trail, a wooded path following the smaller of the two streams that ran through the heart of the old resort and into the woodlands to the north.

It had been a good idea. With the heat wave predicted to continue (John was delighted), the growing but still tolerable early-morning warmth had intensified the sweet, spicy fragrances of the pine forest, so that every breath was thick with cinnamon and vanilla-like scents; markedly different from the cool, cedary aromas of coastal Washington. They had walked hand in hand, quietly, glad to be enjoying the freshness together before the rest of the world had gotten moving. Underfoot, the path lay three inches deep in pine needles as long and golden and pungent as hay. Walking through them made dry, swishing, silky sounds that soothed their ears. And when there was the unexpected, rasping crunch of a hidden pine cone being stepped on, they laughed.

After a quarter of a mile they had stopped and sat down at this pleasant, open spot where the branches filtered the sunlight and the stream lapped at the low bank. They had watched the sparkling water, and sat with their arms around their knees, and chewed wild grass stems, and talked aimlessly about nothing much. It had been too long a time since they'd had a morning like it.

"No," Julie said, "I don't mean generally speaking, I mean right now; specifically."

"Specific bones on the brain?" Gideon said lazily, still beguiled by the water. He tossed in another pebble.

Julie got up, walked two steps to the edge of the bank, and crouched, using a twig to probe gently at the root area of a young willow that overhung the stream. She turned to look at him over her shoulder. "Gideon, I think these are cremains."

"I wish people wouldn't call..."

"Excuse me, cremated remains. Come look."

Gideon got reluctantly to his feet and went to her side, leaning over with his hands on his knees. "Yup."

"But aren't the chunks kind of big? The ones Nellie showed us were almost like powder."

"Well, it depends on the funeral home. Sometimes they pretty much pulverize what's left, and other times they more or less break it up with a hammer, and you get pieces like these." He picked up one of the two fragments; a bit of humerus. "But I grant you, these are bigger than usual.

There seem to be only these two pieces. I imagine someone was throwing the ashes into the stream, and these accidentally fell onto the bank. They don't look as if they've been here very—"

"Gideon!"

Julie had continued scanning the nearby ground, and now she was staring at a small tangle of exposed roots that jutted out from the side of the bank, two or three inches above the water and a couple of feet from the bone fragments.

Gideon saw instantly what had seized her attention. He put down the burned piece and kneeled to look more closely at the bright, granular fleck of white caught among the roots. After a few seconds he sat back on his haunches and looked thoughtfully up at her.

"Jasper?" she said.

"Looks like it."

There wasn't much room for doubt. The fleck was a broken, half-inch-wide particle of white styrofoam; the same kind of plastic that Jasper's remains had been wired to. And, as if the matter needed cinching, there was still a loop of white, plastic-coated wire piercing it, twisted together at one end. It was the loop that had snagged in the roots.

"They must have done it in the dark," Gideon said, thinking

aloud. "After the walk-through at the museum. They wanted to get rid of it in a hurry. They came out here, broke up the display, and tossed everything in the stream."

"Or thought they did," Julie said. "It would have been easy for them not to notice they'd dropped a few pieces."

"Yes. But…"

"What?"

"Doesn't this strike you as an odd place to dump these? Right on the nature trail? I mean, if I'd wanted to get rid of them quickly, I would have maybe tossed them out of the car window on the way back from Bend, a piece at a time. No one ever would have found them."

"Most people didn't go to Bend in their own cars. They went in groups, or took the bus. You couldn't have done it without other people seeing."

"Well, then, I'd have crushed them after I got back—a couple of blows with a hammer or a rock would have done it—and flushed them down the toilet. Crush-and-flush."

"You'd have flushed the Styrofoam?"

"All right, *that* I'd have broken up and tossed in the garbage. Without the bones or one of these wire loops, who would connect it to Jasper? Or maybe I'd have buried it, to be on the safe side. But somewhere out in the woods. I sure wouldn't have left any of it right along the trail like this."

"I agree, it's strange."

He nodded and straightened up. "Julie, I'd better get going. I have to be in Bend at seven. Will you let John know about this when we get back to the lodge?"

"Of course." They began walking back. "What do you make of it, Gideon?"

He shook his head. "I don't know."

"Still think it's just a prank?"

He looked at her. "No," he said, "I don't think it's a prank."

* * *

Miranda was as good as her word. When Gideon arrived at the Justice Building in Bend at 7:00 A.M., the county commissioners' meeting room, which had surely never before been used for such a purpose, was set up and ready with everything he needed.

At the head table the materials he would use were neatly laid out: a somewhat unsettling pair of dark-gray prosthetic eyes; a box of terra-cotta–colored Jolly King modeling clay; a seven-inch length of eraser rubber; a box of round toothpicks; a box of cotton; a tube of Duco cement; an X-Acto knife; a few small rulers; a couple of simple modeling tools (fingers would be the most important tools); some 80-grade sandpaper; and a folder put out by the University of New Mexico called "Tables of Facial Tissue Thickness of American Caucasoids."

And a carton of donuts and a metal urn of hot coffee just perking its last on a long table against the wall. This was especially appreciated by the arriving students. With ninety-degree heat coming, the air conditioning had been turned up to keep the clay from slumping on the skull.

"Need anything else?" Miranda asked.

"No, this is great. You must have gotten here at five." Miranda placed her hand on her heart. "We are here to serve."

She had brought the skull and mandible from the room Nellie was working in and placed it on the table. Gideon quickly filled in the medical examiner's evidence tag: *Released to*: Gideon Oliver. *How:* In person. *Date:* 6-19-91. *Time:* 7:00 A.M.

"Okay, have a ball," Miranda said. "Yell if you need anything. I'll be right down the hall."

"You're going to be working on the postcranial skeleton with Nellie?"

"Uh-huh. Me, Nellie, and Dr. Tilton from the medical examiner's office. Since I'm the one the ME officially released it to, it makes sense for me to be there."

"I suppose so."

"And of course you always learn something from Nellie."

"That's true too."

"And it was either that or coprolite analysis. Hands on." "I hear," he said, "what you're saying."

After Miranda had left and they had stoked up on coffee and donuts, Gideon got started, explaining as he went. First, the skull was firmly locked onto a plastic mount. Then he packed the fragile bones in the eye sockets and nasal aperture with cotton, and covered them with a protective layer of clay. The Duco was used to glue lengths of toothpick to the surfaces of the lower molars to prop the mouth slightly open. Without them, there would be an unnatural, clenched-teeth appearance. After that the mandible was attached to the skull with daubs of clay, an easy-enough process because mandibles fitted into place only one way. Inserting the eyes took more time; eyeballs do not fill their sockets, and getting them placed just right—not too protruding, not too sunken, not too high or too low—was something that took patience.

But by eight o'clock these preliminaries were out of the way. Gideon now had a skull that stared alarmingly back at him with great, goggling, lidless eyes. He explained the rest of the process.

"First of all, despite what you may have read in popular fiction, we don't make a facial likeness by building up the musculature a layer at a time. The Russians may still do it that way, but we've had more success using average skin thickness as a guide.

"The folders in front of you show the average soft-tissue thicknesses of Caucasian males measured at thirty-two points on the face. What I'm going to do is cut the eraser rubber into thirty-two sections to match those thicknesses and glue them to the right places on this particular skull. That's our guide for how thick the flesh is at those points, and we just use clay to fill in between them." He smiled. "Nothing to it."

"Sort of like connect-the-dots," someone said.

"Sort of," Gideon agreed.

What he didn't tell them was that this was the easy part. The basic form of the face, which is what connecting the dots gave you, was relatively simple and reasonably accurate. The trouble was that nobody ever recognized anybody else from his basic facial form. What made you distinguishable from a hundred million other people was not your facial form but your ears and eyes, your lips and nose, the "cast of your eye and your own singular and indefinable mien," as his seminar instructor had put it.

And, as of yet, no one had figured out a way to determine the curve of a lip or the droop of an eyelid from the bone beneath. To say nothing of an indefinable mien.

But that could wait until later, after they understood how the early part was done. First, he would measure and cut the rubber, glue the cut lengths to the skull, then cut the clay into strips and roll them into "worms," which would be laid down from rubber marker to rubber marker, crisscrossing the face until those disturbing gray eyes goggled from behind a tightly fitted grid, like the eyes of the Man in the Iron Mask. And getting it that far was going to take most of the morning.

* * *

The eight students showed a lively interest, which naturally pleased Gideon, but their frequent questions slowed things up. It was almost 1:00 P.M. before the open spaces in the waffle-like facial grid had been filled in and smoothed out. The results, as always at that point, were bland and disappointing, featureless in the literal sense of the word. Without nose, lips, eyelids, eyebrows, and ears, the "face" didn't look like much of anything.

Over take-out pizzas, Gideon explained that, to make it look like something, you had to stop being an anthropologist and start being an artist. Except for providing a few clues on the shape and size of the nose, the skull had nothing further to tell them; there was no way of gauging from the bone beneath how wide the mouth was, or how thick the lips were, or what the form of the eyelids was, or anything at all about the ears. There were lots of artists' rules of thumb, however—the eyebrows were three to five millimeters above the orbital rim; the ears were tipped back fifteen percent and about as long as the nose; the mouth was as wide as the distance between the canine teeth, and so on. They would spend the rest of the day applying them.

* * *

In the tiny sheriff's snack room, twenty yards from where the clay face was slowly developing into something humanlike under Gideon's hands, John Lau was looking at his watch. Nellie Hobert was late for their appointment, not that that was much of a surprise. If Hobert was anything like Gideon Oliver, he went into a trance when you put a skeleton in front of him. You had to nudge him every now and then to make sure he kept breathing.

Idly he contemplated the display behind the glass front of the candy machine, trying to decide if he really wanted anything. Probably so; there were still almost three hours until dinner. Behind him, the door to the room opened.

"Don't do it, John," Nellie called. "Resist all temptation." He came up to the machine beside him and silently scanned the rows. "You'd think they'd have Paydays," he grumbled after a few seconds.

John pointed. "G-4."

Nellie brightened, digging in the pocket of his shorts while John made his selection. A moment after John's Three Musketeers bar clunked into the tray, a Payday followed.

"Peanuts are good for you," Nellie explained. "Loaded with thiamine and riboflavin. Good-quality protein source."

"Yeah, but it's incomplete protein," John said. What that meant he wouldn't have wanted to explain, but he had heard his wife Marti say it, and it always paid to establish your expertise when you were dealing with scientific types.

Not that Nellie seemed so hard to deal with. In a lot of ways he reminded John of an older Gideon: a little stuffy, a little touchy, but with a sense of humor that was never very far below the surface. And under all the technical bullshit there was a likable, unaffected guy who didn't take himself too seriously.

"In that case I'll make sure and have some milk with dinner." Nellie pulled a chair away from the single chipped table, sat down, and unwrapped the candy bar, blissfully twisting off a chunk with his teeth. He looked like a five-year-old with a beard. His T-shirt showed a raised fist, with lettering that said: "Stop Continental Drift!"

John laughed. "So how's it going in there?"

"Just fine, but I'm sorry to say I don't have anything definitive to tell you." Hopefully he eyed the large envelope under John's arm. "I don't suppose that'd be Chuck's file, would it now?"

John handed it to him. "Copy just for you, straight from the ME."

"Aah!" Nellie laid the Payday on the table, brushed crumbs from his fingers, and began riffling through the ten-year-old file. He stopped at what John recognized as the report from Salish's physician. The anthropologist scanned down the sheets with his finger, making a humming noise through his nose. "Mmmmmm… well, hell."

"Problem?" John said.

"No, not a problem, but not much help either. I think you know the skeleton in there's got an old broken arm and some arthritis in one foot. Well, there's no mention of either one here."

John frowned at him. "Are you saying maybe that isn't Salish's skeleton now?"

"Good heavens, no," Nellie said, "not at all. That broken arm was probably fifty years old. Salish probably never even told his doctor about it—assuming he remembered it himself. As for the lack of mention of any arthritis, well, it wasn't very severe, and it's quite possible Salish never complained to his physician about that either. Just one more nagging little ache among the many we all have to start getting used to eventually."

He shrugged. "All I'm saying is that it's not going to be quite as simple as I thought, coming up with a definite identification. It would have been nice to have laid any remaining doubts completely to rest."

He leafed through the rest of the material. "I don't see much else of use here." At a sheet of Salish's photographs he paused, slowly shaking his head.

John had a moment's uneasiness. "That is him in those pictures, isn't it?"

Nellie glanced up. "Yes, certainly."

"You're sure?"

"Of course. They're good likenesses, actually."

"Well, what about using them? Can't you do—what was it, video imposition?"

"Video superimposition. You use a computer program to impose the face from a photograph onto an image of the skull and see if it seems to fit."

"Well?"

"Well, there's some as swears by it and some as don't." He twisted off another hunk of the Payday. "Me, I don't. They're a long way from proof positive, John. Look, have you had any luck turning up those missing dental records? Something tells me we're going to need them."

Let's hope not, John thought. So far, the Albuquerque office hadn't even found out who Salish's dentist was. "We're working on it. Nellie, you have any idea at all who took them out of the file?"

Nellie stopped chewing. "Oh, I can't believe anybody *took* them.

They probably got put back in the wrong file, that's all. It happens every day. I expect a search through the adjacent files would turn them up soon enough."

Not so far, it hadn't. John had spent half an hour in the morning doing just that, and now a clerk was going through the entire file cabinet. Other misfiled items had indeed shown up, but not Chuck Salish's dental records.

"They were there, though?" John asked. "You remember seeing them?"

"You mean ten years ago? Oh, yes, we got his dental records, all right. We didn't get much use out of them, of course, since the remains we thought were his didn't have any...John, your question—why would anyone take those dental records?—implies that you think someone did take them."

"That's right, I do." After a second he added: "Don't you?"

Nellie didn't respond to the query. "And that implies in turn that you think it's one of us, doesn't it?"

"It's a pretty logical place to start."

"And one of us who is here again now."

"I guess," John said carefully. "Nellie, anything you could tell me about that first meeting that might throw some light—"

"Such as?"

"Well, anything that—"

Nellie suddenly thrust himself up from his seat, took the couple of steps that the small room allowed, and stood with his back turned and his arms crossed, facing the Pepsi machine. "You actually think one of us killed poor Salish, don't you?"

This time John wanted to wait him out if he could, but Nellie wouldn't go along. "So? *Do you?* Say what you think, dammit!"

"At this point I wouldn't even want to guess about that, sir." At the word *sir*, Nellie emitted a peculiar growl. John was uneasily aware that he was being cagey with a man the director of the FBI had called the dean of American forensic scientists, a man of spotless reputation who'd already assisted the Bureau on more homicides than John would handle in his entire career.

But, yes, there was something in the air, as Gideon had said last night. He could feel it too. *Holding something back,* those were the words for it, all right. He took a deep breath. "Dr. Hobert, I think you're keeping something to yourself and—"

Nellie spun around, stubby and contentious in his baggy shorts. "I am, am I?"

"—and I think the best thing would be for you to just tell me about it."

"You do, do you?"

Dean of forensic scientists or not, it wasn't the best way to get on John's good side. "Yeah, I do," he said angrily. "And you goddamn well ought to know it too."

Nellie bristled. For a moment it looked as if he were going to stalk out and leave him there. John had unhappy visions of indignant telephone calls to Charlie Applewhite. But then the blue eyes closed. Nellie squeezed the bridge of his nose, rubbing hard. When he opened his eyes the heat had gone. He came back and sat down next to John.

"I seem to be barking at people these days," he said mildly. "Really, I'm very sorry. This miserable business with Salish…"

"That's okay, I understand."

"There's no reason at all why you shouldn't ask me whatever you like. May as well come straight to the horse's mouth. The horse's something, anyway." His smile was tired. "But I assure you I'm keeping nothing under my hat."

John nodded at him. "Okay." He was a long way from convinced. "Let me ask you about something else, then.

You heard about Jasper's remains being dumped in the creek?"

"Yes," Nellie said. "Horrible. Bizarre."

John came close to laughing. Here was the guy who'd cheerfully worked out the plan to keep Jasper's bones in a glass case for everybody in the world to gawk at for the next umpteen years, and now he was talking about bizarre because someone had taken them and put them into that nice, clean, peaceful river. These were weird people.

"Do you have any idea why anybody would do that?"

Nellie spread his hands helplessly. "It's absolutely beyond me. That kind of thoughtless—"

"The idea's come up that maybe Jasper was injured or already dead when he was put on that bus, and that someone wants to make sure no one takes a close look at him now." At least he thought that was what Julie had been driving at.

Nellie laughed shortly. "Well, now, that's a peculiar idea, I must say."

"Did you actually see him get on the bus?"

"Well, no, it left at—I think it was 5:00 A.M."

"When did you last see him alive?"

"The night before. We had dinner together. That is, all of us did."

"What time did it break up?"

"I don't know. Early. Eight o'clock, nine o'clock."

"You're sure?"

"No, I'm not in the least sure. It was ten years ago. John, why all this hypothecating about Albert? I should think you'd have your hands full with Salish."

"You don't think there's some connection?"

Nellie's eyebrows went up. "Connection?" He seemed genuinely surprised. "Between—? Forgive me, but I seem to have missed something in translation here."

"That's okay. We can talk about it later if we need to." They would need to, he thought.

"Fine." Nellie smacked his hands on his thighs and got up again, taking the file. "Quarter to four. I want to go back and check a few things before seeing what Gideon's come up with. Unless you have anything else?"

John shook his head. "I'll see you in there."

Nellie had been gone no more than thirty seconds when Leland appeared.

"Somebody said I'd find you here," he said, closing the door behind him. He looked, to John's eyes, a little uneasy, a little squirrelly. "I wanted to talk to you."

"If you're trying to set up another poker game, forget it. I learned my lesson."

Leland smiled woodenly. "Mr. Lau, there's something you should know. Nobody else is going to volunteer it, so I might as well be the one."

John had heard this opening a good many times in his career, and he had yet to have something useful come out of it. Most of the time, it muddied the waters instead of clearing them. He motioned to the chair Nellie had used, but Leland shook his head. He wanted, it seemed, to say his piece and get out.

"Go ahead," John said.

Leland rearranged his mouth. His thick, old-fashioned glasses made his eyes look like the painted eyes in a doll's head: round, flat, bland.

"Frieda and Chuck Salish were…carrying on."

"Who's Frieda?" John said after a second.

"Frieda Hobert, Nellie's wife."

"Oh, yeah. What do you mean, carrying on? Could you be a little more specific?"

"I mean," Leland said evenly, "carrying on. Loaded glances, odd disappearances together for twenty minutes at a time, whispered remarks no one else was supposed to notice. What else there was, I can only surmise." His lips turned down. "The whole thing was pitiful. And repulsive."

"Did Nellie know about it?"

Leland hesitated. "At the time, I thought he was the only one who didn't."

"And now?"

"Now I don't know. That's something for you to pursue if it seems appropriate. I'm not suggesting," he added with care, "that it will turn out to have any pertinence to…to what we now know."

"Tell me—why wouldn't anyone else volunteer it?"

"Mr. Lau, you have to understand. Nellie Hobert is God to these people. They adore him."

"But you don't?"

Leland colored; a round pink disk beneath each pale eye. "I resent your implication."

"I wasn't implying—"

"I have nothing against Nellie. His reputation may be a bit, shall we say, inflated, but that has nothing to do with anything. For ten years I've kept as quiet about this as anyone else. I would have continued to do so if Salish's body hadn't turned up. But, as it is, I thought it was information you should have."

And so, John admitted to himself, it was. "Thanks, Dr. Roach, I'll look into it. I may want to get some more information from you later."

Wordlessly, Leland looked at him for a few moments. "If you like. It's nothing to me one way or the other." He turned and walked out. John picked up his untouched Three Musketeers and bit in.

Well, it was something to tuck away, assuming it was true. Could it be what Nellie was hiding? Maybe so. And if it was, where did that lead? To Nellie as Salish's killer? John had trouble making himself take the idea seriously. Aside from Nellie's being a nationally known forensic scientist (but then weren't they all?), it was hard to picture the gnomelike little guy murdering someone in a fit of jealous rage. You never knew about those things, of course, but if Nellie had killed Salish, why would he tell Honeyman the skeleton was Salish's in the first place? Why not just let it go, and let everyone keep thinking he'd died in the bus?

On the other hand (just to be fair), was it possible Nellie was trying to be clever? That he felt the skeleton's identity was bound to come out anyway, and he could remove suspicion from himself by being the first person who called attention to it? Possible, yes, but—

"Still here, John?" It was Nellie again, head stuck through the doorway. "What say we join the others and go see what the estimable Dr. Oliver hath wrought?"

With a sigh of satisfaction Gideon finished shaping the soft swelling that formed the middle of the lower lip. The effort was going well; it was going to be one of his better jobs. At what he thought was mid-afternoon he wiped his fingers, stretched cramped shoulders, and looked up to suggest a break. To his surprise the room was filling with conference attendees.

"You weren't due till four o'clock," he said.

"It's four-ten," somebody answered. "The moment of truth."

Gideon put down the modeling tool. "But it's not done. I haven't made a neck, there's no back to the head, the color's off, the—"

"Trying to weasel out, eh?" Nellie said happily. "Come, come, Gideon, time to face the music."

* * *

Those who knew what Salish looked like varied widely on whether the reconstruction was anything like him. Miranda thought it was, especially around the angles of the jaw; Leland, Frieda Hobert, and Nellie said it wasn't even remotely similar; and Les was undecided. John, who had the photographs from the file, couldn't make up his mind either—maybe yes, maybe no.

"Well, it's not finished," Gideon said testily. He had a right to be defensive. He'd put in nine straight hours on the thing. He'd worked painstakingly, and he'd done a damn good job, but the head simply wasn't ready to be viewed, and he told them so again.

The students who had stuck it out with him through the long day—there were six of them left—jumped to his support. A reconstruction wasn't like a photograph, they explained to their elders. It was unrealistic to expect an exact likeness. And, anyway, hadn't Dr. Oliver said last night that there wasn't enough time to do a finished job? Couldn't they see it wasn't complete? Couldn't they let him have a little more time?

"Now, now," Nellie said. "The necromancers have had their chance. I think we'd better let science take over tomorrow."

"Wait a minute, Nellie," Miranda said, "I think Gideon's done a wonderful job so far. It's sure starting to look familiar to me, and I think it'd be a pity not to finish it. How long would it take, Gideon?"

"Not long. A couple of hours, maybe. The hard part's done."

Miranda appealed to Nellie. "Two more hours." The students applauded.

"Why don't you finish up this evening, then?" someone asked.

The students groaned. They'd put in a long day too, and they were as tired of looking at the thing as Gideon was. Ordinarily, working in his lab, he spread this kind of work over a week or more, a few hours at a time.

"No," he said, "I think we're all bushed. If we do it at all, it'd be better to wait until tomorrow."

Nellie used a finger to scratch the side of his beard. "I don't know," he said doubtfully. "I'm sure John here would like a final report as soon as possible."

"Another few hours isn't going to hurt," John said. He gestured at the skull. "This is interesting. I'd like to see the finished job."

Nellie bowed his head. "I submit. All right, Gideon, it's all yours. Finish it up tomorrow."

"Good," Gideon said. "We'll get a good, early start—"

Julie, who had come in with the others, dug an elbow into his side. "Horseback ride," she said under her breath. "Chuck-wagon breakfast. You are going."

"—ah, immediately after the chuck-wagon breakfast. No later than ten."

CHAPTER 11

For the first part of the way back they followed the trail they'd come on, a broad, shaded track of loamy soil that allowed them to go two by two. Gideon rode quietly alongside Julie, relaxed and content, his stomach full, enjoying the creak of the saddle under him, the pungent, gamy smell of horseflesh, the lolling, swaying, gentle gait. They rode slowly alongside Lupine Creek, through a forest of cinnamon-barked pines varied by occasional stands of western larch and aspen, with clumps of manzanita and buckbrush at ground level. (Julie told him the names, which he appreciated learning and promptly forgot.)

He had already admitted to her that the chuck-wagon breakfast had been a wonderful break. Cooked over open fires, the eggs, bacon, burned toast (Leland claimed they burned it on purpose, for atmosphere), and gritty coffee had been served up by authentic-looking wranglers in a shaded clearing, with the morning sunlight illuminating the highest branches of the trees. Tethered horses had pawed and snuffled twenty feet away, and everybody had smelled like wood smoke. It had made Chuck Salish seem like something from an unpleasant dream.

Gideon had expected to see few of the older attendees, but almost all of them were there. Leland, he was surprised to learn, was an expert rider who had requested and gotten an English saddle instead of one of the Western ones—with their big, comforting pommels and horns—which all the others had been glad to accept. Nellie was there too ("Give me the slowest, oldest nag you've got. And the biggest, softest saddle"), along with Les and Miranda. Even Callie, who had arrived back at the lodge at 6:30 A.M. after a red-eye flight from Nevada, had shown up, although the less-resilient Harlow was yet to be seen.

The only problem had been a confusion over time. The head

wrangler, a twenty-year-old named Tracy, with the short hair, fresh, boyish face, and narrow, athletic hips of a youngster who lived for horses, had thought they were due back at the lodge at eleven. When she was told that the sessions began at ten, she had proposed a shortcut.

After twenty minutes of easy riding they came to it. On the way out to breakfast they had turned away from the bank of the stream in a wide arc to avoid this brief stretch of poorly maintained trail that climbed and skirted the flank of a rocky grade at the edge of the water. That was for more advanced riders, Tracy had told them, but now they would save half an hour by taking it.

She called a halt before they started up the grade. "It's not really dangerous," she told them from horseback. "It just looks that way if you're not used to it. Just give your horse its head. They know they're going home, and they know how to get there. Let's go. Oh," she said as she started up again, "and don't let them know you're nervous."

"It's a little late for that," Gideon said half aloud. Earlier, on the ride out, his horse, a placid, good-natured brown mare named Rosebud, had stopped to nibble at the trailside grasses whenever the fancy took her. Twice she'd stopped to doze, ignoring his coaxing. Julie, a competent, confident rider, had had to dismount to help him get her going again. "She's just a thousand pounds of muscle trying to figure out what you want," she had told him. "You have to let her know who's boss, that's all."

"Don't worry," Gideon had said, "she already knows."

Loose rocks now made the footing going up the grade unstable, and several times the horses slipped, bringing a few sudden intakes of breath from the less self-possessed riders, Gideon included. But only Callie's horse gave anything like trouble, skittering abruptly sidewise at one point so that Callie's leg barely missed scraping heavily against a tree trunk. Callie, who hadn't looked very comfortable on a horse to begin with, laughed it off, but seemed shakier and more tentative than ever in the saddle.

At the top of the grade Tracy called for their attention again.

"All right, everybody, now comes the tricky part."

"I thought that *was* the tricky part," Gideon said.

Julie laughed. "Relax, you're doing fine."

"What we've got here," Tracy continued from her saddle, "is a spot where the trail is sort of, uh, washed away for a few yards, so it's only a couple, three feet wide, and not too level, right along the edge, with a rock wall on the other side that sort of, uh, crowds you a little—"

"Wonderful," Gideon muttered.

"Don't worry so much," Julie said. "You really are getting the hang of it, I can tell."

"—but take my word for it, it just looks hard because you're not a horse. I've seen five-year-old kids do it with no problem. If we just take the ledge one by one—"

"*Ledge?*" somebody exclaimed.

"Well, path," Tracy said. "If we take it one by one, and you just let your mounts do all the work, we'll do just fine—close your eyes if it bothers you—and I'll have you back at the lodge in less than ten minutes."

Tracy went first, presumably to show that it could be done, and then the others began, one at a time. The trail, about fifty feet above the stream, was not so much a ledge as an ill-defined shelf in a curving wall of loose, purplish volcanic gravel. Again the hooves slipped on the loose stones, but the slope itself wasn't steep enough to frighten any but the most timid riders, and the first dozen or so crossed easily. Then there was a lull.

"Come on, people, let's get it on," Tracy called from the other side. She pointed at Callie. "Next, please, ma'am."

"Oh!" Callie shook her head. "I'm not...I don't think I'm ready yet. My horse is still a little jumpy."

Tracy shrugged and pointed to Gideon. "You, please."

"Come on, Rosebud," he said, and nudged her gingerly with his heels. Deep in his heart he assumed she would ignore this irresolute request, but with something like a sigh she abandoned the shrub she'd been chewing and started obediently forward. Pleased, he straightened his back and settled more solidly, more commandingly into the saddle. Julie was right. Controlling a horse wasn't anywhere near as difficult as people made it out to be. It was, after all, just a question of letting it know who was boss.

"Atta girl," he said with masterful approval as they moved out from under the trees into the sun and Rosebud began to pick her slow way along the gravel. He leaned forward to pat the moist, muscular neck, wanting to keep her in motion. He didn't want to have to start her up again if he could help it, not being sure of just how long he was going to be in charge.

There was a commotion behind him, from the group still waiting to cross. A horse snorted; another whinnied. Someone yelled "Shit!" Hooves scraped agitatedly. There were shouts of warning. Gideon turned in the saddle to see Callie's horse lurching toward him, its big brown head twisting and heaving. Callie was standing rigidly in the stirrups, her face white and strained, twisting the reins. "Stop! Stop!" she was screaming at it.

"Callie—" he said.

There wasn't time for anything else. She had managed to drag her horse away from the outer edge of the trail, so that when it bucketed wildly into Gideon's, it was on the inside, against the rock wall. Rosebud, forced to the outside, whinnied and kicked at the other animal, at the same time frantically trying to keep her footing on the loose rocks. Gideon, his feet jarred out of the stirrups by the impact, was already beginning to tip helplessly forward out of the saddle and over her left side. He managed somehow to grab the saddle horn with one hand, but it wasn't enough to stop him from tipping further, in what seemed weirdly like slow motion. Her mane whipped his mouth. He had a vivid impression of one wild, chestnut-colored eye a few inches from his face, rolling and showing white, and then he was turning over in the air, wondering immaterially if he still had the reins in his other hand.

He hit on his left side and shoulder, in the dusty purple gravel of the slope, and tumbled downhill, literally heels over head, seeing his legs and feet—one shoe was gone—whipping over him against a hot blue sky. On his back again he continued sliding headfirst down the slope, grabbing at the dry soil with his fingers. To his horror, Rosebud was slipping down the hillside after him in an immense fall of purple gravel. She was sliding on her rear end in a posture straight out of a kids' Saturday-morning cartoon, down on her hindquarters like a sitting dog, her forelegs propped stiffly in front of her in a frantic effort to stop the slide. But down she came anyway, showering him with pebbles and dust, gaining rapidly on him, blocking out the sun.

All thousand pounds of her.

* * *

"Where am I?"

"Now wouldn't you think they only said that in books?" a cheery male voice wondered. "But, no, they always do it."

Gideon pressed his eyes more tightly shut. The sun was sharp against his lids. There was sweat on his forehead. He was lying on his back, on an uncomfortably rough surface. Somebody was pressing on his ribs.

"What happened?" he said. There was dust in his mouth.

"Yes, they say that too. When you think about it, it's fascinating how banal people's remarks are in situations of—"

"Gideon, you're all right." Julie's voice, frightened but trying to be reassuring. "You had a fall."

"A f—?"

Abruptly, he remembered. He tried opening his eyes but winced at the light. Julie shaded his face with her hand so he could open them again. He was still on the slope, head slightly downhill. Above, on the trail, he could see people peering anxiously down at him. At his side, leaning over him, were Julie and a man he recognized as Vern Sauer, one of the few WAFA members who wasn't a professional anthropologist. Sauer was a physician, a coroner somewhere in Nevada.

Gideon wet his lips and spit out sour dust. "How long have I—"

"—been unconscious," Sauer said happily. "I knew you wouldn't disappoint me."

"Only a few seconds," Julie said anxiously. "How do you feel?"

"Okay, I think. I'd like to get up. It's hot." He started to push up.

"Now you just hold your horses," Sauer told him, pressing him back. "Sorry, I'm not much on metaphors," he said with a laugh, and continued his prodding. "Let's just make sure you're all in one piece before you get going."

Gideon lay back without resistance, swept by a billow of nausea. Julie reached for his hand.

"I'm fine, really," he told her weakly. "A little queasy, that's all." He squeezed her hand.

"How many fingers am I holding up?" Sauer asked.

"Two," Gideon said. Below, near the stream, he could hear a

horse stamping nervously, and the voice of one of the wranglers trying to soothe it.

"And now?"

"Three. Is that Rosebud down there?"

"Yes, she's fine."

"Did she fall on me?"

Sauer laughed. "If that thing landed on you, you wouldn't have to ask. No, you got out of its way, but apparently you hit your head on a stump." He probed some more, gently moved Gideon's limbs, asked a few questions. Then he leaned back. "Well, it looks like he'll live," he told Julie.

Getting up was easier than he expected. The queasiness was uncomfortable, but he seemed to have suffered nothing worse than some abrasions on his back and shoulders. They were only now beginning to sting, and he thought he could feel a few small tracks of blood. The back of his head hurt, but the skin didn't seem to be broken. There was going to be a hell of a lump, though.

Sauer brushed pebbles from him. "Going to be able to walk? We're only five minutes from the lodge."

"Sure."

"Good. When you get back I want you to take a bath, get into a pair of pajamas, and climb into bed. Then I want to have another look."

"Vern, I appreciate it, but I'm fine now. I don't need a doctor."

"Be a sport, Oliver. When do I ever get a chance to work on a live body anymore?"

"I'll have him ready for you," Julie said.

"I have to finish that reconstruction," Gideon said. Sauer shook his head. "Not today."

"I just—"

"I'll have him ready for you," Julie said again, this time more firmly, for Gideon's benefit.

He was too unsteady to argue. With their help he climbed slowly back up the slope.

Tracy, taut-faced and anxious, ran to them from a knot of people comforting a noisily distraught Callie.

"Are you okay?"

"Fine," Gideon said. "How's Callie—the other rider?"

"All right, I think. She never—she never fell off. Oh, God, I *knew* we shouldn't have come back this way!" Tracy was close to tears. "I was supposed to have people sign waivers before we started out. I—"

"Don't worry about it, Tracy," Gideon said. "I don't think anybody's going to get sued."

Sauer cut in. "Do you suppose we could start back, please? I'd like to get this man off his feet."

Tracy practically snapped to attention. "Absolutely. Right now. Sir?" she said to Gideon. "Did you want to mount up again, or would you rather walk?"

Gideon managed a smile. "I think," he said, "I'd just as soon walk."

CHAPTER 12

"I can't find anything to be concerned about," Sauer said, sitting back. "I'd take it easy for a day or so if I were you. And let me know right away if you have any vision problems or anything of the sort. Need anything for the pain?"

"No," Gideon said, "the scrapes sting a little, that's all." He buttoned his shirt and gingerly felt the lump behind his left ear. "My head's not too bad. I'll take a couple of aspirin if it bothers me."

"Good thinking. Well, then, I'll be on my way." He zipped up his bag and stood. "Julie, those dressings can come off tonight. They're just to sop up any bleeding, of which there shouldn't be much. Just stick on some Band-Aids if you think he needs them."

"Thank you, Doctor," she said.

"Vern, thanks a lot," said Gideon.

Sauer grinned at them. "Believe me, the pleasure's all mine. Autopsies are no end of fun, but one gets bored after a while."

As he left the cottage he passed John Lau coming in. "He's perfectly all right; nothing to worry about," Gideon heard Sauer say in response to John's murmured question.

John came into the bedroom. "How ya doin', Tex? Little trouble in the saddle?"

"He was doing beautifully," Julie said loyally. "It wasn't his fault."

"Right," John said. "How many other people fell off their horses?"

Gideon sighed. "None, just me."

John dropped into the rattan armchair that Sauer had vacated and looked at Gideon. "So I guess that's it for the reconstruction."

"Well, as a matter of fact, I do feel okay now, and I hate to just leave it, and I was thinking I might, um, head over there and put in a couple of hours…" He paused to permit a reaction from Julie, who tended toward a forceful and despotic maternalism at times like this.

Surprisingly, she failed to come roaring out of her chair. "I think that's a good idea," she said quietly. "If you feel well enough."

Gideon was speechless.

Even John was surprised. "You do?"

"Gideon—John—I think that—now will you let me get this out before jumping all over me? I'm not so sure this was an accident," she said, speaking rapidly to keep from being interrupted. "I was only a few feet away from Callie when it happened, and I didn't see anybody else jostle her, or anything at all. Nobody was even moving. All of a sudden she just took off, yelling. I think she knew darn well what she was doing, and 1 think—well, that's what I think." She drew a breath and waited for a response.

John, his arms crossed, leaned back, tipping the chair onto its rear legs. "I suppose I could ask around, see if other people saw it the same way."

Julie stared at him. "You mean you're not going to try to argue me out of this? You think I might be right? I'm stunned. Gideon, you too?"

"Sorry, I don't see it."

"What's wrong with it?"

"Why would Callie want to kill me?"

"Kill you?" The idea obviously distressed her. Gideon hadn't much liked it either. "Who said anything about killing you? I think she wanted to keep you from finishing the reconstruction, that's all."

"By scaring my horse? It's way too iffy. How could she know she'd get a chance to do it? How could she know for sure it'd throw me off? How could she know I'd be hurt at all? Besides, Callie's horse was giving her trouble the whole morning. I just don't think—"

"All right, all right," Julie grumbled, "I gather you don't think it's highly probable."

"And why would it matter to anyone whether I finished or not? You know a reconstruction isn't that critical. It's just not that reliable. The dental records are what's going to count in this one."

"Yeah, but who's got dental records?" John said, taking up the argument. "That reconstruction could turn out to be the closest thing we've got to proof that it's Salish."

"God help us, then," Gideon said. "Look, we're ninety-nine

percent sure it's Salish right now. What difference would a little more evidence make one way or the other? Why would Callie or anybody else care?"

"I can think of a damn good reason," John said. The front legs of his chair hit the floor with a thump. "Let's assume for a minute that Callie's mixed up in Salish's murder somehow, okay?"

"Okay."

"Okay. Well, then, she'd care plenty, because if we can show this is Salish for sure—for absolute, positive sure the Bureau's gonna jump into this with both feet. If it's not, if it just *might* be Salish, then Applewhite maybe gives me another day or two here to see what I can come up with, and that's it. It's all Honeyman's again."

Gideon frowned. "So?"

"So if you killed somebody, who'd you rather have on your tail, Farrell Honeyman or the Federal Bureau of Investigation?"

After a pause Gideon said, "I see what you mean."

"Right. Hey, I'm not knocking Farrell, you understand."

"But look, John, it still doesn't figure. In the first place, you could never use a reconstruction as 'proof that anybody was anybody. It's the first step toward an ID, not the last one—which all these people know perfectly well. Second, what good does it do anyone to stop me from finishing? You can always get somebody else—somebody really good at it—to do one later if you want it."

John sighed. "Listen, Doc, I don't know what the hell is going on any more than anybody else does. I don't know if Julie's right or wrong. I just think it'd be a real good idea if you went ahead and finished the thing. Let's see where that gets us."

"Well, I'm not going to argue with you about that. John, would you mind dropping by the meeting room and letting the kids in my class know we'll get started again down at the justice building in half an hour?"

Slowly and stiffly, Gideon swung his legs over the side of the bed. He was not in any real distress, now that the headache and nausea had receded, but there was no mistaking the fact that he'd taken a pounding. "Better tell them forty minutes," he said. "I'm not going to be setting any speed records."

"If it's all the same to you, Doc, we'll just get on with it and leave everybody be. You can explain what you did later. How long you figure it'll take?"

"Couple of hours, once I get there."

"One o'clock," John said. "Tell you what, let's just have Nellie and the others—the ones who knew Salish—come see it then. I'd kind of like to see what they have to say."

"Gideon, are you sure you're up to this?" Julie asked, frowning. "Maybe it isn't such a good idea."

"I'm perfectly fine. I feel like I fell off a horse, that's all."

"Well, you're not driving to Bend by yourself. And I can't drive you because I got myself talked into leading a hike to Metolius Springs this afternoon."

"I'll drive him," John said. "No problem."

"And you'll be with him the whole time?" She was starting to sound more like the old, familiar Julie.

"I won't let him out of my sight, Julie."

"Not that I don't appreciate all this concern," Gideon said, "but do you really think I'm going to be in all that much danger working at the sheriff's office?"

"You never know," John said, getting up. "If things get too exciting you might fall off your chair."

* * *

Completing the reconstruction was basically cosmetic, an effort to make the final product more like life and less like a horror-movie prop. Ears were molded and stuck on, eyebrows were etched into the forehead, and the back and sides of the skull were covered with modeling clay. More clay was used to form a neck, and the whole was mounted on a clothing-store bust originally made for displaying ties and shirts. Gideon added a few wrinkles and sags to the jowls, befitting a man in his late fifties, and patted down the clay with a square of sandpaper to give it a grainy, skinlike texture. Then came a thin layer of pancake makeup and a little rouge, an artfully draped shirt, and an unfortunately youthful brown wig that looked as if Miranda had picked it up in a drugstore.

Gideon used his own comb to tuck a few stubborn plastic strands into place and stepped back. All things considered, he was reasonably pleased.

No one else was.

Everyone but Harlow had shown up, and once they'd examined it, they all expressed the same opinion. There were, they said, a few things about the reconstruction that reminded them of Salish, and a few things that didn't, but nothing either way that was close to persuasive. In other words, the reconstruction was essentially useless, a judgment with which Gideon had to agree once he'd looked at Salish's photograph for himself. Whatever the reason, he had missed the boat, and he freely admitted it.

"Oh, I'd hardly say that," Nellie said, generous in his small victory. "Given the intrinsic fallibility of the process, I'd say you've done wonderfully well"

"I guess that's a compliment," Gideon said, "but—"

Miranda, who had been meticulously comparing Salish's pictures to the reconstruction, spoke wonderingly. "Am I crazy," she said, "or am I crazy?"

Leland pursed his lips. "A question worth pondering."

Miranda was squinting at the reconstruction, framing different parts of the face with her hands. "Gideon, can I make a few changes in this?"

"Changes? Sure, why not?"

She studied the clay head silently for a few more seconds, her round face pensive. "Scissors," she said, like a surgeon about to go into action. John found a pair of shears and handed them to her. Miranda removed the wig, snipped away some of the front, put it back on the naked scalp, took it off again, and cut away some more of the now-receding hairline. The others watched in attitudes of doubt or puzzlement.

Before replacing it she went to the other side of the table and turned the reconstruction so that its back was to everyone else. "I think this'll work better if you see it all at once." She found a thick black marking pen and made some judicious dabs on the face, out of sight of the others.

A mustache? Gideon looked again at one of Salish's photographs. No mustache. No receding hairline either.

"What's she supposed to be doing, Doc?" John asked.

Gideon shook his head. "Who knows?" And yet, dim and barely formed, there was the shadow of a disturbing and fantastic idea.

"Leland, lend me your glasses," Miranda said.

"I beg your pardon?"

She held out her hand. "C'mon, Leland, give."

Reluctantly, Leland gave. Without the massive horn-rims he was a startlingly different man, fragile and defenseless, like some squishy night creature caught unexpectedly in the glare of automobile headlights.

Miranda put the glasses on the uncomplaining clay face and studied it some more. "Gideon, you don't mind if I smush the nose up a little?"

"What? Uh, no, smush away." Gideon was staring uncertainly at what he could see of the reconstruction. Surely, even from this angle, there was something about the way the thick brown earpiece of the glasses lay against the broad temple, about the way the slightly depressed zygomatic arch rode low and flat on the cheek...but, no, he had to be imagining it. Miranda pushed delicately on the nose with her fingers, then stepped back to see the result better, her lips pressed together in concentration. She pushed again, picked up the shears one more time, cut away a few more tufts of hair, and disarranged what was left.

Then she turned it to face them. "You have to imagine that the hair is more gray."

That was all she said, and all she had to say.

It seemed to Gideon that sound and movement stopped as suddenly and utterly as if they'd all been caught by the freeze-frame button on a VCR. For two or three seconds this taut, electrified stillness gripped them, and then Leland snapped it.

"Oh...dear...God," he whispered, and followed this with a soft, nervous titter.

Gallic jerked convulsively, staring pop-eyed at the reconstruction. Her mouth was working but nothing came out.

Next to her, Nellie mumbled vaguely to himself. He looked stricken, almost as if he might faint. One hand clenched and unclenched.

Only the consistently unflappable Les remained in character. "What," he murmured with an only slightly incredulous smile, "is wrong with this picture?" John, on the periphery, seemed not to know what was going on, as of course he didn't. Even Miranda seemed stunned by her own handiwork.

And so it looked as if it were going to be up to Gideon to speak the words. A tiny shiver, like the touch of a spider, crawled up between his shoulder blades. He cleared his throat.

"It's Albert Evan Jasper," he said.

CHAPTER 13

But saying it didn't mean he was ready to believe it. And yet, what else was there to believe? So convincing, so utterly inarguable, was the likeness, that it would have been absurd for him to keep telling himself that this couldn't be, that Albert Jasper had been killed in a bus crash, not stealthily buried in the floor of an unused storeroom; that his remains had been identified with absolute certainty by an expert and reputable team of forensic experts—by, in fact, the very people now staring with such seeming perplexity at that unmistakable, bulldog-like face.

Like tumblers clicking in a complex lock, questions, answers, and surmises turned over in Gideon's mind, rearranged themselves, slid smoothly if bewilderingly into new niches. The uppermost uncertainties of the last few days—Was this or wasn't this Special Agent Chuck Salish? Was he actually killed during the first WAFA meeting? Were any of the WAFA members really involved in his murder?—had suddenly become nonquestions.

It wasn't Salish, it was Jasper. And, oh yes, he was killed during that meeting; he'd damn sure never left it alive by bus or any other means. And if the WAFA attendees had been logical suspects from John's point of view before, they were in it up to their eyebrows now. Who else was there to suspect?

A brief exchange of glances with John showed him that the big Hawaiian's thoughts were running in much the same groove. Despite all the professions of astonishment, one of the stupefied expressions in that goggling half circle of anthropologists was a sham. One of them—at least one of them—hadn't been in the least surprised to find out that Jasper's end had come via garrote, not highway disaster. It was Callie whom Gideon naturally found himself studying hardest, but she seemed as genuinely confounded as anyone else. Which didn't mean much when he thought about it.

But, he realized, it wasn't necessarily someone in the room. Where was Harlow Pollard? John had contacted or left messages with everyone about being there. Why had Harlow failed to show up? Harlow...

"Preposterous," Nellie croaked abruptly, breaking a second lengthy silence. His face, waxy only a moment before, was flooding with a dull red—visibly, from the neck up, like a pitcher being filled. "It can't be Albert and everyone here damn well knows it!" He stared challengingly at them.

They didn't look as if they knew it, Gideon thought, and no wonder. Preposterous as it might seem, no one could seriously doubt whose skull was propped on the table in front of them.

Except Nellie. "Gideon—if this is some—some joke...?" he began, half angrily, half hopefully.

"There's no joke, Nellie."

But in a way there was. It was on him, and Jasper himself was playing it, so to speak. Here Gideon had *made* the damn thing, and he'd *known* Jasper. He'd spent going on twelve hours bent over that skull, memorizing every groove and irregularity; he'd somehow gotten just about everything right in the modeling process—which was amazing in itself—and still, in the end, it was a colossal blunder. He hadn't come close to recognizing who it was and probably never would have, if not for Miranda's sharp eye. Yet now, with just a few swift, superficial changes, there, beyond any possibility of doubt, was Jasper gazing at them through those bland, prosthetic eyes—or did they look just a little more amused than they had before? Surely this was a situation the old man would have relished.

"But how could we have screwed it up so royally?" Callie murmured from a faraway daze—Real? Concocted? Who knew any more?—"We were so positive it was Jasper. We had the teeth, remember?" she asked abstractedly, and then her eyes cleared, her voice firmed. "We had the damn dental report! There was never any question about it."

"Of course there wasn't," Nellie said, heartened. "We were right."

"I don't think so, Nellie," Gideon said quietly. "I don't know how you all could have made a mistake like this, but there can't be any doubt about this being Jasper's skull. Coincidences like this don't happen."

Les laughed. "This is fantastic. The guy that was in that drawer for all those years, the guy we all looked at so solemnly in that museum case, the guy somebody stole out of that museum case, wasn't Jasper all along. Can you believe it?"

"This is not funny," Leland snapped. "It's horrible. We have to try to—to make some sense out of this."

"Nosir," Les said. "Yessir."

Leland turned on him in a shrill little spasm of outrage.

"You—you *nitwit!* Don't you see what this means? Albert was *murdered!* We—we—"

"Goddamn it, Albert was not murdered!" Nellie interrupted hotly. "I don't care who this...this fucking thing looks like, it isn't Albert!" He banged the table so hard with his fist that the reconstruction tottered and would have fallen if John hadn't caught it.

Gideon looked at him with surprise. Histrionics were Callie's department, not Nellie's. Nellie could be a little touchy on occasion, but in all the time Gideon had known him, this was the first time he'd ever heard him use profanity, the first time he'd heard him shout in anger at anyone. It was true that Nellie had been closer than any of the others to Jasper, so that today's unsettling events would have had to be deeply disturbing to him, but all the same—

Leland swallowed, his naked eyes blinking. "Excuse me, Dr. Hobert," he said stiffly, "but I beg to differ. And there's something else too..." He quailed momentarily under Nellie's ferocious scowl, but then drew himself up, darted his tongue at each corner of his mustache, and continued. "Don't you think it's high time this—this absurd secret we've all been keeping so religiously—"

"No, God damn you, I don't!" The arteries at Nellie's temples were bulging, something else Gideon hadn't seen before. As if aware of them, Nellie massaged them, one hand on each side, and blew out a long breath.

"Leland, I'm truly sorry. I don't have any call yelling at you or anyone else. Look, everyone, it's easy enough to settle this. I'll go over to the ME's office and get Albert's file right now. Everything's in there, and I'm sure it'll refresh our memories. We did a good job, you'll see; a careful, professional job. Our identification of Albert is incontrovertible."

"This is pretty incontrovertible too," Les said, pointing at the reconstruction. "Now that I look at it, it even has that nasty smirk we all remember so well."

Nellie summoned up a frail smile. "You'll see," he said again. "Just wait here, I'll be right back. It's just over on Greenwood Avenue."

"I don't think we can," Miranda said. "Harlow's odontology round table comes on at three back at the lodge, and most of us are on it."

"Odontology round table?" Callie echoed with a laugh. "At a time like this, we're supposed to worry about an odontology round table?"

"I think so, yes," Miranda said simply. "A lot of the people here have paid their own way. I think we owe them the best we can give them."

"Miranda's right," Nellie said. "You all go on back to the lodge. I'll see you there later. I've got my own car."

"I think I'll go along to the ME with you," John said, his first words in a while. "I'd like to see that file too."

There was a fractional pause. "Well, I'm bringing it back."

"I know," John said pleasantly, "but I need to talk to Dr. Tilton anyway. Come on, I'll give you a ride."

Nellie began to say something, then changed his mind. "Thank you, John."

As Nellie bustled to the door, John spoke to Gideon. "Meet you back here." He leaned closer. "Probably be a good idea if you didn't leave anybody alone with that skull."

Gideon nodded. "You better believe it."

CHAPTER 14

"What secret?" Miranda asked when she was sure the door had clicked closed behind Nellie and John.

"Yes—" Gideon chimed in, and caught himself. In the second that Miranda's face had been turned toward the door he had caught a furtive, flickering play of glances between the others. Of caution? Guilt? Concealment? What was going on here? What did they all know that he and Miranda—and John—didn't? Why had Nellie jumped all over Leland about it? What was the connection to Jasper?

Gideon was suddenly struck with the odd, unwelcome feeling that he didn't know any of these people very well; hardly at all, in fact. He'd been associating with them off and on for years, but how much of what he thought about them was real and how much had he constructed to fit his notions of what they ought to be like? Affable, laid-back Les with his DR BONES Porsche; droll, dry, harmless Leland —

"Forget it, Miranda," Callie said, "you don't want to know."

"Me not want to know a secret? Somebody's kidding. Gideon, are you in on this?"

He shook his head.

"Good, at least I don't feel so left out. Now is anybody going to spill the beans or not?"

"Ah, what the hell—" Les began amiably.

Leland cut him off. "Why don't you ask the great Dr. Hobert," he said curtly to Miranda, "since he's the one who seems to feel so passionately about it."

For a moment Les looked as if he were going to continue anyway, but he shrugged and let it pass. In Les's view, Gideon knew—or thought he knew—there wasn't very much that was worth hassling about.

"All right," Miranda said, unoffended, "I'll ask Nellie. Well, if we're going to have a chance to get a bite before the round table, we'd better get going. Leland and Callie are driving with me, Gideon. There's room for you if you want."

"No, thanks, I'll find my own way. If I'm a few minutes late, tell Harlow to get started without me."

"Begin without the Skeleton Detective?" Leland said. "Somehow it hardly seems worth the doing." With the return of his horn rims, he hadn't taken long to become the old Leland again.

Gideon held Les unobtrusively back as the others left. "Give me a minute to stow the skull in the evidence room. I'll be right back."

"What's up, Gid?" Les said when he returned. "Want a lift back with me?"

"In the Red Terror? Do I look that crazy? No, I wanted to ask you something."

Les nodded. "Yeah, I figured as much."

"What's going on, Les? What's this big secret?"

Les lowered his heavy body into Gideon's chair behind the work table. "Well, I tell you," he said. "As far as I'm concerned, it's a new ball game now. All skeletons out of the closet."

For a few seconds he concentrated on the rubber band around his ponytail, looping it a couple of times and getting it readjusted to his satisfaction. Gideon could see that he was arranging his thoughts as well.

"The thing is," he said, "we had a roast."

"Come again?"

Les smiled. "No, not that kind of a roast. Like they used to have at the Friar's Club. We had a dinner for Jasper, where everybody got up and made these smart cracks, these jokey little speeches about him. We even did this dumb little skit—I was supposed to be Jasper, if you can believe it—and they bring me this femur, which I brilliantly deduce is the remains of a murder victim, only at the end it turns out to be the remains of last night's leg of lamb dinner." He laughed easily. "Dumb."

The smile slowly faded. "How well did you know him, Gid?"

"Not very." Was it too late to tell Les he didn't much like being called "Gid"? Probably so, considering he'd let it go for almost ten years now.

"You're lucky. Among other things, the guy was not very big on what you might call self deprecating humor, you know? We should have realized that a roast was not the greatest idea in the world."

Les picked up a strip of unused modeling clay and began slowly rolling it between his palms. Gideon pulled up a chair and sat opposite him.

"Aside from that, he was an on-again, off-again lush, and he was already about six times more sloshed than anybody realized when the roast started. The guy had been in a fairly good mood up till then, you know, wallowing in all that obsequious veneration crap. So at first he just sat there and took it, but then he turned real hostile. I mean *real* hostile. And then he starts *crying*—slobbering, his nose running, the whole bit." He grimaced. "Can you imagine it? Albert Evan Jasper?"

"It sounds pretty awful"

"Yeah." Les squeezed the strand of clay into a ball and started rolling it out again, this time between his palm and the table. "Of course, when you get right down to it, all of us had a few that night. Well, not Harlow—you know Harlow and his stomach—but I know I was sozzled. I guess we were trying to get our courage up, you know? That old bastard could be pretty intimidating."

He tossed the clay onto the table. "And the fact is, all the cracks weren't as friendly as they might have been. Things got pretty bitter once we got into it. Everybody turned the knife. Jasper was brilliant, no doubt about that. He was even a good teacher—I learned more from him than anybody I ever knew—but he was so damn…insensitive, so mean, even to people who worshipped the ground he walked on. I'm telling you, to know him was to want to punch him out."

"I know," Gideon said. "I've seen him in action."

"Well, it got away from us. Once things got started, a lot of bottled-up feelings came out and Jasper just couldn't deal with it. I don't think he'd ever been on the receiving end of shit like that. So, finally, he just blew up; I mean, he was running at the mouth, literally. And then he stomped out." He shrugged. "Never saw him again. At least *I* didn't; obviously, somebody did."

"And that's it?" Gideon asked. "I understand that it wasn't very pleasant, but why all the secrecy?"

"No, that isn't it. You see, right up until today, until half an hour ago, we all thought we were responsible for his death."

"For his death? Why?"

"You have to remember, Gid—up till now we thought he was on that bus."

"Yes, I know, but why—"

"Well, he wasn't supposed to be; not originally. He was going to leave the day after, like everybody else. The first clue we had that he might be on the damn thing was when he didn't show up around the lodge that morning. And when we checked, we found out his clothes were cleared out of his room."

Gideon watched him pick up another lump of clay and start rolling again.

"We figured he must have been so pissed at us that he took off early, with his pal, just so he wouldn't have to look at our faces anymore. And then we did find his remains—what we thought were his remains. You can imagine how great that made everybody feel."

"With his pal? Salish, you mean?"

"Yeah, Salish was catching the morning bus anyway, if I remember right—he had to be back at work—and we figured Jasper just got on it with him without telling anyone."

"Did he check out of the lodge?"

"You didn't have to check out. It was like now; you paid for everything in advance." He curved the strip of clay around his wrist and pressed the ends together. "Sonofabitch," he said softly.

"Les, all that doesn't make you responsible for his death. Maybe it's nothing to feel good about, but it's no reason for a—well, for a conspiracy to keep it quiet."

"Hey, tell me about it. That's exactly what I said—I mean, the guy was over twenty-one, he made his own decisions, right? We didn't have anything to hide—but nobody would come right out and agree with me. I guess no one liked disagreeing with Nellie."

"You mean Nellie was pressing to keep it a secret?"

"Pressing? Yeah, I think you could say that. Funny, the whole roast business was his idea in the first place, and then later he was the one who was so hot to keep it a secret."

And who was still so hot to keep it a secret. "Why?" Gideon asked.

"I guess he just thought it made everybody look pretty terrible. Which it did. Besides, you know, we were all feeling rotten about it—about being the reason he got on the bus. I mean, there he was—these greasy, burned chunks of garbage on the table right in front of us. Not your basic happy time."

"But now we know those weren't his remains; Jasper wasn't killed on the bus. Why would Nellie still be so eager to keep it a secret?"

"I guess he honest-to-God doesn't buy this reconstruction thing. As far as he's concerned, nothing's changed."

"I don't know, Les. Does that make sense to you?"

"Hey, what can I tell you?" He looked uneasily at Gideon. "Personally, he was being weird about it from day one. This hush-hush crap—you know that's not Nellie's style. I couldn't believe it; I was, like, what is the problem here?"

"Les, are you trying to tell me you think Nellie had—" it took an effort to get the words out "—had something to do with Jasper's murder?"

Les's low forehead folded into parallel creases. "Hell, no, when did I say that?" He looked as close to irritated as he ever did.

Gideon liked him the more for it. "You never did." He leaned forward, elbows on the table. "Les, I'm still trying to understand how that misidentification could have happened in the first place."

"*You're* trying to understand? Hell, I was there; I was part of the team—and I'm here to tell you we did it right; by the book, man. I just don't—"

"It was basically a dental identification, is that right?"

"It was a dental identification, period. You saw what was left. If not for the dentition we'd have been lucky to come up with 'male' and 'adult.' But we had half a mandible, with the teeth and the alveolar border in reasonable shape. So we got the reports from Jasper's dentist, matched them to what we had here, and that was it."

"Who matched them? Was it Harlow? Did he do the analysis?"

"Well, yeah, sure, he was our odontologist, but we worked as a team; everybody got in on it. That's the way Nellie likes to do it— hey, where is Harlow? I haven't seen him since he got back from Nevada."

"Neither has anybody else, as far as I know."

Their eyes locked for a second. "No, forget it, Gid. There was no way he could have flimflammed us. I'm not talking about any tricky odontological formulas. It was completely straightforward—a simple postmortem-antemortem comparison. Jasper's charts had a lot of fillings anybody could recognize, and a, what do you call it, an extra tooth, a supernumerary tooth in there somewhere. It was just a matter of comparing."

Gideon frowned. "A supernumerary tooth…"

There was, he was certain, no extra tooth in the clay-covered mandible now in its wooden cubbyhole in the evidence room; the mandible that had so startlingly transformed itself from Salish's to Jasper's less than an hour before. A first faint glimmer of illumination showed itself, an indication of just how they had come to make so freakish an error a decade ago. Except that, if he was right, there wasn't any error. They had been flimflammed, all right. With a vengeance.

Les backed off. "Well, I wouldn't swear to a supernumerary tooth. I've looked at a lot of skulls since then. But whatever there was, you didn't have to be an odontologist to see there was a match."

"And you personally compared the charts to the remains yourself? You saw that they matched? You didn't just take Harlow's word for it?"

"Of course I compared them. We all did." He tilted his head, pulled on an earlobe. "Well, I think we did. Who remembers now? But, look, that mandible was right there in front of us the whole time. Anybody who felt like it could check it against the charts anytime he wanted. Harlow or anybody else would have been out of his mind to try to fudge anything."

Not if it had been done the way Gideon thought it had. It was becoming clearer, but there were still some fuzzy edges, some pieces that didn't fit. "Let me ask you this, Les. How positive are you those records were really Jasper's?"

"What kind of question is that? About as positive as you can be. We found out who his dentist was, Harlow got in touch with him for the charts—you know the drill—and back they came, just like for anybody else. Well, except for the x-rays."

Ah. Gideon's eyes narrowed. "What about the x-rays?"

"There weren't any. Jasper was scared of them." He laughed.

"Weird when you think about it. Here's the number-one bone expert in the country—"

"How do you know he was scared of them?"

Les shrugged. He was beginning to tire of the conversation, or perhaps to wonder what they were talking about. "I don't know. It wasn't any secret."

"I never heard about it."

"So? What does it matter now?" Les yawned and shook himself, bearlike, the undulation seeming to roll slowly up his big torso under the skin. He took off the clay bracelet and dropped it on the table. "I guess head for—oh, hey I remember. Harlow told us. When he contacted the dentist. The guy told him Jasper was scared to death of x-rays. Okay? Satisfied?"

With a gratifying *clunk,* the last piece dropped tidily into place. Gideon leaned back in the chair.

"Satisfied," he said.

CHAPTER 15

"Hello, welcome to McDonald's; may I take your order, please?"

John stuck his head out the car window to get closer to the microphone-speaker. "Hamburger, large fries, strawberry shake." He turned back into the car. "Doc, you sure you don't want something?"

"No, thanks." Gideon's stomach still wasn't quite settled, and the heat wasn't helping. But he was thirsty. "Well, maybe a shake. Chocolate."

"And a chocolate shake," John yelled into the mike.

"Yo," the speaker said metallically, and then a moment later: "That'll be $3.54 at the first window, please."

John drove twenty feet to the first window and paid.

"Thank you, drive to window number two and await your order," he was told, this time by a living person.

John drove to window number two and awaited. "And so that's what the big secret is?" he said to Gideon. "They had a roast and Jasper took it the wrong way?"

"According to Les."

"So what's the big deal?"

Gideon explained some of what Les had told him.

John shook his head. "Hell, I don't know what to make out of that. I asked Nellie about it twice and both times he told me he didn't know what Leland was talking about." He turned away to collect their order. "I just wish the guy would level with me," he muttered.

As John got the car moving north on Highway 20 toward Whitebark Lodge, Gideon continued going through Albert Jasper's old file, which John had copied at the Medical Examiner's office.

After three or four miles, John glanced over at him. "What do you think?" He was getting restive. The hamburger had been consumed in a few bites; the french fries were being plucked one at a time from the bag beside him on the seat.

"Tell you in a minute," Gideon said.

Side by side on his lap he had set two forms, slightly different in their layouts, but each diagramming the same thing: a set of all thirty-two human teeth, "folded out" to show the five surfaces of each. One of the forms bore the logo, "Victor MacFadden, D.D.S., 333 Montezuma Avenue, Santa Fe, New Mexico 87504." Under it, alongside "Patient Name," was "Jasper, Albert E." The diagram had been crosshatched and shaded to show a variety of dental problems and treatments; to judge from them, Jasper had spent a lot of time in the dentist's chair, as Les had implied.

And crammed in between the lower-right canine and first bicuspid was an extra tooth that had no business being in anybody's mouth: Les's supernumerary.

The other form, plainer and more cheaply printed, had Harlow Pollard's finicky signature at the bottom, and a date of June 13, 1981. This was a standard odontological postmortem diagram, and it had apparently been filled out after the crash, directly from the remains. Naturally enough, only the part representing the eight teeth in the right half of the mandible had been marked up.

And those markings, as Les had told him more than once, perfectly matched those on Dr. MacFadden's chart: five fillings, all on the identical surfaces of the identical teeth, one gold inlay, one missing molar with its space closed…and one highly unusual supernumerary, between canine and bicuspid.

"I can tell you what Nellie said," John volunteered. "What'd Nellie say?" Gideon murmured, studying the charts.

"He said you're nuts," John informed him cheerfully. "He took one look at MacFadden's chart, that one you've got right there, let out a yelp, and said it proves once and for all that Jasper died on that bus."

"Mm?" Gideon said without looking up. "And how does he account for the reconstruction looking so much like Jasper?"

"I can give you his exact words." John took out the notepad he carried in his shirt pocket and glanced at it from the corner of his eye as he drove. "'Occultism…humbuggery…subliminal suggestion…hocus—'"

Gideon laughed and took his milkshake from the opened lid of the glove compartment. "Well, he's wrong, John. Sharp as he is, Nellie's got a blind spot when it comes to reconstructions. The fact is, Jasper never got on that bus. He was buried at Whitebark, and what's left of him is now sitting on a shelf in the sheriff's evidence room."

"What about these charts?" John asked. "They match, don't they? And this one's from Jasper's dentist, right? How do *you* account for *that?*"

"Faked," Gideon said. "Or rather, one of them is. The postmortem one that Harlow filled out after the crash is accurate, all right. It shows exactly what was in the burned mandible that came from the bus. But this one—" he held up the form with Dr. MacFadden's logo on it "—is a fake. It isn't really Jasper's chart, John."

"Now wait a minute, Doc. You know I don't argue with you when it comes to bones and things—"

"Oh, ho, ho," Gideon said.

"—but you need to know I already checked this out. While I was with Nellie. I put in a call to MacFadden's office in Santa Fe. This guy is definitely a bona fide dentist, he's still in practice, and Jasper was his patient. He remembers the accident, he remembers getting a call from Pollard—and he remembers sending out the chart. So—"

"I'm sure he did send one out. But this isn't it."

"This isn't...?" John flicked a finger at Jasper's name, at MacFadden's logo. "What the hell are you talking about?"

"The logo's real," Gideon said, "but the chart isn't Jasper's."

John was beginning to show signs of exasperation. "Is that MacFadden's form or isn't it?"

"It's a photocopy, not an original. "To be more exact, it's a photocopy of the photocopy that MacFadden sent. What Harlow did was the simplest thing in the world: a cut-and-paste job. Look, those ME files are full of forms from dentists, right? There were thirty-some-odd people on that bus and most of them were unrecognizable. But there were ways of coming up with almost all the names: bus reservations, unburnt pieces of ID, calls from people who were expecting to pick up other people, and so on."

"Right, so?"

"Well, what the forensic team was trying to do was match these piles of bones and teeth to the names, so Harlow would have contacted every one of their dentists he could reach, right?"

John made an impatient, rumbling noise. "Yeah, so?" "So one of the forms that came back was for the guy who they eventually identified as Jasper—call him Mr. X. What Harlow did was take off Mr. X's name and the name of Mr. X's dentist, stick on MacFadden's logo, type in Jasper's name on the Patient's line, and run it through a copy machine. Presto-chango, Mr. X's chart is now Albert E. Jasper's chart—and naturally it matches Mr. X's dentition, since that's what it's a picture of."

John chewed this skeptically over. "Assuming that it really happened that way."

"I'm pretty sure it did, John. And so Mr. X is duly identified as Jasper, and the question of what happened to the real Jasper never comes up. It doesn't compute. And somebody gets away with murder; Harlow, it looks like."

John remained doubtful. "I don't know, doc. If this Mr. X wasn't Jasper, who was he, where'd he come from? Where'd Harlow find him?" He leveled a french fry at Gideon. "Everybody on the bus got identified, remember? Everybody's accounted for."

"Not exactly. Take a guess."

"What do you mean, guess? How the hell am I supposed to know that?"

"Come on, take a stab," Gideon said, beginning to enjoy himself just a little.

John folded the stick of potato into his mouth and shook his head. "How the hell am I—oh, shit. Salish?"

"That'd be my guess. He had a bus reservation, right? And he had to be back at work in Albuquerque that afternoon, so there's every reason to think he was on it."

"Only they never ID'd him," John said thoughtfully. "Not for sure."

"That's right. But they did identify Jasper—from eight teeth and a handful of burned debris. Let me tell you, John, with the shape those bones were in, Harlow wouldn't have had any trouble convincing the others they were the remains of Genghis Khan—not if he had a perfectly matched dental chart to prove it."

John chewed mechanically, looking straight ahead through the windshield. "So it was Salish in that drawer all these years? Salish in the museum case?"

"I think so."

John laughed unexpectedly, a brief splutter. "I know it's not funny, but…Christ."

They let a few miles go by without talking. In the east, but still far away, bands of clouds were beginning to form in the Cascades; the first clouds in several days. Maybe, Gideon thought hopefully, relief from the hot spell was on the way.

"Doc," John said, "you're not saying Harlow engineered that whole bus accident, are you? Because that's just—"

"My God, no. I'm assuming, that he must have killed Jasper some time the night before, after the roast. Probably buried him then too. The bus crash happening the next day was probably just a lucky break. He saw a great way of disposing of Jasper for good, with no awkward questions, and he took it."

Gideon sipped' his shake, thinking. "Or, you know, it could be the other way around. Maybe the bus crash happened first, and when Harlow heard about it, he knew he had a chance to kill Jasper then and there—"

"Why? I don't suppose you've got a motive all cooked up too?"

"—with nobody ever finding out about it, so he went to Jasper's room—"

"Wait a minute, hold it."

Gideon waited.

"Listen," John said, "are we talking facts here? Or are you making it up as you go along?"

"About which came first, the crash or the murder? I'm making it up, what else?"

"No, about the whole thing, the switch of the dental charts. You got anything at all to support it? Or is this all, you know, just—"

"Unverified supposition?"

"Yeah, exactly, unverified supposition."

"Uh."

"I knew it."

"But there's some circumstantial evidence to support it."

"Oh, great, now I feel better."

"For example, this would explain why Salish's dental chart is missing from the file. Harlow removed it, probably back in 1981, to use as Jasper's. And he didn't have to bother about replacing it with still another fake, because nobody was interested in Salish's teeth right up until yesterday."

"Why wasn't anybody interested in Salish's teeth?"

"Because the remains that they tentatively ID'd as Salish back then didn't have any teeth."

John chewed for a while. "Okay," he said slowly, "I see what you're saying. I think."

"Look, there's a simple enough way to verify this. Just ask Dr. MacFadden to send Jasper's chart again. We'll see if it's the same one we have here—which it won't be—or if it matches what's in the skull in the evidence room—which it will." He laughed. "I think."

John grunted. "Okay, I will. We'll see what happens."

"There's something else. When a dentist sends in records, some x-rays usually come with them. But there aren't any here. According to Les, that's because Jasper was afraid of them. So said Harlow."

John glanced at him. "This is supposed to tell us something?"

It told them, Gideon explained, that Harlow had been lying. Gideon recounted how the hapless Casper Jasper had been knocked cold by an awning rod, and how his solicitous father had immediately hustled him off to the hospital to be x-rayed. Did it stand to reason that a man leery of fluoroscopic radiation would unhesitatingly put his son through it?

"Maybe not," John admitted. "So why is that important?"

"John, if you photocopy x-rays onto ordinary paper, they're not much good because so much of the clarity is lost. So dentists use a special copying machine to reproduce them onto transparent film. Well, that's what MacFadden would have done—and that would have been hell for Harlow to fake. You're not talking about a simple cut-and-paste job to change the names anymore. And he would have had to get access to the right kind of machine himself. Not easy to do without anybody knowing."

John nodded, finally beginning to come around. "Easier just to say there weren't any x-rays, and invent a reason for it."

"That's right. I'm betting MacFadden actually did send a set and Harlow just tossed them. Any dental reports corning in would have gone straight to him, so who would know? And there wasn't a chance in a million MacFadden would ever find out about it. He'd just read in the newspapers like anybody else that Jasper was identified from his teeth, period. And maybe he'd get a nice, polite thank-you call from Harlow."

"Yeah, but what about the rest of the file?" John said. "There's a report from a doctor, something from a physical therapist. How could he fake all that stuff and hope to get away with it? He'd be bound to slip up somewhere,"

"He didn't have to fake anything else. The rest of the file is really Jasper's, Look."

He thumbed through the folder until he found the physician's report, a three-page form signed with a looping flourish by Willa Stover, M.D.—"'Post-traumatic osteoarthritis, right first and second metatarsophalangeal joints,'" he read. "That's the big toe and the one next to it. And here: 'Fractured left ulna, childhood fall.'"

John nodded slowly. "Just like on the skeleton Nellie dug up."

"Sure, because the skeleton's really Jasper. But at the time, it was buried under the floor of the shack where nobody knew about it—and the remains Harlow said were Jasper's were nothing but those teeth and a few splinters of bone that were just about unreadable. Every damn joint in the body could have been arthritic, and nobody would have known the difference. So there wasn't any risk. All Harlow had to fake was the dental stuff. And that's what he did."

"You think."

"I think."

They pulled off the highway and into the graveled parking area at the entrance to the lodge. Even in the shade of the ponderosas, getting out of the car was like stepping into a smelter. Gideon glanced at the rusting metal Dr. Pepper thermometer nailed to the bulletin board. Ninety-four, it said, and it felt as if the relative humidity was about the same.

"God, what weather."

"Yeah," John said absently, "great, isn't it?"

They began walking toward the main building. John had a ruminative look on his face. "Harlow," he said, as if he were testing the name on his tongue. "Seems like such a meek, harmless little guy. Kind of hard to see him as a killer."

Gideon nodded. "It's a surprise. I was starting to wonder if Julie might not be right, if you want to know. About Callie."

"Let's concentrate on Harlow. Any idea why he'd want to do in Jasper?" He looked up at Gideon's laugh. "Did I say something funny?"

"John, let me quote Les Zenkovich on Albert Jasper: 'To know him was to want to punch him out.' That would have applied to Harlow as much as any of them."

"Why? What'd they have against him?"

"Well, he wasn't the kindliest man in the world. From what I know about him, he was short-tempered, spiteful, contentious… inconsiderate…"

John waved an impatient hand. "Doc, you don't usually kill people because they're inconsiderate. Or even inconsiderate and contentious."

"John, you asked me what they had against him, and I'm trying to tell you."

"Right, sorry."

"I'm doing the best I can."

"Right, go ahead."

"I mean, don't expect me to solve your whole case for you."

John emitted a rolling growl. "Will you go ahead?"

"With pleasure, if you'll let me. The thing is, they were all his graduate students at one time or another—"

"All of them? Even Nellie?"

"All of them. Nellie was the first. And from the war stories I've heard, none of them had an easy time. If I remember right, it took Harlow eleven or twelve years to get his Ph.D. Jasper kept changing the ground rules on him. It was the way he was with them all, I guess."

"But he finally got his degree?"

"Oh, he got it, but his marriage came apart during the struggle, and I understand Harlow's always blamed Jasper for that. In his own quiet way, of course. Had two kids, I think, but he never talks about them. Never remarried either, as far as I know."

John weighed this. "Well, I guess it's a place to start."

With Gideon, he stood at the entrance to the lodge building. "This where your round table is?"

"Yes, it started ten minutes ago."

"Well, don't let me hold you up. When's it over?"

"Five o'clock. But the later it gets in the week, the earlier the sessions seem to let out. It's a natural law. I'd say four-thirty."

"Good enough. I've got some stuff to write up, and Harlow'll keep till then."

"I guess so. He's kept for ten years."

"Yeah." John took the last, cold french fry from the bag he'd carried from the car and crumpled it into his mouth. "Boy, am I ever gonna spoil his day."

* * *

With blinds drawn against the sun and air conditioners groaning, the meeting room's temperature was wonderfully cool, but the atmosphere was heated with hypothesis and conjecture. The startling news about Jasper had quickly spread, and knots of academics had turned their chairs around to face each other, the better to argue over what it might mean.

Gideon made his way to the front, where seven of the nine participants in the odontology round table were seated: Miranda, Les, Leland, Callie, and three others. Gideon, taking the empty chair next to Leland, made eight. The ninth, Harlow, had yet to arrive to take his place as moderator.

"HAAAR-lowww," Les was singing softly to the ceiling, "where AAARRRE you?"

Leland looked irritably at the wall clock, then at Callie. "Yes, where *is* he?"

It took a few seconds for Callie to look up from her notes. "What are you asking me for?"

"Well, he came back with you, didn't he?"

She laid down her notebook and concentrated on getting a cigarette out of its slim metal case. "From where?" she asked absently.

Leland looked at her. "From *where?*"

They stared at each other with the bafflement of communication gone askew.

"From Nevada," Leland finally said. "Where else?"

Callie had gotten her cigarette going. She squinted at him through the first acrid explosion of smoke. "Leland, Harlow didn't go to Nevada with me."

"Of course he did."

"Are you telling me?" Her voice was beginning to rise. "I'm telling you, he didn't go. He didn't feel well, he didn't want to fly." She had taken only two puffs of the cigarette, but she jammed it out angrily against a flat metal ashtray, smoke pouring from her nostrils. "A year's planning, and he misses the whole damn thing. How is he going to hold up his end of the reciprocal contracting if he doesn't share ownership 'for the development process, tell me that."

"I really couldn't say."

Leland had a way of looking at people as if he were examining them through a lorgnette. Callie was briefly subjected to this scrutiny before he spoke again.

"Well, then, where's he been?"

Callie's attention had returned to her notes. With a sigh she closed the binder. "Leland," she said between set teeth, "I already told you—"

Gideon got up and left the room, crossing the lawn and taking the footbridge over the pond toward Harlow's cottage. Halfway there he hesitated, changed his mind, and made for John's cottage instead.

"Harlow hasn't shown up at the meeting," he told him. "I think we ought to check his cottage."

John had come to the door with a legal pad in his hand and his mind obviously elsewhere. "I don't know, maybe he's—"

"Nobody's seen him since Tuesday. Two days."

"I thought he went to, where was it, Utah, with Callie."

"Nevada. And she says he never went."

"Well, maybe he—"

Gideon blurted it out. "John, I've got a hunch he's killed himself. I think he may have realized it was all over when we found the burial."

John eyed him. "What's this, another 'feeling'?"

"I guess that's what it is, yes. I'm telling you, he looked like absolute hell when we found the grave. And he practically started shaking when we talked about bringing in the police. Nobody's seen him since, and—look, I'm probably making too much out of it, but let's check it out anyway, all right?"

John looked gravely at him for another moment, tossed the pad onto a sofa, and closed the door behind him. "Let's go. We'll get a key from the office first. Just in case we need it."

Most of the cottages at Whitebark Lodge were on the main lawn, in a cluster that curved around the big pond, but an additional half-dozen trailed away from these along the first few hundred feet of the bridle path; into a clump of woods, then out again into the sun, beside the stream. Harlow's cottage was the last in this row, all alone on a grassy, creekside bank, forty feet from its nearest neighbor on one side, and with nothing but ponderosa forest on the other.

"He sure got himself an out-of-the-way place," John said as they approached it.

"That's why we had our poker game there, remember?"

"How can I forget?"

As if by agreement, they stopped before climbing onto the porch. Behind them the creek burbled happily over stones and gravel, and from the woods on the opposite side floated a lovely, fluid trill of bird song, but the cottage itself seemed hunched in its own aura of torpor and decay. Sunlight glinted dustily from dirty windowpanes. Around the knob on the door a flyspecked "Please— do not disturb" sign had been hung.

"Who'd he think was gonna disturb him?" John said. "We're not getting any room service."

Gideon pointed to a stack of linen on top of the firewood box. "They changed the towels and things yesterday."

"That's right. Except it looks like they didn't get in here." He blew out a long breath. "Well, we better have a look."

They stepped up onto the porch and John thumped on the door. "Harlow! Hey, Harlow!"

The footsteps, the thump, John's voice all seemed unnaturally loud. There was no answering sound from inside, and none expected. Had Harlow actually answered John's call, Gideon would have jumped.

John tried again. "Harlow, you in there?"

Gideon went uneasily to the front window beside the door, putting his hand against the dusty pane to shield his eyes from the glare. Near his ear a comatose fly roused itself, buzzed thickly, and fell back into a crack in the casement. Gideon's view into the room was hampered by a basket of dried flowers at eye level, just on the other side of the window. Whatever color they had originally been, years of exposure to the thin mountain sunlight had bleached them a ghostly white. They looked as if they might crumble to dust at a touch.

He moved his head to try to peer around them. "See anything?" John asked.

"No, I…oh, Christ, yes."

Wordlessly, he stepped back to allow John room. The FBI agent took a long, sober look, his mouth tight.

"Well, I tell you one thing," he said. "He sure as hell didn't commit suicide."

CHAPTER 16

The armchairs in the cottages were of walnut-stained rattan, with white seat cushions and relatively high, broad backs. In one of these battered but handsome chairs, about fifteen feet from the window and in full sunlight, Harlow Pollard was sprawled, head thrown back and to one side, eyes closed, mouth hanging open.

In the immediate aftermath of death, Gideon had noticed, people tended to look smaller than they had in life; shrunken, imploded, somehow less substantial. "As if someone let the air out of them," he'd once heard someone say. But in Harlow's case the opposite was true. The anthropologist's limbs were outflung with an expansiveness never exhibited when he was alive. His legs were extended, feet spread, heels on the pine flooring, one brown shoe half off. One hand lay in his lap, palm up; the other dangled extravagantly over the arm of the chair, the loosely curled fingers almost resting on the floor.

Gideon's eyes shied instinctively from the bloodied head, but even glimpsed briefly through the unwashed window and the screen of dried flowers, the cause of death was unmistakable. His skull had been bashed in with sickening force. The right-front upper quarter of his head simply wasn't there. Where it should have been was a bowl-shaped, stomach-turning concavity, almost down to the eyebrow.

"No," Gideon said tersely, "he didn't commit suicide."

"Let's have a look," John said, turning the key in the lock. "Don't touch anything, doc. Especially the body."

"Don't worry," Gideon said under his breath.

He steeled himself as the door swung open. If Harlow had really been lying there since Tuesday morning—well over fifty hours in ninety-degree temperature—the decomposition process would be well along. They stepped over the threshold.

More flies buzzed, their bright blue bodies shimmering handsomely in the sunlight. Bluebottles, he'd called them when he was a kid, and he'd had fun catching them in his hand and letting them go. Now he knew them as blowflies or flesh flies, and he no longer caught them in his hand. He shuddered as he brushed them away.

"There's the weapon," John said matter-of-factly. He pointed at a heavy table leg lying on the floor a few feet from the chair. There was a similar one in Gideon's cottage, propped against the fireplace to serve as a poker. This one, like his own, was coated with ash at both ends. One end, however, was overlain with ugly smears that left little doubt about what it had last been used for.

"Mm," Gideon said. He hadn't yet gotten himself to look directly at the body again, but he drew a tentative breath as they neared the chair. He smelled nothing but a general staleness. That and a faint residue of insecticide, barely perceptible. And no longer doing its job, judging from the flies.

"He hasn't been dead two days," Gideon said.

"How do you know that?"

"If this body'd been sitting here two days, you'd know."

"Oh, the smell. Yeah, that's true."

John was leaning over the corpse, peering attentively at the ruined head, his wide back blocking Gideon. "Blood's pretty well dried out, though," he said. "And there are some maggots here. Doesn't that mean he's been dead a while?"

"Eggs, or larval stage?"

"How the hell do I know?" He looked more closely, getting his face nearer to Harlow's than Gideon would have cared to do. "Gray little guys. They don't have any legs. Does that tell you something?"

"Hard to say."

John turned irritably. "Are you gonna come and look, or not?"

Gideon sighed. "Yes, I'm going to come and look." But he moped over, taking his time about it.

"Jesus," John said, "you are the most squeamish guy I know. How'd you ever get into this line of work?"

"I was just wondering the same thing. As I recall, you had something to do with it. And those are eggs," he said, finally looking but not quite focusing—an ability he'd perfected only since getting into this line of work. "They haven't hatched yet."

"Which means what, timewise?"

"John, my line is bones, not bugs. Aren't you going to call in the ME?"

"Yeah, or rather you are. I don't want to touch the phone in here, so I want you to go over to your place and call Honeyman. But first tell me what you think. About the bugs."

"Well, I'm not sure how long these things take to hatch either. A day or so, I think. If that's right, he's been dead less than twenty-four hours."

"Uh-huh." Crouching, John pushed experimentally against the freely hanging arm with a finger. It swayed limply back and forth. "Maybe a lot less?" he suggested knowledgeably. "Rigor mortis hasn't set in yet."

John, whose many strengths did not include forensics, never gave up trying. Unfortunately, he rarely got things altogether right.

"Um, not exactly," Gideon said. "I think it's already set in and gone."

"In less than a day? How the hell could—"

"It's hot, John. In this kind of weather all the degenerative changes are speeded up. Besides, look at his hand."

He gestured at Harlow's dangling hand, suffused with the bruise-like purple of well-advanced liver mortis, the slow after-death settling of the blood due to gravity. "That'd take eight or ten hours at least."

John nodded and straightened up. Hands on his hips, he studied the body. "Boy, that is what you call a massive head wound. Three separate blows. Look at that; you can see the damn dents, one, two, three."

Gideon stood a couple of feet away, studying the toes of his jogging shoes. "I guess I ought to go call Farrell."

"Right." John began walking with him toward the door. "So he's been dead eight hours minimum, twenty-four hours max, is that what you said?"

"About," Gideon said uneasily. "But go with what the ME says."

"So he got killed somewhere between yesterday afternoon—Wednesday—and early this morning."

"I guess."

"So where was he from Tuesday morning to Wednesday? Nobody saw him all that time."

"According to Callie, he was sick."

"Is that right?" John strode into the kitchen, inserted a ballpoint pen into the handle of the refrigerator, and pulled it open. He did the same with the two cabinets. All were empty of food. There were no used plates or silverware in the sink or dish drainer, no wrappers in the lidless kitchen garbage can. There was no sign of anything edible in the cottage.

"So sick he didn't even come out to eat?" John said. "For over a day?"

Gideon shrugged. "Maybe he came out and nobody saw him."

"Yeah, sure."

"Well, what do you think?"

"I think we've got something funny going on here, Doc. I think if he was that sick he wouldn't be sitting up in a chair, dressed in his clothes, wearing his shoes." He gestured with his head toward the open bedroom door. "I think his bed wouldn't be all made up."

Gideon nodded. "You're right. That is odd." John might misconstrue a forensic indicator here and there, but all the same he never failed to notice some things that got by Gideon.

John's eye was caught by something else. "Now what the hell is that?"

Gideon followed John's line of sight. At the back of a small table near the door, caught between the edge of the table's surface and the wall, was a foot-long strip of cardboard about a third of an inch wide, with scalloped edges and a slight curl to it. One side, the outside of the curl, was plain gray cardboard with some dabs of dried glue on it. The other was bright yellow, with a few printed messages in blue and red: "Clingier, clearer, stronger"…"250 sq. ft. (1 ft. x 83.3 yds.)"…"E-Z Open. Just pull off, starting here."

They leaned over it, not touching it. "It's just a tear-off strip from a box of plastic wrap," Gideon said.

"Yeah," John said thoughtfully. "Now that's interesting."

Gideon looked up. What was getting by him now? "What is?"

"Well, for one thing, does Harlow strike you as a guy who'd just tear open a box and toss the strip onto a table? I mean, look around."

John was right, of course; Harlow wasn't the kind of man who had much effect on his surroundings. Except for the table leg—and Harlow himself—nothing was messy, nothing was disturbed. Even the living-room wastepaper basket was empty.

"For another thing," John said, "what would a guy who doesn't have any food want with a box of plastic wrap?" After a moment he added: "And where's the box?"

"I don't know, but what does it matter? For all we know, this has been here for months. Whitebark isn't the best-maintained place in the world."

"Mm."

"John, does this have some sort of significance I'm not seeing?"

"I don't know, Doc. It doesn't fit, that's all."

Gideon straightened up, his head swimming. He'd been leaning over too long. He felt suddenly empty, drained of energy and acutely aware of Harlow behind them, of the caved-in skull and the wide-open mouth, and the hideous splatter.

He moved wearily toward the door. "I'd better go call Farrell," he said.

* * *

As soon as he'd given Honeyman the unwelcome news, Gideon did what he'd been wanting to do since the moment he'd stepped into the bloody nightmare of Harlow's cottage. He got under a hot shower, his second of the day, and scrubbed himself remorselessly down, sparing only his scraped shoulders. This urge to wash was something that asserted itself whenever his work took him away from dry, brown bones and brought him anywhere near the more gruesome bodily remains that too often came along with forensics. Gooies, anthropologists called them among themselves in moments of macabre but sanity-saving levity; gooies, or greasies, or sometimes crispy critters, depending on the particular kind of messiness involved.

Harlow most assuredly fit into the gooey category, but he was far from the worst case Gideon had seen. Yet the need to get himself clean had been unusually strong, a crawling, physical itch. He'd have tried some sandpaper on himself if he'd had it, and he'd never even touched Harlow. He stepped out of the shower stall and toweled himself dry, feeling better. Then, also for the second time, he changed clothes, unwilling to put back on what he'd been wearing. He shivered slightly when the cool, fresh cloth of the shirt touched his skin, and turned the air conditioner down a little.

It hadn't been just the physical ugliness of the scene that had gotten to him, he thought, although that had been awful enough in its own right. But this time there was more. The butchered corpse was no stranger, but someone he'd eaten with, laughed with, played poker with. True, Harlow had never been one of his favorite people, but a day or two ago he could have truthfully described him as an old friend. Today, of course, things had changed. In less than two hours the bumbling, plodding Harlow had metamorphosed into a cunning and resourceful murderer—and now into a murder victim himself.

Which brought up an almost equally disturbing thought. Whoever had killed him was surely an old friend as well, or at least an old acquaintance. There couldn't be much doubt that Harlow's murder was connected with Jasper's, and the list of suspects in Jasper's death was a small and circumscribed one.

And getting smaller. There was Callie, there was Leland, there was Les, there was Miranda, there was Nellie. That was it; all the people who had been at Whitebark Lodge when Jasper had been killed, and who were here now. Nobody else met both those all-important criteria. One of them, it would seem, had somehow been involved with Harlow in Jasper's death and the subsequent cover-up, had realized Harlow was starting to come apart, and had killed him before he gave it all away. That, at least, was the best guess of the moment.

Callie. Leland. Les. Miranda. Nellie.

Some were better bets than others. Miranda, he was glad to think, was among the least probable. If it hadn't been for her, they'd still all be under the illusion that the garroted man was Chuck Salish. And even if they'd eventually discovered that it wasn't—which probably wouldn't have taken long—the outlandish idea that it might be Jasper would never have crossed anyone's mind. Without Miranda, the skeleton would have remained an unidentifiable John Doe, and that would have been the end of it. No uncomfortable old questions raised about Jasper or anything else.

And Callie would seem to be off the hook too, assuming his guess at Harlow's time of death was anywhere near correct. Despite what Julie saw or didn't see during the trail ride, Callie had left for Nevada on Tuesday, a full day before he'd been killed. And she hadn't returned until this morning, long after it had happened. Or could she have planned it all ahead of time, made an unannounced, unseen return visit on Wednesday, killed Harlow, flown back to Nevada, then returned here on Thursday morning...? No, that was getting too fanciful. People might do such things in books, but he'd never known an actual killer to try it.

That left Les, Leland...and Nellie. Reluctantly, it was Nellie he kept coming back to. Nellie, who had pressed everyone to keep the disastrous roast a secret from the beginning; Nellie, who had headed the forensic team after the accident and signed off on the final report; Nellie, who had been so quick to suggest—to insist— that the skeleton was Salish's and not Jasper's; Nellie, who was even now maintaining that Jasper had been killed in the crash; Nellie—

He jerked his head with irritation, angry at himself. Nellie Hobert garroting Albert Jasper? Bringing down that table leg on Harlow's collapsing skull, not once but three times? No, he could hardly make himself imagine it. It simply wasn't credible. Not for any of them, really, but especially not for Nellie. True, he'd been a little cranky lately, but who could blame him, with the formidable Frieda hovering protectively around him, straightening his collar for him, stuffing frayed Kleenex down into his pockets when they stuck out, holding her hand out for his keys or coins when he unthinkingly jingled them...

Well, wait a minute. Combing his damp hair in front of the mirror, he paused. What about Frieda? She'd been there for the first meeting too, hadn't she? According to John, Leland had come to him with a story about her having a thing with Salish. Was it possible that Jasper had found out about it, and she had killed him to keep him from telling Nellie? For a moment he managed to seriously consider it, but even if he could make himself believe it, how did Harlow figure into it? Why had he been killed? Why would he have engineered—as he surely had—the dental-chart fakery that had led to the misidentification of Jasper?

"Hi, there," Julie said. "Gorgeous, isn't he?"

Buried in thought, he hadn't noticed her come into the cottage. She had found him in front of the bedroom mirror, stock-still, staring at himself.

He turned to smile at her. As always when she came in from the outdoors, she had a way of bringing some of it in with her; some indefinable freshness of skin and hair and fragrance. His spirits lifted.

"Did I ever tell you you're extremely wholesome-looking?" he said.

She laughed. "Just when you get carried away on the wings of passion." She came up behind him, hugged him gingerly, avoiding the scrapes, and stretched to kiss him on the back of the neck. "Do you feel okay?"

He reached around, drawing her head closer. "I love you."

"Mmm," she said, nuzzled him a moment longer, gave him a final hug that made him grunt, then flopped into an armchair and kicked off her shoes.

"So," she said, "how'd it go this afternoon? Anything interesting happen around here?"

CHAPTER 17

"And that's about it," Gideon said, summing up. They were standing on the footbridge over the pond, their elbows on the railing. After three blistering days, the layer of streaky clouds in the west had risen to veil the late-afternoon sun, and with it had come a moist breeze. The temperature had dropped a few degrees to marginally tolerable. They had walked slowly around the grounds while he told her what had been going on, finally stopping on the bridge while he concluded.

Julie had been quiet through the recital, asking few questions, making few exclamations; merely shaking her head occasionally. They began walking again. At the end of the footbridge was a weathered wooden sign that said, "Limit 3 Per Day." Three what, Gideon wondered. The pond was all of four inches deep, and he had yet to see anything move in it.

"So the skull was Jasper's," Julie said. She was chewing on a grass blade she'd picked up somewhere. "That explains a few things, doesn't it?"

He looked at her, surprised. All he seemed to have was questions, not explanations. "Not to me, it doesn't."

"Well, it explains why those remains were taken out of the case and destroyed. Someone was afraid one of you would somehow spot that they weren't Jasper's."

"Yes, that's probably true." The fate of those burned shards of bone had plummeted to a lower priority this afternoon. He'd forgotten all about them.

"And it gives us a reason for Callie to knock you off your horse."

"It does?"

Now it was Julie who stopped to look at him. "Of course, don't you see? It's what I said—or at least it could be. She was trying to keep you from finishing the reconstruction. She was afraid you'd find out it was Jasper. Which you did. Gideon, I'm telling you—"

"Julie, we've already been through this. If I didn't finish it, somebody else would have, so—"

"But they wouldn't have; that's what I'm getting at. You explained yourself—very publicly—why there wasn't any real point in doing a reconstruction on that skull: If it was Salish, there were better ways of proving it; and if it wasn't, then who was there to show it to? The only reason you were doing it was as a demonstration of the technique."

"Well, yes—"

"So if you didn't finish it, if she could put you out of commission just for this one afternoon, that would have been the end of it. It would have gone back to Nellie for analysis and wound up in a box somewhere, or wherever they keep unidentified skulls. There would have been no reason to reconstruct it, and certainly no reason to think it might be Jasper's."

They had circled the pond a second time and begun to head back toward their cottage. "Well, what do you think?" she said.

"Well—"

"In fact," she went on excitedly, "she would have had the same reason for getting rid of Harlow to keep him from telling whose skeleton that was. Both of them could have been involved in Jasper's murder, and she could have seen that he was starting to crack. After all, you did."

"You know," Gideon said, "you're starting to make a certain amount of sense."

"Why, thank you. It's about time."

"Except..."

She sighed. "I knew it."

"Except that Callie couldn't have had anything to do with Harlow's murder. She was four hundred miles away."

"Oh." The grass blade was nibbled and discarded. "Are you sure about that?"

"Pretty much, unless I'm way off on the time Harlow was killed."

"Oh," she said again. "You don't suppose she only pretended to go away? Or that she snuck back, or—no, I guess not."

"I sincerely doubt it. It'd be awfully easy to check."

Julie shrugged and smiled. "Well, it was a pretty good theory anyway, don't you think? I mean, except for that little detail?"

"It's a great theory, Julie."

At the porch of their cottage she stopped him. "Gideon, can I ask you something?"

"Sure."

"If that reconstruction you made was such a good one—"

"Which it was, but the skull gets all the credit. The bony landmarks were all in the right places, for a change." He smiled. "Not that I'd expect anything else from the skull of Albert Evan Jasper."

"And if all you people are trained professional anthropologists—"

"Which we are, certifiably."

"Then how come none of you certified experts knew it was Jasper until Miranda revamped everything you did?"

He laughed. "You've put your finger on the problem with reconstruction. That's what bothers people like Nellie so much. No matter how right you get the bony stuff, the rest of it involves a lot of guesswork, and that's the most critical part."

"I'm not following you. What's the most critical part?"

"Look at it this way. Forget about reconstructions. Do you think you'd recognize me on the street if I changed just a few inconsequential, soft-tissue details on my face?"

"What kind of details?"

"Oh...different nose, different mouth, different hair, different eyebrows, different ears, different eyes—"

"But those aren't inconsequential details. They're what make you you."

"Exactly. Well, I got most of them wrong, which is what usually happens—there's no way to tell from the skull—but Miranda was sharp enough to pick up the similarity in the basic shape of the face. She just altered a few of those details and Albert Jasper jumped right out at us."

"Hm. Impressive, but I think I'm starting to come over to Nellie's side."

Inside the cottage the telephone rang. "I'll get it," Julie said. "You're being brave about it, but I can see you're still stiff." She took the three steps at a leap.

"What a hot dog," Gideon called after her. But she was right. He was glad to let her make the run for the telephone.

The call was from John. The on-scene processing was done, the body was on its way to the morgue. Dr. Tilton, the deputy medical examiner, had come to his preliminary conclusions. Would Gideon like to join them for a drink in the bar to talk about them?

* * *

"Hot enough for you?" Dr. Tilton asked. He pulled the toothpick from the left corner of his mouth, put it in the right corner, twirled it as if to set it in more firmly, and with a noisy sigh rearranged himself more deeply in the wooden lawn chair. "Great God-o-mighty."

Forensic pathologists, in Gideon's experience, tended to be lively sorts, and Deschutes County Deputy Medical Examiner Floyd Tilton was no exception. A sweating, balding cabbage of a man with a hopelessly scroungy beard that failed to disguise the absence of discernible chin, he was a nonstop talker with the astonishing ability to gnaw on a toothpick, chew gum, and eat popcorn at the same time. All without missing a word.

They had gotten their drinks in the bar—Scotch and soda for Gideon, beer for John, rum and Coke for Tilton—and taken them outside, to a shaded spot on the edge of the lawn, near a rust-mottled children's play set that looked as if it hadn't seen any use for a decade or two.

"I tell you," Tilton said, "when I heard we had ourselves a deceased in some out-of-the-way cabin in this heat, I expected the worst. You know, everybody gets used to looking at decomposing bodies after a while—"

"Not this guy," John said, directing a thumb at Gideon. "—but nobody ever gets used to the damned smell. God-o-mighty. So I came armed."

He lifted a small plastic bag halfway out of the pocket of his damp plaid shirt. Oil of wintergreen, Gideon saw, and a couple of gauze plugs to saturate and insert into the nostrils. A lot of people in the field did that. Others preferred Noxzema, or Vicks Vapo-Rub, or strong cigars. Most, like Gideon, found that nothing really helped.

"As it was," Tilton continued, reaching into the cardboard bucket of popcorn he'd carried from the bar—did he chew the popcorn and the gum on different sides of his mouth? Tuck one of them in a cheek while he worked on the other?—"the putrefaction process'd hardly gotten underway. Whoo. Thank the Lord for small favors. Well, what can I tell you gentlemen?" He raised his glass to Gideon. "Much obliged."

"Cause of death?" John asked.

"Blunt-force trauma, it would appear, inflicted by the table leg. The blows were delivered from behind, the victim being seated at the time. Either three or four of them, any one of them sufficient to cause death."

John nodded. "Can you give us a TOD estimate?"

"Ah, time of death; every policeman's favorite question. Well, there's lab work to be done, but I think you'd be on pretty safe ground assuming it happened sometime yesterday."

"You couldn't make it any more specific?"

Tilton closed one eye and squinted at John with the other. He fiddled with the toothpick, sliding it in and out between two teeth.

"Maximum, twenty-four hours; minimum, eighteen hours. That's counting back from four o'clock today."

"Between 4:00 P.M. and 10:00 P.M. yesterday," John said.

It was what Gideon had guessed, but narrowed down to a degree that surprised him. Time-of-death estimation was tricky work, especially when it came to establishing the early part of the range, and most pathologists would have been leery of pinning themselves down to a six-hour span.

"That's cutting it pretty close, isn't it?" he asked.

He could see that Tilton was happy to get the question. "Most of the time it would be, yes," he said spiritedly, "but we've got a few things going for us here, and what they add up to is eighteen to twenty-four hours." He chuckled. "Between us, nineteen to twenty-four, but I hate to sound cocky."

First of all, Tilton explained, there was the rigor mortis to be considered, or rather the passing of it. A notably unreliable indicator, but it was surely safe enough to conclude that Harlow had been dead a good twelve hours or more, putting the latest possible time of the murder at four that morning. The other extreme was established by the general lack of putrefaction; there had been no bloating yet, no overall discoloration of the abdomen; merely some blue-green marbling of the lower-left quarter. Under ordinary circumstances, that would mean that the death had occurred less than thirty-six hours ago. Given the heat, it was reasonable to make that thirty hours in this case. Would they agree with that?

They agreed.

"So," Tilton said, "that puts it somewhere between twelve and thirty hours, are you with me? This is supported by the ocular changes—advanced corneal cloudiness, but nothing like opacity yet. Now, let's see if we can narrow it some more. Let us consider..." He paused. "...carrion insect activity."

That was another thing about forensic pathologists. To a one, they loved to lecture when they got a willing audience. Possibly that came from the infrequency with which they got hold of willing audiences. Julie, for example, although invited to this conversation, had known enough to beg off and have her predinner glass of wine with some of the others.

"You noticed the arthropodal deposits in the nostrils, the mouth, the wound?" Tilton asked.

Gideon nodded, fighting off a shudder. He was beginning to think he should have gone with Julie.

"Sure," John said, "all over the place." He helped himself to a fistful of Tilton's popcorn.

"Well," Tilton went on, "I'm sure you observed the stage of development of the deposits—"

"Eggs," John said knowledgeably. "Not larval stage yet."

"Right, yes, true. Bluebottle fly, *Calliphora vicina*. And I think we can take it for granted they were laid about the time he died, because in this kind of weather, with those kinds of nice, juicy wounds, the flies would have found him and started laying in about five minutes. Kapish?"

John and Gideon both nodded.

Tilton nodded back at them. "So what does that tell us, hm?" Bright-eyed, chipper, in his element, he looked at them, twirling the toothpick, his jaw muscles working vigorously. He chewed the gum in the front of his mouth, Gideon noticed, like a hamster, repositioning it with quick, twiddly movements of his lips. Was that his secret? Popcorn on the molars, chewing gum on the incisors?

"It tells us," he continued, as Gideon had no doubt he would, "that those li'l suckers were laid sometime in the last twenty-four hours because that's how long the egg stage lasts, and even that's pushing it. Well, now; we can knock twelve hours off that straight out, because we already know your man was killed more than twelve hours ago, that is, before four this morning—"

"We do?" John said.

"Rigor, rigor," Tilton said. "It's already had time to loosen up."

"Right, I forgot."

"And, likewise, we can rule out any possibility of those eggs being laid *after,* oh, mm, nine o'clock last night—"

"We can?" said Gideon.

"Sure, because the lights in the cottage were off, and that's about the time it gets dark, and flies don't lay eggs in the dark. They don't do anything in the dark."

"They don't?" Gideon said.

Tilton laughed. "You ever hear a fly buzzing around in a dark room?"

"I guess not."

"I *know* not," Tilton said. "So there you have it, my friends. Death occurred no earlier than four yesterday afternoon, no later than nine yesterday evening. Nineteen to twenty-four hours." He grinned happily at them and mopped his forehead with a wadded handkerchief. "Whoo. God-o-mighty. Ain't science wonderful?"

"How positive are you about all this?" John asked. One of his more frequently employed questions.

"Let me put it this way. On a scale of one to ten, we're up at about a forty, okay? I mean, maybe—*maybe*—I'm off by three or four hours at the far end, but that's it. And I don't think I am."

John tilted the bottle for a thoughtful swig of beer. "Scratch Callie," he said to Gideon.

"Unless she wasn't really in Nevada," Gideon said. He told them about his talk with Julie and raised the possibility of Callie's trip being faked.

John was more receptive than he'd expected. "It's possible," he said reasonably. "She could have fudged it. Julian Minor's going to give me a hand from up in Seattle. He loves to get into stuff like that. If there's anything funny about it, he'll dig it out."

Gideon agreed. Julian Minor was another special agent who was often teamed with John. A reserved, methodical black man of fifty who spoke like a 1910 secretary's handbook ("At the present time…" "At a later date…" "In regard to your request…"), he was a whiz at unearthing facts and pinpointing contradictions. And somehow, he did it best from his desk on the seventh floor of the Federal Building in downtown Seattle.

Tilton had followed the conversation restlessly. "Who's Callie, one of your anthropologists?"

"That's right," Gideon said, "one of the few who was here for both murders."

"Nope, uh-uh, forget it. If a forensic anthropologist did this, I'll eat my hat. My fur-lined hat with earflaps, the one I wear when it snows."

"What makes you say that?" Gideon asked.

"Well, the method," he said, as if it were obvious. "I mean, really— simple blunt-force trauma?" His mouth curled contemptuously around the toothpick. "What kind of way is that for a forensic scientist to kill somebody?"

"Too unsubtle?" Gideon asked.

"Too physical, too risky, too much likelihood of getting caught. All that blood. Whoo." He shook his head. "No, sir, these people are trained, just like you and me. They know things your everyday killer doesn't." He leaned forward, jiggling the gum between his front teeth. "Knowing what I know, I could come up with half-a-dozen ways to commit an absolutely perfect murder if I had to. Untraceable. Couldn't you? And don't tell me you haven't thought about it."

"I haven't," Gideon said truthfully, "but I see what you're getting at. If I wanted to get away with murder, I certainly wouldn't bludgeon somebody with an old table leg and then just leave him sitting in his chair, waiting to be found. Along with the table leg."

"You're darn tootin' you wouldn't. And neither would any of the rest of them." Tilton twirled his toothpick, brushed popcorn from his paunch, and got to his feet. "Well, gentlemen, I leave you to it. John, I'll have a report to you by tomorrow afternoon."

"Okay, thanks, Dr. Tilton. I'll be in touch."

John watched him go. "Doc, you buy this expert-murderer bit?"

"I think he's got a point."

"Well, I don't." He stood up and yawned, stretching. "Let me tell you, smart people do the goddamn dumbest things all the time."

"You said a mouthful there," Gideon said with a smile. "Great God-o-mighty."

CHAPTER 18

"No, the last time I saw Harlow would have been…oh…" Callie jutted her long chin out and up, and whooshed a sizable lungful of smoke at the ceiling. "…a little after noon. Probably about twelve-fifteen."

"This was Tuesday?" John asked.

"Tuesday. In his cottage."

"Would you mind telling me what you were talking about?"

"No, why should I mind? We were discussing his reason for not flying back with me for the curriculum meeting."

"Which was?"

She looked at her hands, running her thumb over the tips of her polished fingernails. "He said he wasn't feeling well."

"What was the matter with him?"

"What was always the matter with him. His stomach."

The guy's just been murdered, John thought, and she's mad because he didn't make it to a meeting.

"Did he seem pretty sick to you?"

"Do you mean generally speaking, or Tuesday afternoon in particular?"

"Both."

"No and no."

John didn't like it when interviewees got cute. It led to misunderstandings. "You want to explain, please?"

"Frankly, I think the main thing wrong with his stomach was all the worrying he did about it. He didn't have anything worse than an intermittent generalized gastritis."

That sounded bad enough to John. "Are you saying he could have made the meeting if he wanted to?"

"If he wanted to," she said.

"Why wouldn't he want to?"

Her upper lip bulged as she scoured the inside of her mouth with her tongue. "I don't believe in speaking ill of the dead."

"Uh-huh," John said. He'd heard that a whole lot of times in his career. Nine times out of ten it was followed by a "but."

"But I don't think it's any secret that Harlow was thoroughly burnt out. He was serving out his time; he didn't give a damn. Frankly, his being on the curriculum committee was my idea. I hoped it might create some interest in the educative process—you know, as a synergistic function and as a source of personal renewal as well. But of course that kind of interest has to come from within."

"Yeah, I can see that," John said. "Were the tickets nonrefundable?"

"What?"

"The flight tickets to Nevada and back. Were they nonrefundable?"

"Well, I don't—yes, I suppose they must have been. Mine were, and the same secretary made the arrangements for both of us."

"Who paid, the school?"

"Of course it did." A glimmer of defensiveness. "It was university business, wasn't it?"

"The reason I'm asking about them—"

"I understand the reason. And you're right. Harlow wasn't the kind of person who would throw away several hundred dollars— of his money *or* the school's—because he wasn't in the mood to attend a meeting." She brushed her hair back with a tentative flick. "It's conceivable I may have been wrong."

"About what?"

"About his being ill. He may have been sicker than I thought."

"But that wasn't the impression you got?"

"To be perfectly candid, no," she said, frowning, "but he did seem…"

John waited.

"…worried…frightened…almost as if he sensed what was going to happen to him. But he didn't say anything." She drew thoughtfully on her cigarette, staring through the window over John's shoulder at the soft gray rain that had broken the heat wave during the night and had been drifting down all day onto the Whitebark Lodge lawn. "My God, maybe if I'd been more receptive, more empathetic, instead of being tuned in to where *I* was coming from, I could have done something to prevent it."

Her dark eyes, earnest and glowing, settled on John's face. "I cared about him, you know, John. We had our professional differences, but I cared about him as a human being."

Lady, you're a phony, he said to himself. Right down to your socks. Harlow was a pain in the butt to you, and you couldn't be happier about the guy's being out of your hair.

He leaned back, studying her. Happy about it or not, she hadn't killed him. That was one of the things Julian Minor had already established from his Seattle desk. The man at the Budget car-rental counter in the Bend-Redmond Airport had verified by telephone that Callie had turned in her Dodge Colt at 2:10 P.M. on Tuesday, sat around the airport lounge drinking coffee and working on her laptop for half an hour, and boarded the commuter plane to Portland. He'd reserved another car for her and had it waiting when she got off the first plane from Portland at 6:00 A.M. Thursday. And yes, he remembered seeing her actually get off. It wasn't what you'd call a real big airport.

On top of that, her presence in Carson City as late as 5:00 P.M. on Wednesday had been confirmed. Unless she'd taken a private plane, there was no way she could have gotten back to Whitebark Lodge inside of Tilton's 9:00 P.M. time-of-death deadline. And Julian had found no such flight.

Whatever Julie had seen or not seen on the trail ride—and John's own brief interviews with several people who'd been on it had turned up nothing to support her—Callie was several hundred miles away when Harlow had been murdered.

So, once again: scratch Callie.

"Would you have any idea where he was between the time you saw him and late Wednesday?" he asked.

"No, I don't. What's so important about late Wednesday? Is that when he was killed?"

John nodded. "Between four and nine o'clock."

Callie shuddered suddenly. "Is it true that his skull was crushed?"

It was true, all right, John said. Did she have any idea what might be behind the murder?

She dragged hard on her cigarette. "It has to have something to do with this bizarre thing with Jasper—with Jasper's murder."

That was true too. "Tell me a little about Jasper."

"Jasper?" Her mouth thinned and set. "Jasper was a son of a bitch."

Not just your everyday sonofabitch either, John noted, but a son of a bitch; three fat, separate words dripping with venom.

Well, Callie had good reason for hating him. According to Gideon, Jasper had made her life as a graduate student miserable. He had chipped away and chipped away at her doctoral dissertation, making her process big chunks of her data over and over, until she had quit in frustration after four years and transferred to Nevada State. Thereunder the less-demanding Harlow—she had her degree in a year and a half.

"Enough of a sonofabitch for one of his ex-students to want to kill him?" he asked Callie.

"Albert Jasper was awful," she said. "Cynical, condescending, ruthless, uptight, paternalistic in the worst sense of the term..." John thought she had run out of words, but she was only pausing for breath. "Arrogant, inauthentic, self-centered...all in all, a horrible person. You don't have to take my word for it either; the others will tell you exactly the same thing."

So they had, so far. "And yet you put on a big party for him when he retired."

"Nellie put it on. He did the organizing, and I think most of us came to please him, not Jasper. And, well, to tell the truth, in my case I was flattered to be invited. I wasn't a very big fish at the time. And I was excited about the idea of a forensic anthropology conference. But the whole retirement-party bit was Nellie's concoction; no one else's."

"And yet you all came."

Callie laughed shortly. "A big mistake."

Especially for Jasper, John thought.

Callie drew herself up. "Are we done? There's a session I'd like to attend."

"Just one more thing," John said. "I'd like you to take a look at this." He removed a sheet of paper from the folder at his elbow and passed it to her. On it was a copy of Albert Jasper's telephone bill for June 1981—more of Julian Minor's work, obtained by Telefax a couple of hours earlier.

"Look at the circled number, the call to Nevada." She looked. "Yes?"

"Do you know that number?"

"Well, it's the university's prefix—"

"I know that, but the extension isn't in use anymore, and so far no one's been able to tell us what it was. You don't recognize it?"

"No. Wait, yes. It's the old anthropology department extension. We haven't used it since 1989."

"So it would have been a call to the department switchboard?"

"The department secretary. There were only six or seven faculty offices back then, and a secretary could handle it."

"The call was made just two weeks before the meeting—two weeks before Jasper was killed. You wouldn't happen to know what he was calling about?"

"No."

"He wasn't calling you?"

She laughed. "Jasper wouldn't call me."

"All right, who would he call?"

"Well, Harlow, probably. I mean, I don't think he knew any of the others. They were all cultural, or linguistics, or archaeology. But I'm just guessing."

"What would he be calling Harlow about?"

"I have no idea. They weren't exactly in close contact, so it's a bit of a surprise, actually."

John looked up as a head poked through the open doorway of the lounge.

"Manager said you wanted to see me." It was one of the lodge staff, a sleepy-looking teenager with a bad complexion and long, stringy blond hair under a turned-around baseball cap. He took an unwilling step into the room.

"Thanks, be with you in a second."

"I can come back later."

"No, I'm just leaving," Callie called to him. She ground out her cigarette and stood up. "I really think I would have heard about that phone call if it were anything significant," she said to John. "I can't imagine it was anything important."

Maybe not, John thought, but it was the only call listed on Jasper's bill to any of the people John was now concerned with.

And they had talked for thirty-nine minutes. That was a long time for a long-distance call. Especially for people who weren't exactly in close contact.

John pulled out his small notebook as the kid eased warily into Callie's chair. "What's your name?"

"Vinnie."

John looked up.

"Stoller."

John wrote it down. "And you're the one who changed the sheets and towels Wednesday?"

"Not all of 'em. I did Cottage 18."

Harlow's cottage. "Do you remember what time that was?"

"About 4:57."

John put down the pad. *"About* 4:57?"

"I remember because it was the last one in the row, and I was like back for my dinner break at 5:00."

John wrote down *4:57p.* "Tell me exactly what you saw at the cottage, exactly what you did."

The boy shrugged. "I didn't do nothing. There was a do-not-disturb sign on the door, so I left everything on the wood box, under the eaves." His hands were circling one another. They were already the hands of a man; square, work-scarred, thick-jointed.

"You didn't have a passkey?"

"Sure I did, but we're not supposed to go in if there's a sign. So I left it, that's all."

"You didn't knock?"

"Well, yeah, I think I did."

"And?"

"I told you. Nothing."

"You didn't look through the window?"

"There wasn't no point. I'm telling you, you couldn't see nothing. Can I go now? I gotta get back to work."

"Sure. Thanks for your help, Vinnie."

Vinnie ran his tongue over his lips as he got up. "Was the, uh, guy already, like, dead when I was there?"

"Looks like it," John said.

And that was about the only concrete thing he'd learned in over four hours of interviews: The do-not-disturb sign had been put out

by 4:57 P.M. Wednesday. Assuming that the killer had hung it
there to put off the discovery of the murder, that had to mean
Harlow was already dead by then. And with 4:00 being the earliest
possible time of death—Tilton was awfully damn sure of that—
the murder had to have happened after 4:00 and before 5:00.

He picked up a molded-glass paperweight that sat on the table
as a decoration. Inside was a miniature desert scene with cactuses, a
tiny bleached steer skull, and a rail fence. He shook it, and instead
of the usual snowstorm effect, there was a swirl of brown particles;
a sandstorm. Very Western.

He held the weight in his palm and watched the particles settle.
One thing he had no shortage of was motives for wanting to see
Jasper dead. Callie wasn't the only one. As Gideon had told him,
they all had similar stories. Jasper had told Les Zenkovich flat
out—after three years of graduate work—that he didn't have the
brains to make it as an anthropologist and he'd do better looking
for a field that made less stringent intellectual demands on its
practitioners. Like Callie, Les had transferred too, and wound up
getting his Ph.D. at Indiana with little difficulty.

Miranda Glass had been told much the same thing, also after
three or four years under his thumb, but she had lost heart and
thrown in the towel on her doctorate. She'd become a big name in
museum work, but in this crowd, with only an M.A. to her credit,
she was one of the undereducated.

Leland Roach had a different kind of grievance. Although
he'd suffered the usual hard time under Jasper, he'd stuck it out
and managed to get his degree without having to go elsewhere,
and to do it relatively quickly. All the same, he had been unable
to get a satisfactory academic appointment for five years. Then
he had learned that it was because Jasper had been blackballing
him behind his back, smilingly agreeing to serve as a reference
whenever Leland had asked, then denouncing his competence,
his resourcefulness, his personality, and, at least in one case, his
sense of humor. When Leland had dropped Jasper from his list of
references, he had quickly landed an assistant professorship at San
Diego State, then moved on to the prestigious Colorado Institute
of Technology.

All these accounts, Gideon had reminded John, had to be taken with a grain of salt. The sources, after all, were the aggrieved parties themselves, and the tales had been told during various late-night rounds of war stories at one conference or another through the years. But whether accurate in their specifics or not, they left no doubt that there hadn't been much love lost on Albert Evan Jasper in this group.

Only Nellie Hobert, Jasper's first student, had gotten through his apprenticeship with his admiration for the old anthropologist intact. Maybe it was because Jasper had been kinder in those days, or maybe it was because Nellie had been the best as well as the first. Either way, Nellie had never, in Gideon's hearing at least, expressed the hard feelings the others had.

But seen from another angle, it was Nellie who'd had the best reason for wanting him dead. Not out of revenge or bitterness, which had never been high on John's list of homicidal motives anyway, but from personal ambition, a much more likely incentive. For it had been on the older man's death that Nellie's own career had bloomed. He had, as everyone had expected him to, succeeded his mentor as Distinguished Services Professor of Human Biology at Northern New Mexico, as president of the National Society of Forensic Anthropology, and, in effect, as top gun in his field.

So none of them could be ruled out. Not on grounds of motive. Not by a long shot.

He upended the paperweight one more time and set it swirling back on the table. The one bright spot in all this was that nice, tight little time range; one hour, from four to five o'clock Wednesday afternoon. A little checking on who was where at that time was going to narrow things down, speed things up.

And speeding up was in order. Applewhite had given him until Monday, three more days, to do what he could to help Honeywell. After that, the case would be handed back to the Deschutes County Sheriff's Office. John wasn't going to solve it for them in three days, but it'd be nice to tie things up a little more for Farrell, who would still have another week to go before his sergeant of detectives got back.

He stood up, yawning, and slid his papers into his folder. Jasper's telephone bill caught his eye again. That unexplained call to Harlow was interesting too, a link between two men murdered a decade apart. He needed to call Julian Minor and pass on what little Callie had told him about it, then let Julian run with it. The guy was amazing. You never knew what he'd turn up.

Mrs. Gelbert, the resort manager, tapped on the doorjamb. "Mr. Lau, telephone. Gideon Oliver. You can take it up front."

CHAPTER 19

"Hi, Doc, whatchagot?"

Gideon took the receiver from the crook of his shoulder, where he'd wedged it while pouring himself a cup of coffee and waiting for John to come on the line.

"It checks out, John. It's Jasper, all right. No surprises this time."

He had spent the last two hours in the Justice Building's small conference room, scraping the clay from Jasper's skull, comparing the dentition against the newly received chart (and x-rays) from Dr. MacFadden, and going over the skeleton as a whole.

"Good," John said. "I've had enough surprises for a while."

"And Nellie's report is fine, as expected. I agree with everything in it."

"Glad to hear it. All the same, I'd appreciate it if you'd do one up yourself."

"Why? It'd say just what his says."

"Yeah, but we better have it anyway. I mean, what if Honeyman winds up charging him? Is he supposed to use the guy's own report as evidence? Does he call him as an expert witness to describe those broken neck bones? It wouldn't work."

"Okay," Gideon said resignedly. It would mean getting the bones back out of the evidence room, out of the labeled paper sacks in which he'd put them, laying them out on the table again, and going over them one more time. "I'll take care of it. I just wish you'd told me before."

"I wish I'd thought of it before. Thanks, Doc. See you later."

When Gideon brought the first armful of sacks back to the conference room, he found Nellie sitting at the table dressed relatively conservatively—in full-length trousers and a red T-shirt with nothing written on it but "Go, Broncos!"—and looking subdued.

"I was driving around in the rain, thinking about things," he said, "and decided to stop in. I thought you might be working on the bones."

Gideon felt himself flushing. He understood perfectly well why John had wanted him and not Nellie to complete the skeletal analysis, but it didn't stop him from feeling rotten about it. He had planned to use the drive back to the lodge to think up some way of broaching it tactfully with the older man, but Nellie had beaten him to the punch.

"Uh, Nellie, actually, the reason I'm doing this is—well, I'm sure you know it's not a question of trust, or of—of competence. I mean, there's certainly no question, no question at all—"

With a wave of his hand, Nellie put a merciful end to his babbling. "Don't worry about it. Of course I understand. I'm a potential suspect; how can I have anything to do with the investigation? I approve completely."

Gideon was happy to see that he gave every sign of meaning it. "Thanks, Nellie."

"My boy, don't give it another thought." He sobered when he looked at the sacks in Gideon's arms. "Is that Albert?"

"Yes." Gideon laid them on the table, then looked up sharply. "You mean you agree it's him now?"

A rare sheepish look dragged Nellie's features down. "Yes, yes, you were right about it, of course. You all were. It just took a while for me to admit it. I can, on occasion," he said dryly, "be a wee bit stubborn. Or maybe we'd better make that 'pigheaded.' I simply wouldn't accept having made so colossal an error."

Gideon was more relieved than he showed. Nellie had seemed more than pigheaded to him; he'd seemed fixated, almost fanatical.

"That's really what I came to say," Nellie said. "I wanted to apologize for being so obstinate."

"There's nothing to apologize for."

"I assume you've made the identification definite by now." Gideon nodded.

"Simply astounding," Nellie said, shaking his head. "I still can't conceive of how we came to make such a botch of it, can you? It's not as if—" One wiry eyebrow went up. "Or *do* you know how it came to happen?"

"Well, I think so, yes—"

Nellie held up a hand. "But you can't tell me. Of course not. Tell me this much, though. Was it simple error or were we bamboozled?"

"You were bamboozled."

Nellie banged his palm softly on the table. "That's what I thought. It makes me feel a little better, if you want to know. But by whom, do you know that? Do you know if poor Harlow's death is related to it somehow? It is, isn't it?" The hand shot up again before Gideon could say anything. "No, I'm putting you in a difficult position. Never mind, I can wait to find out along with everyone else."

He stood up. "Look, I've said what I had to say, and I want to thank you for being so damned decent about all this. I wouldn't have blamed you if you'd accused me of something worse than sloppiness."

Gideon didn't feel so damned decent. And although he hadn't accused Nellie of anything, had never suspected him of anything really, there were still unanswered questions, a remaining reservoir of doubt and uncertainty.

"Can I ask you something, Nellie?"

Nellie looked amiably down at him. "All right."

"Why did you make such a secret of the roast?"

"Apparently it isn't much of a secret anymore. It seems to be all over the place."

"But why did you try so hard all these years to keep it one? Why did you shut Leland up the way you did yesterday?"

"Well, you have to understand—until yesterday we thought we'd caused his death. We thought he'd gotten on that bus because we'd driven him to it. We were—we were ashamed of ourselves. So we talked it out, and we agreed that no purpose would be served by telling anyone else about it. And we haven't. Childish, perhaps, but that's the way we saw it."

Gideon shook his head. "Nellie, I'm sorry, but it doesn't ring true. I can see some of the others going along with covering it up, but it just doesn't sound like you. I mean you, personally. It's not your style."

"I suppose I should take that as a compliment," Nellie said gruffly. "Well, damn it, you're right, it's not my style." He slid back down into the chair. The pipe came out of his pocket, and the Latakia, but once they were in his hands he seemed to forget about them.

"Do you know what it was, really? It's not very deep." He looked up at Gideon from under his eyebrows. "You know what happened at the roast, I gather?"

"I know it got out of hand, I know Jasper took offense—"

"Yes, well, that's it right there. Jasper took offense."

He began stuffing the pipe methodically with tobacco. "You certainly couldn't call Albert a model human being, Gideon. I know how the others think of him—a slave driver, a martinet—and there's some truth to it. But you know what it is they're really complaining about without even knowing it? His standards. Mortifyingly high, true; uncompromising, true—but if you could meet them, if you could deliver, then, my God, the man could stretch you! Everything I know about this profession of ours stems from him. Without him, there wouldn't *be* any profession. He made it a science, Gideon." A match was struck and held to the bowl of the pipe. It was trembling very slightly.

"I realize all that—" Gideon began, but Nellie, sucking on the bit, shook his head: There was more.

The match was shaken out, the first smelly cloud of smoke expelled. "All of us owe that man a great debt, me more than anybody, and the fact of the matter is, I couldn't stand—still can't stand—the thought of his last recorded moments being so—so—squalid. Drunk, ranting, bawling...I felt I owed it to him to protect his memory."

"His memory," Gideon said.

"Yes, and so I—well, I suppose I imposed my will on everyone else. I made them promise to keep that last awful scene to themselves. And they, good souls that they are underneath it all, humored me." He hesitated, looked awkwardly down at his lumpy knuckles. "And that's all there was to it. I hope you believe me."

"I do," Gideon said. Loyalty. Fidelity. Obligation. It sounded like the real Nellie Hobert, all right, just slightly askew.

Nellie smiled wryly at him. "I guess it was pretty dumb, wasn't it?"

"Pretty dumb."

"Well, you know what they say: *'Mit der Dummheit kämpfen Götter selbst vergebens.'*"

Between Gideon's rudimentary German and Nellie's impenetrable accent, not much got through. *"Mit der...?"*

"'With stupidity the gods themselves struggle in vain.' Schiller said it."

"Ah," Gideon said. Schiller wasn't the only one. John Lau said it too: Smart people do the goddamn dumbest things.

* * *

At 5:00 P.M. that afternoon, Miranda convened a special meeting of the FMs to consider an unanticipated problem: the Whitebark Lodge catering department, not having received instructions to the contrary, had begun preparing for the traditional Friday-evening Albert Evan Jasper Memorial Weenie Roast, Singalong, and Chugalug Contest. With the rain having stopped, the mesquite fire in the cookout area had been started and the tables were in the process of being set up. However, having belatedly learned of the recent tragic events that had befallen WAFA, the caterer now wished to know if the cookout should be canceled.

"I would say so, yes," Callie said with a dismissive laugh. "This is hardly the time for a weenie roast."

"It is steaks we're talking about," Miranda reminded her gently, "not weenies."

"Whatever. The longer we put off dealing with the trauma and depression associated with what's happened, the longer it will be before we can get on with our lives in a constructive way. As a matter of fact, I've been thinking that this evening would be a good time for some co-supportive grief work sessions for those who'd like them."

"I don't know that I'd go as far as all that," Leland said, "but it's certainly not the time for a biennial picnic. It would be entirely out of place." It was the closest he'd come to agreeing with Callie in Gideon's or anyone else's memory.

"Well, but that creates a small problem," Miranda said. Leland gave her the lorgnette look. "And what problem is that?"

"They've already gone ahead and bought the supplies. Forty-five T-bone steaks, ten chickens, wine, beer, charcoal, plastic plates, the works. The bill comes to $432. We'll have to pay for it in any case."

"Oh," Leland said after a moment. "That's different." He considered. "Well, perhaps we could think of it as a joint memorial picnic—for Harlow as well as Albert? That might be more appropriate. In fact, we might think about keeping it as the Jasper-Pollard Memorial Dinner in the future."

"Hey, at the rate we're getting knocked off, we better just start calling it the General Memorial Weenie Roast," Les said.

Callie glared at him. "One of our members has been murdered. Two, if you include Jasper. The murderer or murderers are still at large and would almost certainly be in attendance, have you thought of that? Under those circumstances, I think it's repellent even to be discussing this."

"Yes, I think so too," Nellie said. "You know, if the wastage is what's bothering people, we can always have the food served in the dining room as the regular dinner tonight."

"Turn forty-five choice T-bones over to the regular kitchen staff?" Miranda cried. "To the same people who were responsible for Rhoda's Meatloaf? Instead of having them grilled over an open mesquite fire? Please, are we sure we don't want to give this some serious thought?"

"Why don't we just go ahead and have it outside if they've already gotten started?" Gideon suggested. "We don't have to make a big deal out of it. There's nothing that says we have to call it a picnic or a memorial or anything else."

"Fine!" Miranda said. "Excellent idea. I'll settle for that."

"Simply an alfresco dinner," Leland said. "A picnic. That sounds like a reasonable compromise to me."

It did to the others, too, and the matter was settled.

"Well, I'll be there," Nellie said to Gideon as they got up to leave, "but I can't say I'm looking forward to it. I'm afraid it's going to be an awfully gloomy affair."

CHAPTER 20

But Nellie turned out to be wrong. Although it was true that the general level of hilarity wasn't up to that of previous years' Weenie Roasts, Singalongs, and Chugalug Contests, there was an unmistakable crackle of lively interest in the air as people gathered in the cookout area near the crumbling, weedy tennis courts at seven o'clock. Even the qualmish presence of Farrell Honeyman, who had come to confer with John and had been induced to stay for the cookout, failed to dim the sparkle. The eyes of the younger members, in particular, returned again and again to the faces of the Founding Members, not so much with outright suspicion as with a kind of curious and speculative relish.

Julie, John, and Gideon, off to one side, surveyed the scene from the small rise on which the tennis courts were set. Below them the line at the barbecue pit, which Honeyman had just gone to join, was beginning to shorten as people got their steaks and found seats.

"Well, look at the bright side," Julie said. "You're not going to have any trouble getting a big registration for the 1993 conference."

Gideon smiled. "Wouldn't you love to have a booth selling buttons and T-shirts? 'I survived 1991.' You could make a fortune."

He turned to John, who was looking glum. "No progress?"

John shook his head and sipped beer from a bottle. "Anything from the fingerprint people?"

"What can they tell us? There aren't any fingerprints on the weapon, and finding prints on anything else doesn't prove a thing. Everybody and his grandmother was in there playing poker Monday night."

"Everybody but Frieda," Julie said.

"Wrong," John said. "She came in to drag Nellie out of there at about two in the morning, so she's got an excuse for her prints being there too. Oh, one thing: we pinned down the time of death a little closer. Now it looks like Harlow bought it somewhere between four and five o'clock Wednesday afternoon."

"How did you come up with that?" Gideon asked.

"One of the employees, the kid who brought around the towels." He gestured with the bottle at a tall, skinny boy with a turned-around baseball cap, one of three people who were working at the barbecue pit and who was at that moment serving Honeyman his steak. "Him. He was there a couple of minutes before five, and the do-not-disturb sign was hanging on the door. I figure that's got to mean Harlow was already dead, don't you? I mean, why would Harlow put the sign out? He wouldn't know anybody was coming around with towels."

Gideon nodded. "True."

"The employee," Julie said. "Did he see anything?"

"Nah, just the sign. He couldn't see anything through the window. Come on, they're starting to run out of steaks over there."

They walked to the stone barbecue pit and got utensils and plastic plates from a table alongside it.

"Why couldn't he see anything through the window?" Gideon asked. "I could see through the window."

"Well, there were those flowers right in front of it. They made it hard to look in."

"But I looked in. I saw Harlow."

John shrugged as he helped himself to a roll. "I guess he didn't look as hard as you."

"Were those his exact words? He couldn't see anything?"

"Look—" John lowered his voice; they were approaching the boy. "This is not a particularly swift kid, you know? Words are not his thing. But go ahead and ask him, if it's worrying you."

"It's not worrying me. I was just wondering."

John had reached the boy, who was standing at the ready, tongs in hand, having just served Julie. "How're you doing, Vinnie? Let me have that one on the side there."

"It's pretty well-done."

"Great, that's the way I like 'em." He held out his plate. "And my associate here has something he wants to ask you."

What he really wanted to ask him, Gideon thought, was why so many kids walked around with their baseball caps on backward, a fashion that had mystified him since the first time he'd seen it. Instead he said: "I understand you're the one who left the linens at Cottage 18."

The boy regarded him suspiciously.

"I understand you said you couldn't see anything through the window."

"That's right. You want a steak? I'm not supposed to be talking to the customers."

Gideon held out his plate while Vinnie dropped a huge T-bone into it. "What did you mean when you said you couldn't see anything? You must have been able to see *something.*"

"I already told him," Vinnie said, indicating John. "I didn't look. There wasn't no point."

"Why wasn't there any point?"

"Because," Vinnie said, showing a streak of adolescent impatience with slow-minded adults, "the blinds were down. I already told him that."

There was a moment of startled silence before John said, "Uh, actually, I think you missed that little detail."

"Well, they were," Vinnie said sullenly.

"You're absolutely positive?" Gideon said. "They were down?"

"Well, jeez, I know what blinds look like."

"All the way down?" John asked.

"Yeah, all the way down. I gotta go back to work. There's more people."

"Why all the fuss?" Julie asked as the three of them moved away from the pit. "Why is it so important that the blinds were down?"

"Because," John said, coming to a standstill, "they were up when we found him. And if he really was dead when Vinnie was there, that means somebody must have come back later—before we found him—and raised them. Is that the way you see it too, Doc?"

"Mm."

"Oh," Julie said, chewing gently at her lip. "But that doesn't make any sense. You mean somebody *wanted* the body to be found?"

"Looks like it," John said.

"But then why not take down the do-not-disturb sign too?"

"You got me."

"And why would the killer want the body to be found anyway?

Wouldn't he want to put it off as long as possible? Don't all those gruesome pathological clues get harder and harder to figure out as time goes on?"

"Yeah, they do," John said thoughtfully. "Everything does. You know, maybe it wasn't the killer. Maybe—maybe what?"

John and Julie looked at each other and shook their heads. "Gideon," Julie said, "you're being awfully quiet."

Gideon was being quiet because his mind was racketing along another track entirely, one that hadn't even vaguely occurred to him before.

"I was just thinking..." he murmured. "What if those blinds didn't really have anything to do with keeping people from seeing in? What if...I don't know; I don't quite have it worked out..."

"Hey there, you three," Miranda called from a few feet away, "we can squeeze you in here if you don't mind consorting with known suspects."

And indeed, there they all were, lined up at a single table: Miranda, Callie, Les, Leland, Nellie, and Frieda.

"Thanks," John said, "but I've still gotta talk to my compadre about a couple of things. You guys go ahead." He headed for the next table, where Farrell was sitting.

Callie slid over so Julie had room next to her. Gideon sat around the corner from Julie, on her right, next to Leland. Frieda and Nellie were across the square table from him, with Les and Miranda on the fourth side.

"We have been driven to band together," Leland said, "by the unrelenting scrutiny of our peers." He looked sourly across at Callie. "We are now hard at work providing each other with a caring, nurturing environment in which to initiate the mind-body healing process." Something in his voice suggested that the glass of white wine at his elbow was not his first.

Callie glowered briefly at him. "Do you suppose we could get the potato salad started around, please?"

Julie began to cut into her steak, then stopped and touched the back of Gideon's hand. "Everything all right?" she asked quietly.

"What? Yes, fine, I was just thinking." He sliced a wedge from his steak and began chewing.

The blinds, the blinds. Down shortly after Harlow's death, up twenty-four hours later when he and John had found the body. All the way up, letting the sun pour in...

Julie passed him the big blue bowl of potato salad. "Thanks," Gideon said absently and put it down without spooning any onto his plate.

The blinds—yes, sure, the blinds could have fooled them all; especially with a little help from the air-conditioning. But what about those *Calliphora* eggs? Surely there was no way to fake them, no way to alter the—

"Hey, if you're not going to have any of that stuff, cover it up, will you?" Les said to him from the other side of Leland. "The flies are having a field day."

"Oh—sure," Gideon said. Mechanically, he began to tug at the plastic wrap that still covered half the bowl, pulling it down over the rim.

And then, suddenly, he was on his feet, almost upsetting the bench and Leland with it. "Plastic wrap!" he blurted.

Faces at nearby tables as well at their own turned toward him with varying expressions of astonishment.

"What did he say?" Frieda asked.

"I believe," Miranda replied drily, "that he said 'plastic wrap.' I may be mistaken, however."

But it was Callie that Gideon was looking at, and Callie who stared rigidly back at him, her long face frozen and waxy, her nostrils pinched. For a second their eyes locked, and then she was up too.

"Oh, no," she said. "No, no, no. No, no, no."

Even while rising she had been groping in her shoulder bag, and when her hand came out, it was clutching a squarish, compact handgun of dully gleaming black metal.

"This won't do," she said wildly, but not so wildly that she forgot to slide back the safety. "I can't have this."

The pistol's muzzle swept the table erratically. A wave of flinches followed in its wake. Leland made a peeping noise, either of outrage or fright.

Callie said something unintelligible. The pistol came up a few inches, sleek and wavering, like the head of a snake homing in on its prey.

My God, Gideon thought, she's going to kill herself. Right now.

"Callie, this is a bad idea," he said calmly. He didn't feel calm. His pulse was thumping in his temples. "This can be worked out, believe me. Just put—"

"Goddamn you, shut up!" she screamed. The pistol jerked spasmodically at him. Gideon, who hadn't flinched before, flinched now.

Christ, it's me she's going to shoot, he thought, dry-mouthed. From five feet away the muzzle's trembling aim fluttered from his throat to his chest. His mind groped sluggishly for action, for words.

"Callie, look—"

"Oh, you bastard," she said. Her arm extended the gun closer to him, quivering but aiming directly at his left eye. He tensed himself to make a grab for her hand. It had to be now. The gun was four feet from him. He coiled, his stomach muscles tightening. Now—

Without warning, Julie, sitting on Callie's right, brought her hand sharply down on Callie's forearm in a concise, chopping movement. Callie's fingers flew open. Her hand hit the table with a thump and bounced up, the pistol dangling by its trigger guard from her forefinger. With a grunt she tried to force it into her hand again, but Gideon had already launched himself over the table, arms extended, scattering plates and glasses.

His hand swooped down on the pistol, snaring it on the fly, like a brass ring on a merry-go-round, and flinging it away in the same motion. The other hand caught Callie at the base of the rib cage, and down she went like a bowling pin, hooked behind one knee by the bench. John, with one of those bursts of speed with which he sometimes amazed Gideon, was behind her the moment she hit the grass, hauling her roughly to her feet, practically on the rebound.

"What the hell is going on here?" His grip solidly encircled her upper arm. Somehow he'd picked up the pistol too, holding it not like a gun but like a parcel or a book, in his other hand.

Callie glared back at him, ashen-faced and twitchy, her lipstick askew. She said nothing.

An anxious Honeywell had appeared at the table, somewhat twitchy himself. "What is it? What's going on? What's happened now, for God's sake?"

"Lieutenant, you'll want to put Dr. Duffer here under arrest," John said brusquely.

"Why?" the agitated Honeyman demanded. "What charge do I use? What the hell happened?"

"Hell, carrying a concealed weapon, ADW, intent to commit bodily harm, I don't know; you come up with something." He held the gun out to Honeyman, who looked as if it were the last thing in the world he wanted anything to do with, but took it anyway.

"And check her bag," John said. "She might have another one stowed away."

"But what the hell *happened?*" Honeyman asked. "What was this all about? All I saw was—I don't know what I saw. What did I see?"

"Just do it, okay, Farrell? Trust me, I'll explain later." He glanced sideways at Gideon. "When I know what the hell happened," he said under his breath.

When the dubious but eventually cooperative Honeyman began to read Callie her rights, before a subdued, growing crowd, John gestured with his chin toward the open lawn, away from the others. "Let's go someplace where we can talk. My cottage."

Gideon and Julie followed him there, Gideon wiping potato salad from the sleeve of his shirt. He caught Julie's hand. She turned to look at him.

"Thanks," he said.

She laughed, her face flushed and excited. "I'll never complain again about having to take a forcible-restraint class. Oh, boy, my heart's still in my mouth."

John smiled at her. "You did good, Julie."

"We all did pretty good," she said, laughing.

Nobody said anything else until they got to the cottage. Then John closed the door behind them and studied Gideon for several seconds, his hands on his hips, head cocked.

"Plastic wrap?" he said.

CHAPTER 21

The plastic wrap, Gideon explained, was what had made it all come together. But it was the blinds, those up-and-down blinds, that had been the key. Those, and that twenty-four-hour period during which Harlow had dropped from sight. And of course that faint smell of insecticide in Harlow's cottage.

"What smell of insecticide?" John asked.

"Well, I didn't bother to mention it," Gideon said. "I didn't think it was important."

John leaned forward. "You didn't—!" He fell back in his chair with a wave of his hand. "Ah, what the hell, it wouldn't have told me anything anyway. It *still* doesn't tell me anything. What does insecticide have to do with anything?"

"The blowflies," Gideon said. "She had to get rid of that first infestation."

John made a visible effort to process this. "Doc, just what are you telling us, that Tilton had it wrong—that you had it wrong—that Harlow wasn't killed when you said he was, when Callie was in Utah?"

"Nevada," Gideon said. "And, yes, that's right. She killed him before she ever got on the plane. He was murdered on Tuesday, not Wednesday. The time of death was faked. Brilliantly, I might add."

"The time of death was faked," John echoed woodenly. "Brilliantly, he might add." He sighed. "I can't wait for Applewhite to read my report."

"Well, it was brilliant. Let me tell you just what I think happened, just how I think she did it, and see if it makes sense to the two of you."

"This involves blowfly infestations?" Julie asked.

"Yes, it does."

She reached for her sandwich. "I think I'd better finish this. I have a strong suspicion my appetite is about to disappear."

They were sitting around the table in John's tiny dining area, an exact duplicate of Julie's and Gideon's. Spread out in front of them were the meager but welcome results of foraging in both their refrigerators: Cheerios, milk, baloney, Wonder bread, a six-pack of ginger ale. They had thought briefly of retrieving their barely touched steaks from the cookout area, where the picnic now continued in even higher spirits than before, but had decided that it would be better for them to keep to themselves for the time being. Besides, John had the impression that Gideon's headlong dive across the table might have knocked their plates to the ground, a possibility also suggested by the condition of Gideon's shirt.

"First of all," Gideon said, "I think Callie decided Harlow had to go as soon as she saw how shook up he was when we found the burial—and we know Harlow had good reason to be shook up; he was the one who fudged the dental charts to cover up Jasper's murder. I think it's pretty safe to assume Callie was involved too, and that she got rid of Harlow before he cracked completely and gave everything away."

"Ahem," said Julie.

They looked at her.

"I believe I expressed this very hypothesis only yesterday, and was told by a certain eminent authority that it was out of the question."

"Well, it was. Yesterday it made no sense at all. Today it does."

"Yesterday it was my idea. Today it's your idea."

He laughed. "All right, credit where due. For the record: it was Julie who first fingered Callie, within hours after Harlow was found."

"It was Julie who fingered Callie before Harlow was found," she pointed out. "I knew right away there was something fishy about that horse thing, didn't I? Even if the aforementioned authority took pains to point out the impossibility of that too."

"That's right, I'd forgotten. You sure did, Julie. We should have paid more attention."

She nodded gravely. "Thank you."

"But you have to admit that at the time it really didn't stand to reason."

"Oh, sure, that's easy to say—"

"Look, folks," John said, "can we straighten out who gets credit for what later? I've got to get over to Bend and tell Farrell what the hell is going on, and at this point I still don't have a clue." He looked pleadingly at Gideon. "Doc? Please?"

Gideon slowly chewed thick-sliced baloney and soft white bread while he got his thoughts together. "All right. Understand, I don't know whether she had all of this planned ahead of time, or came up with it after she killed him, but I think I know how she pulled it off."

Not, he explained, that he had everything straight yet himself. She really had been extraordinarily clever, coming up with a plan that had missed being foolproof by a hair. First, she'd realized that her best bet for getting away with it was to make it seem absolutely certain that she'd been hundreds of miles away, at her prearranged meeting, when Harlow had been killed.

"My guess is that she made sure a whole lot of people saw her in Nevada, and on the airplanes," Gideon said, "and probably at the airports too."

"Yeah," John allowed, "a lot of people saw her. Look, Doc, I need to know *how* she did it. How could she fool a pro like Tilton? I mean, you're saying he was off by over twenty-four hours. How could that be?"

"She fooled me too, John."

"Yeah, well, I didn't want to mention that."

Gideon got up to wrench some ice from the freezer tray for his ginger ale. "Let's go back to basics for a minute," he said.

And the most basic axiom of forensic pathology was that the processes of decay began at the instant of death and advanced through time in a reasonably regular and predictable progression until decomposition was finished. The second most basic axiom was that this progression could be altered by—

"When did you learn all this stuff about forensic pathology?" John said irritably. "Every time you get near a fresh corpse, all I hear is how it's not your field."

"He's just making up that business about axioms," Julie said matter-of-factly. "He thinks that's how professors are supposed to talk. Admit it, Gideon."

"Okay," Gideon said, smiling, "but what I was about to say is true anyway. Decomposition can be affected by a lot of things, with temperature being number one. The hotter it is, the faster it goes; the colder it is, the slower it goes.

Which is why refrigeration keeps things fresh, of course."

It was this principle that Callie had applied. The blinds had been lowered not just to keep out prying eyes, but, more important, to keep out that blazing sun. She had lowered them as soon as she had killed him. No doubt, she had also turned the air conditioner on full-blast. Then she had hung out the do-not-disturb sign to keep unwanted visitors away. Then she'd left for Nevada.

"And when she got back on Thursday morning she went to his cottage, raised the blinds, and turned off the air conditioning. Then she went horseback riding."

John rolled up a slice of baloney and bit off half of it, "So in came the heat, in came the sun, shining right on him. Tilton naturally went on the basis that it'd been like that all along, that the body'd been sitting there in that heat since the murder."

"Right, we all were. But it was only that way for about ten hours. The rest of the time, another forty hours or so, it'd been under refrigeration, so to speak. All those changes Tilton talked about— bloating, discoloration, everything else—were slowed way down during that time."

He leaned against the sink, sipping ginger ale, wrinkling his nose at the bubbles. "So naturally Tilton's estimate of the TOD was quite a bit more than ten hours, but a whole lot less than the fifty that it really was. Nineteen to twenty-four hours, remember? Between four and ten P.M. Wednesday."

"During which time Callie was provably off doing her thing in Carson City," Julie said pensively. She fingered her can of ginger ale. "But where does the plastic wrap come into it?"

"Oh, that was even trickier. You can slow the internal bodily changes way down by lowering the heat, but there isn't much you can do—not with just an air conditioner about the fly larvae. And there was no question the flies were going to find Harlow in a hurry."

"In about five minutes, according to Tilton," John said.

"That's right. And finding fly larvae at the two or three-day stage of their development, instead of the one-day egg stage, would have given it away. So she—"

"Do I really want to hear this?" Julie said nervously. She had stopped eating, but she stayed where she was.

"It's not that bad. She wrapped him—probably him and the chair both—in plastic before she left, to keep the flies off. When she came back to turn off the air conditioner two days later, she took off the wrap, and the flies got right to work. Result: eggs in their first-day level of development when we found him ten hours later."

"Ugh!" Julie said emphatically.

"I knew there was something funny about that tear-off strip; I just couldn't figure out what," John said regretfully. "She must have taken the box with her, but she forgot about the strip. It'd fallen into the crack between the table and the wall, remember? Easy to miss."

He downed the rest of the rolled baloney slice and wiped his fingers. "Hey, what about the insecticide smell, what was that all about?"

"Well, I'm guessing she had to run over to the general store at Camp Sherman to buy the plastic wrap. That's a good twenty minutes, back and forth, and she knew the flies would probably start laying in that time. So she had to kill that first batch. She probably picked up the spray at the store, too, along with the plastic wrap."

"Yeah, good point," John said. "I can check over there, see if someone remembers her."

"Wouldn't that mean it wasn't planned ahead of time?" Julie suggested. "If she knew she was going to use it, she'd have had it with her when she went to Harlow's cottage. And she wouldn't have needed the insecticide at all."

"What, walk in with a box of plastic wrap all ready to seal him up in?" Gideon said. "Right in front of him?"

"Yes, why not? Normal people don't jump to the conclusion they're about to be murdered because somebody comes in carrying a box of plastic wrap."

Gideon smiled. "You're right. Normal people don't."

"Wild stuff," John said. He drained his ginger ale and crumpled the can. "Well, I guess I ought to go fill Farrell in and see what kind of a case we can make."

"Wait a minute, John." Gideon came back to the table and sat down. "What kind of a case can you make? Look, we're assuming

Callie killed Harlow to keep him from talking about Jasper's murder, right? But what evidence do we have to connect her to Jasper's murder? No credible motive or anything else. No more than anyone else had. For that matter, we don't have any proof it was Callie who actually killed Harlow. Any of the rest of them could have done it the same way."

"She pulled a gun an hour ago," Julie said. "That's not bad for starters. And the whole thing—the blinds, the plastic wrap, everything—revolved around juggling the time factor. Callie is the only person who benefits from that."

Gideon looked at John. "Is that enough, do you think? In a court of law?"

"In a court of law, who knows? That's Farrell's problem, or rather his DA's, but I think we're doing okay; the investigation's just revving up. Oh, and we do have something on motive. For killing Jasper, I mean."

Julian Minor's research skills had paid off again, John told them. Minor had hunted down Marie Tustin, the retired secretary of the anthropology department at Nevada State, who remembered Jasper's mysterious telephone call very well. Jasper had demanded that Harlow mail him the department's copy of Callie's workbook— the record of measurement data and statistics for the dissertation project she'd begun under Jasper and completed under Harlow. Harlow had asked Ms. Tustin to retrieve and mail the copy for him, and Ms. Tustin had done so. She remembered, however, that Callie had been extremely obstructive, even underhanded, in unsuccessfully trying to keep Ms. Tustin from carrying out her commission.

And why, Minor had asked her, would Callie have behaved that way? At this, Ms. Tustin had emitted a condescending flutter of laughter. She was revealing no secrets in telling him that Harlow Pollard was not the most exacting or interested of dissertation supervisors. Those students lucky enough to draw him tended to go their way without unduly rigorous guidance. And it had been remarked behind the back of many a hand—Ms. Tustin could not say if it was true or false—that Callie Duffer had taken more advantage than most of this circumstance and had been somewhat free in statistical manipulations. Did Ms. Tustin mean that Callie had faked her dissertation, Minor had asked. Ms Tustin had coughed discreetly. Well, as to that, she was hardly in a position to say. She was merely reporting what was common gossip.

"So what do you make of it, Doc?"

"Interesting," Gideon said. "You think Jasper suspected that Callie fudged her results? Maybe went over her workbook and satisfied himself that she had? Confronted her at Whitebark?"

"Could be. The workbook disappeared, along with his clothes and everything else. Everybody figured they were burned up in the bus crash. But of course he never got on the bus, did he?"

"You're saying she *killed* him for that?" Julie said. "Why? She already had her degree. Jasper couldn't take it away, could he?"

"Maybe not," Gideon said, "but she was just beginning her career. She had a new assistant professorship at Nevada State. Her dissertation was being published as a major monograph. If Jasper went public—and he was the sort of man who would have—it would have ruined her, right at the start. No decent university would touch her."

"All right, I can see that, but why would Harlow get involved? He was already established. Being a little careless wouldn't have cost him his career."

"You know," Gideon said, "my guess is that Harlow had nothing to do with the actual killing, that Callie came to him afterwards and got him to fake the dental records."

"Why in the world would he agree to that?"

"Well, she could easily have cornered him the next morning, after they heard about the bus crash, and told him: 'Look, I gave him a little push and he hit his head and died. Now help me! I saved your reputation too—you were supposed to be overseeing my dissertation. Anyway, he's dead, isn't he? What difference does it make?'"

"Yeah, I could see it happening like that," John said. "In fact, it could be she really never did mean to kill Jasper. Maybe she went to see him after the roast to make a last try at keeping him quiet; you know, throw herself on his mercy."

"With Jasper?" Gideon said. "Good luck."

"Well, that's what I mean. Maybe she just lost control; shoved him or something. Or maybe he fell; he was pretty drunk, from what everybody says. You said those cracks in his head were from a fall, didn't you? Could have been unintended."

Gideon nodded. "But not the garroting."

"No, not the garroting. And not what happened to Harlow." John stood up. "Thanks a million, Doc. I'm gonna get over to Bend and see where we go from here." Gideon stood with him. "John, this thing about her motive, the dissertation. It sounds good, but, you know, at this point it's just—"

"Unverified supposition."

Gideon laughed. "Well, yes. Maybe even unverifiable, what with the workbook gone."

John grinned back at him, the skin around his eyes crinkling. "Well, as a matter of fact, the great Julian has turned up a little something that might help. A copy of her dissertation in the library stacks—with a 125-page appendix full of statistics. In small print. I was hoping I, uh, might convince some trustworthy, public-spirited anthropologist to, uh, sort of go through it in the next few weeks and see if he could turn up anything. You know, see if the statistics match what she says, or whatever the hell you do."

"I hate statistics."

"It'd really be helpful. It might make or break the case, Doc."

Gideon wilted. "How long is the dissertation?"

"Long."

"What's it about?"

"Good question." John took his notebook from his shirt pocket, opened it, and handed it to Gideon. "Here's the title,"

It was printed in careful block letters. *Cephalometric Sexual Dimorphism in Four Related Populations (n= 572): A Multifactorial Study Using Discriminant Function Analysis.*

Gideon sagged back down into his chair with a moan of self-pity. "Great God-o-mighty."

* * *

By the time they walked slowly back to their own cottage it had gotten dark. Another rainstorm was building; they could feel it in the heavy, damp air and see occasional pallid flickers of lightning in the northwest, probably up around the stark, lonely lava flows of McKenzie Pass. It was a long way off. The rolling booms of thunder were like echoes, faint and grumbling, and reached their ears long seconds after the lightning had flared.

They stood on the porch, looking out toward this distant display, Gideon's arm around Julie, Julie's head tipped to his shoulder, her hand resting in his back pocket. To their left they could see the shimmer of firelight through the trees and hear night-muffled murmurs of conversation and laughter. A few diehards were still in the cookout area, perhaps unwilling to leave before they were sure that every weird thing that was going to happen, happened.

"Gideon?"

"Mm?"

"Do you really have to stay through tomorrow?"

He tilted his head to look at her and smiled. "Had enough rest and relaxation already?"

"I don't know if I could stand any more. Wouldn't it be nice to go home tomorrow morning?"

"Mal."

"Is that yes?"

"Yes."

She hugged him. "Let's get an early start, so we can drive in the morning. How about eight?"

"How about seven?" Gideon said.

CHAPTER 22

By morning, the sky over the Cascades had cleared, but about the time they crossed the Columbia into Washington, the rain started again; not the mountain thunderstorm of the previous night, but the normal, misty, cool, gray-green rain of the coastal lowlands. Even to Gideon it looked good. He'd had enough heat and sun to last him for a while.

And you didn't get bluebottle flies in this kind of weather.

"How would she have gotten a gun on the plane?" Julie said suddenly.

"Oh, I talked to John just before we left. She probably never did have it on the plane. She's had a permit for a long time, and she had the gun with her in the car when she drove to the conference in the first place. That's what she says, and John believes her."

"She's talking to the police, then?"

"Nope, that's about all she'd admit to. She's waiting for her lawyer before she says anything else."

"Or maybe for the true-crime writers to come buzzing around. What a book this will make."

Gideon laughed. "Probably so. Listen, I have a question for you; two, really. I can't understand why Callie—or, who knows, maybe it was Harlow—stole those burnt bones out of Miranda's display. What would be the point?"

"Obviously, to keep you from finding out they weren't really Jasper's."

"Julie, there wasn't a ghost of a chance I'd have figured that out, not just from seeing them in the case. They knew that."

"I don't mean you alone, I mean all of you. Put yourself in Callie's and Harlow's place. How would you feel with those telltale bones sitting out there under the beady-eyed gaze of forty professional anthropologists—people like you and Nellie—"

"Hey, thanks."

"Wouldn't you worry that maybe you'd forgotten *something* that somebody would see, something you hadn't even thought about? You wouldn't want to take that chance."

"You know what? You're right."

"Well, you don't have to sound so amazed. What's your other question?"

Gideon pulled over to let a seventy-five-mile-an-hour logging truck scream by, spewing chips and dust. "This one's harder, I think. Assuming it was Callie who stole those bones, why would she have dumped them in the creek where she did, right alongside the nature trail? She could have gotten rid of them someplace where no one would ever find them."

"Why didn't she crush-and-flush, you mean?"

"Exactly."

"Oh, I think I know the answer to that."

He looked at her. "You do?"

"Sure. It was a kind of insurance policy, just in case anyone was able to trace the theft to her. She picked a place where she could take people later on and say: 'Don't you see? The only reason I removed them from the museum was to give him a decent burial—here in the outdoors he loved so well, in this rippling brook among the whispering pines...oh, and *look!* Here are a few fragments that just happened to catch on this bush, thereby verifying my claim.'"

He nodded his approval. "Could be. I never thought of that."

"But you notice that none of the teeth—the only parts that could prove it wasn't who it was supposed to be—happened to catch on the bush, did they? No, they were nowhere to be found."

He smiled and shook his head. "You used to be such a nice, unsuspecting type. When did your mind start working like this?"

"Well, it didn't before I met you, that's for sure."

Just before Port Angeles they rounded a broad curve that opened into a stupendous view of the Olympics, looking up the wide, densely treed Elwha River Valley to the vertical green wall of Klahane Ridge in the national park; Julie's turf.

"Isn't it good to be home?" she said with a sigh. "My God, what a week. WAFA will never live it down."

"Oh, I don't know. There's one good thing to be said for it. Aside from wildly increased registration in 1993, I mean."

"What would that be?"

He laughed. "I don't imagine they're going to have any problem picking the wildest, weirdest case of the last ten years."

About the Author

Aaron Elkins is a former anthropologist and professor who has been writing mysteries and thrillers since 1982. His major continuing series features forensic anthropologist-detective Gideon Oliver, "the Skeleton Detective." There are fifteen published titles to date in the series. The Gideon Oliver books have been (roughly) translated into a major ABC-TV series and have been selections of the Book-of-the-Month Club, the Literary Guild, and the Readers Digest Condensed Mystery Series. His work has been published in a dozen languages.

Mr. Elkins won the 1988 Edgar Award for best mystery of the year for *Old Bones*, the fourth book in the Gideon Oliver Series. He and his cowriter and wife, Charlotte, also won an Agatha Award, and he has also won a Nero Wolfe Award. Mr. Elkins lives on Washington's Olympic Peninsula with Charlotte.

OPEN ROAD
INTEGRATED MEDIA

Open Road Integrated Media is a digital publisher and multimedia content company. Open Road creates connections between authors and their audiences by marketing its ebooks through a new proprietary online platform, which uses premium video content and social media.

CPSIA information can be obtained at www.ICGtesting.com
Printed in the USA
BVOW04s0931110516

447651BV00001B/40/P